MIDNIGHT CREED

Prairie Wind Publishing
Omaha, Nebraska

MIDNIGHT CREED

Emily Dickenson's poem, "I'm Nobody," is in the public domain.

Attention: Permissions Coordinator
Prairie Wind Publishing
15418 Weir Street
Box 207
Omaha, NE 68137

This is a work of fiction. Names, characters, places, and incidents are a product of the author's imagination. Locales and public names are sometimes used for atmos-pheric purposes. Any resemblance to actual people, living or dead, or to businesses, companies, events, institutions, or locales is completely coincidental.

Ordering Information:
Quantity sales. Special discounts are available on quantity purchases by corpora-tions, associations, and libraries. For information, please email the Sales Department at sales@pwindpub.com

Interior design and formatting: Prairie Wind Publishing
Book cover design: Prairie Wind Publishing & Shae Marcu
Original Cover Photo: Rafael Barquero

FIRST EDITION

ISBN: 979-8-9852513-1-9 Hardcover
ISBN: 979-8-9852513-2-6 eBook
ISBN: 979-8-9852513-3-3 Paperback
ISBN: 979-8-9852513-4-0 Large Print

Printed in the United States of America

10 9 8 7 6 5 4 3 2 1

ALSO BY ALEX KAVA

RYDER CREED SERIES

Breaking Creed
Silent Creed
Reckless Creed
Lost Creed
Desperate Creed
Hidden Creed
Fallen Creed

MAGGIE O'DELL SERIES

A Perfect Evil
Split Second
The Soul Catcher
At The Stroke of Madness
A Necessary Evil
Exposed
Black Friday
Damaged
Hotwire
Fireproof
Stranded
Before Evil

THE STAND ALONE NOVELS

Whitewash
One False Move

NOVELLA ORIGINALS

Slices of Night
Storm Season

SHORT STORY COLLECTION

Off the Grid

DEDICATION:

To my dear friend,
Marlene Haney

AND

In Memory of my boy, Scout,
who is the *true inspiration* for this series

"Most hours of the dark
feel like midnight
when you're seven."

—Ani Baker, Handsome Vanilla

1

Friday, December 1
Washington, D.C.

Peter Gregory knew the exact moment that changed his life forever.

The incident had been seared into his mind and had blackened his soul. The memory of that night—almost twenty years ago—constantly played in his mind. There was no way to control it. Anything could trigger it. A barista handing him coffee instead of the latte he'd ordered. A driver cutting him off in traffic. A homeless person on the sidewalk. All it took was a flash of anger, and his mind started skidding off the rails.

The horrific images had been stamped on his brain. They came full force in bright technicolor, like starting a movie at the action scene. Only in slow motion. Every detail highlighted. It played out. When it finished, it began all over again.

That incident, twenty years ago, it followed him. Haunted him. Drove him to madness. Made him the man he was today.

Standing here on the dark street corner, Gregory watched the flashing red and blue lights and listened to the high-pitched sirens.

He did enjoy the chaos. He could practically feel the vibration through the concrete. His pulse raced. Palms and forehead were sweaty, despite the cold. Over the years, he became fascinated by why some people ran away from danger while others ran toward it.

His father had run toward it. But his mother? She couldn't drive away fast enough.

Now, watching the urgency of the first responders had almost a soothing effect on him. It calmed the rattle in his brain. It paused the images. Maybe he could see something more horrific to replace them. And if he didn't find anything, perhaps he could create it all on his own.

In the meantime, he soaked in the chaos like big gulps of fresh, cold air. He reveled in the satisfaction that he'd created it. He brought all of first responders, law enforcement officers and bystanders…they were all here because of him.

He did that.

But even with this brand new turmoil, the memory raised its ugly head.

It had been dark that night, the sky ink-black with thousands of tiny star pricks. The long drive home seemed endless, especially in the backseat. Back then, he was prone to motion sickness, and the dark only made it worse.

If he concentrated, he could still hear the words of his parents' argument. Most of the time, his mind played it back in a low monotone, their voices merging. The sound droned on and on. It was part of the movie he couldn't mute.

Noise brought his attention back to the present. Cops were pushing him and the others back, trying to keep people out of the way as an ambulance wailed through. Gregory leaned against the brick building, girding himself for the nausea, but it was too late.

Snow fell on the streets of D.C., but Gregory could smell the musty Florida air coming through the family car's air vents. He was a boy again, sliding down farther into the backseat, ignoring the potato chip crumbs and the damp spot from where he'd spilled his soda. His mom would be mad about the new stain tomorrow. But that night, she was mad at his father.

Why didn't they have enough money? And why didn't his father care?

As long as she was angry with his father, nothing else mattered.

Gregory remembered closing his eyes, but only pretending to sleep. They hadn't paid attention to him or his brother for the last hour. And that was a good thing.

Darkness engulfed the vehicle. There were no other cars on the old country road. Trees lined both sides, so it looked like they were driving through a tunnel. Gregory squinted enough to see the blue dashboard lights. The inside of the car glowed like a spaceship.

Back then, his imagination could get him through almost anything. He remembered turning their rundown car into a sleek spaceship being propelled through the star-studded sky. He imagined the bumps in the road were from stray meteors instead of plain old potholes. His dad's face was washed in blue from the dashboard light, and the scowl made him look more like a comic book villain. Certainly not the captain of a spaceship.

Still squinting, Gregory stole a glance at the curled figure pressed against the other door, feet pulled up, arms crossed and hugging his body. Pretty soon he'd start crying. His brother was a crybaby. It didn't take much, but he especially hated the yelling. Maybe he thought they were mad at him. He was a little kid. He really didn't know better.

A wider squint and he could see the quivering lip in the blue glow. The outburst was on its way. And the worst part? It would only make their parents angrier. The subject of this argument would be forgotten. The new battle would be which of them made their son cry. His mother's precious golden-haired boy.

He slumped down farther but not so low his eyes couldn't see the passing landscape. What would happen if he opened the car door and slid out? It would probably hurt. But maybe just in the beginning like when he fell off his bicycle.

Flew off his bike was more like it.

The scraped knees and elbows healed though he still had some awesome scars. Back then, his mom was just relieved he hadn't knock out any teeth, but she was pissed that the bike's front wheel got bent.

"We're not buying you anymore new bikes or toys or computers," she told him when she realized his injuries wouldn't require a trip to the emergency room. Never mind that he was still bleeding.

"All you know how to do is break things."

That last part stung him more than his raw knee with gravel embedded in the bloody wound. How many times could she say hurtful things and still expect him to not be crushed under the weight of those words?

That's when he started thinking about opening the car door. What would she say when he rolled out and actually broke an arm or a leg? He bet she'd be sorry for being so mean to him then.

More sirens screamed on the street in front of him, but he could feel his ten-year-old fingers searching the door latch. Could he open it then tuck and tumble like he'd seen in the movies?

And what if he did break his arm?

The thought still made him smile, twenty years later.

How guilty would his parents feel? Or would they only be angrier because then they would need to take him to the ER? And it would cost a fortune and they were already arguing about money. Still, he imagined white bone sticking out of his skin. Would it get their attention? Could he actually steal a couple days of attention away from precious Mickey?

His mother would feel bad. Wouldn't she?

Or would she say, "See, you're always breaking things and making a mess."

But he didn't open the door that night. The boy-coward scrunched down again. His imaginary escape defeated. A quick glance at his brother told him their parents' argument had died down for now. No more quivering lip. Mickey's eyes were closed, and he looked like he was sleeping. He envied his brother's ability to soar from tears to sleep. The words hadn't left bruises on him yet.

Why couldn't he do that?

In his mind, he imagined his ten-year-old self dressed in an armor of steel like a superhero. Words would ricochet off the metal like bullets. The sparks igniting everything around him, but none of it affected him. None of it touched him. Not a single scratch. He'd be invincible with powers no one could stop. And he'd decide who to crush and who to save.

The car swerved suddenly, and he still felt that unexpected motion. His father had driven around a curve and on-coming headlights blinded them through their windshield. A pickup was parked on the side of the road.

"Someone's stalled," his father said and slowed then braked. He pulled onto the right side of the road, tires bumping off the edge and skidding in the grass and clay.

That was where the horror movie began. It happened so quickly, yet twenty years later it always played out in nerve-wrecking slow motion.

His father opened his car door, but left the engine running.

"They probably ran out of gas," he said, getting out of the car and leaving the door open.

In some versions, his mother protested.

Sometimes he hears her scream.

There are screams, but he's never sure if they'd come from Mickey or his mother. But he was certain that when the man alongside the pickup started hitting his father, Gregory couldn't believe it was real.

It had to be a game.

Or maybe the dark was playing with his eyes.

Later, his mother told the police officers that his father waved and yelled for her to go. They all were in danger. His father wanted them to run. Go get help.

But Gregory didn't remember any of that.

He didn't hear his father yell to her. How did she know? How could she be so certain?

But one thing he remembered clearly—remembered it the same every time since—was the last view of his father through the back window. Gregory could never forget that look on his father's face.

Surprise? Pain? Shock? All of that. But mostly, what Gregory saw was disbelief. His father looked like he couldn't believe they were leaving him behind.

A police whistle startled him back to the present. Back to the cold, dark street. By-standers had gathered. Others who looked like him. Gawkers of the night. The police told them they needed to step back, again. Step away from the flashing lights.

One of them looked directly at Gregory, never once suspecting he was the reason they were here. He was the reason for this chaos, bringing them out in the middle of a frosty, dark night.

And he was still capable of breaking things.

2

Santa Rosa County, Florida

Ryder Creed had a bad feeling about this search.

It started as a prickling sensation raising the hair at the back of his neck. He couldn't ignore it even as he raced to catch up with his dog. Already he regretted not putting Bolo on a leash.

The dog's sleek, lean body weaved through the trees, sprinting into the woods. The Rhodesian Ridgeback had long legs that leaped and glided. He slowed to drag his nose over some shrubs. His glances back at Creed were only a courtesy to see if his handler was keeping up. He huffed as if to say, "Nope, not here." Even then the dog didn't stop and trotted on, this time faster.

Creed struggled to keep the dog in sight. His boots crashed through the prickly undergrowth that snagged his jeans and threatened to trip him. He could no longer hear the sheriff and deputy behind him.

Hell, he couldn't hear anything over the pounding of his heart and the tromping of his feet.

When the crunch underfoot switched from snapped twigs to broken glass, his stomach fell to his knees.

Bolo's paws.

Creed's gut instinct was right. He should never have let Bolo off-leash for this search. Not here in unfamiliar territory.

Fallen leaves barely concealed the garbage dumped on the forest's floor. Bottles, cans, plastic takeout containers littered the area. Chunks of concrete, a rusted dishwasher, a ripped-up recliner—the trash heap was deeper here. None of it slowed down his dog.

Then suddenly, Creed couldn't see him at all.

"Bolo!" He tried to level his tone, but the panic spilled into his voice.

A handler never sends his dog into a dangerous terrain, no matter how capable and sturdy the dog was. What was he thinking?

There was a surprised yelp. And Creed skidded to a stop.

He held his breath, not an easy task with his chest heaving and his heart pounding.

Another shriek. High pitched.

But it was human. Not dog! He was certain.

It didn't matter. Creed's pulse began racing faster. That prickle at the back of his neck was on fire.

"Bolo, heel," he shouted though he still didn't see his dog.

This was not good.

Creed tripped over a discarded microwave tangled in the brush. He caught himself before he fell. Hands outstretched to take on the impact smacked against a tree trunk instead. The stitch in his side suggested he stop. The same place where a recent knife injury was still healing. And despite the pounding that had moved from his chest to his head, he could hear his business partner, Hannah saying, "Rye, you really don't understand what rest yourself means, do you?"

Beyond the branches, Creed could clearly see a mattress teetering on the debris pile beneath it. On the other side was the Ridgeback. Bolo stood in front of a man who had obviously just minutes ago sprung from the dirty mattress, and now was pressed up against a huge live oak.

"Bolo," Creed called to him. His voice hitched as he sucked in air and tried to catch his breath. "Bolo…heel."

It wasn't the correct command, and the dog pinned his ears as if waiting for Creed to get it right. Bolo cut his eyes toward his handler without moving the rest of his body and without taking his attention away from his target.

Behind him, Creed heard voices and footsteps. Sheriff Norwich and her deputy were finally catching up. The man against the tree stayed put, arms dropped to his sides. Legs spread. Eyes wide. Creed suspected Bolo had frightened him awake. He was feeling sorry for the guy until he saw the man's arm slowly rise.

How had Creed missed seeing the knife in the guy's hand?

"Hey, stop! The dog's not gonna hurt you. He's a scent detection dog. He's not a police dog."

"What's going on?"

It was Norwich. Creed could hear the snap of a holster.

"Sir, drop the knife."

But the man wasn't listening. He hadn't even acknowledged their presence. Instead, he glared at Bolo, his body frozen in place. He leaned awkwardly against the tree. Without warning, he launched himself forward, swiping the knife at Bolo.

The dog yelped, and Creed broke into a sprint. He dived over the dirty mattress between them, knocking the man backwards. The guy sprawled over a holly bush, but he hadn't dropped the knife.

Creed struggled to get to his knees. That stitch in his side told him to wait. Bolo brushed against him, his nose lifting Creed's arm, checking on him. But now, Bolo's ears pitched forward. His eyes shifted to the man with only a glance back to Creed as if asking, *You want me to take this guy down?*

"No, Bolo. Stand down."

Creed grabbed the dog's vest. He wanted to see if the knife had cut his dog, but instead, he dug his fingers around a strap, getting a tight hold and pulling back just enough to let Bolo know to stay put.

The dog was overly protective of Creed. He was thin, but lean, all muscle and stronger than he looked. He had taken down bigger men than this guy, all in defense of his handler. But the man didn't seem to get the message. He scrambled back to his feet. His eyes wild and focused on the dog. His hand ready to swipe.

Bolo began to tug. Hard. A low growl started deep in his throat.

"Drop the knife," Norwich yelled.

Creed felt the deputy behind him. Out of the corner of his eye he saw the service revolver, steady and leveled at the guy's chest, center-mass. And yet, he still ignored her.

"Drop the knife. Now," Norwich said, coming in closer.

The man was young, maybe early twenties. His hair flopped around his face, thick and unruly. It was hard to tell what color his dirt-gray T-shirt used to be. There was something about his eyes that Creed didn't like. They darted around and kept skittering back to Bolo. It was more than just being startled awake, and Creed wondered if he was high on something. Which made him even more dangerous.

"I wasn't trying to hurt nobody. I was aiming for the dog."

Creed wanted to yell that was why he tackled him, but Norwich beat him to it.

"Well, sir, this dog is an officer of the law." Norwich sounded calm but very much the voice of authority. The man's eyes immediately flicked to hers, a glimpse of concern floated across his face. "Attacking him," she continued, "is no different than attacking one of us."

That wasn't exactly true. Creed and Bolo weren't law enforcement. They were independent contractors hired to conduct a search. But after dozens of searches over the years, he knew Sheriff Norwich considered him and his dogs a part of her team.

"The stupid dog attacked me. I was just minding my own business. Taking a nap. That dog attacked me." He gestured with the knife to make his point as if forgetting it was still in his hand.

"Hold on." Creed heard Norwich say as he readjusted his own body to protect his dog.

It wasn't until the sheriff stepped forward that Creed realized she wasn't telling the guy with the knife to "hold on." She held her hand up to her deputy in a "stand down" motion. She did, however, have her own weapon in her other hand, dropped at her side and ready.

None of this seemed to matter to the guy with the knife. If anything, it made him more anxious. Ten feet away, Creed was close enough to get cut with another lunge. Close enough, he smelled the guy's sweat. The right side of his face twitched, and so did the fingers around the knife's handle.

Creed could sweep the guy's feet out from under him if he didn't have to worry about Bolo. The dog vibrated with his own pent-up energy, but he tapped the ground with his big front paws. His approach was always a straight-forward approach. Nothing fancy. Pure and simple. Bolo was alerting, telling Creed, *Here you go. I found what you wanted.*

But it wasn't possible. This guy was definitely not the teenager they'd set out to find. Now, Creed regretted putting them in this predicament.

Then suddenly, Bolo tilted his head. His body went rigid. He heard the incoming threat before Creed could notice. It wasn't until he saw the top of the tall grass rustling back in the distance.

Behind the guy with the knife. Behind the tree. Shrubs separated. Twigs snapped. Something was running toward them. And it was coming fast.

3

"Sheriff!" Creed yelled and pointed.

At first Norwich didn't see it. By now, the crashing and rustling in the dry undergrowth grew. She raised her service revolver just as someone shouted, "Gunner, stop!"

The voice was a deep bass reverberating through the woods and filled with urgency.

"Please, don't shoot." The man who yelled was only a blur, thrashing through the trees, arms swinging as if it helped propel him forward. But clearly, he was too far back to control the situation.

"Bolo. Sit and stay," Creed told his dog in almost a whisper, and Bolo obeyed. He saw the young guy drop the knife to his side as he turned to watch.

Creed got to his feet and shot a glance back at Norwich then the deputy. "It's probably just a dog."

Neither law officer dropped their gun.

"I've seen an alligator come that quickly," Norwich said, adjusting her stance and taking aim.

"It's Gunner," the young guy told them. "That dog wouldn't attack nobody. Not like yours did." Then he noticed their guns, and his eyes went wide. "Hey! Wait a minute. Don't shoot!"

By now, Creed had quietly inched forward and inserted himself in front of them all.

"Mr. Creed. Norwich noticed. "That's not a smart thing."

"Gunneeeeer!! Stop!"

That's when the crashing came to a sudden halt. The grass and foliage went still less than fifty feet away. Too far for Creed to see.

The man could be heard in the distance, breaking branches and sending birds flapping. But the force charging through the shrubs had listened to him and went silent.

Waiting now. Listening for the man's voice.

Creed glanced back at Bolo. The big dog didn't look concerned. He glanced at the spot where the intruder was hidden from the rest of them. His eyes sought Creed's, but only briefly. Then his attention went back to the young guy with the knife as if to say, *this is who we need to watch.*

But that man didn't appear to be a threat right now. He shifted only to get a better view of Gunner's owner while keeping an eye on the law enforcement officers.

"Old Sully wouldn't hurt nobody either," he told them.

Creed had to agree. Gunner's owner had slowed considerably. His pace had petered out to a stumble-run. The cartwheeling arms now stretched in front of him as he grabbed onto and leaned against trees, using them to pull himself along.

"Maybe I'd believe you if you'd put that knife away," Norwich said.

"Will you put your guns down?"

Creed looked over his shoulder. Bolo sat calmly, still watching the guy, but not with his earlier urgency.

Norwich looked at Bolo, too, then caught Creed's eyes. Slowly, she lowered her weapon. To her deputy, she said, "Let's stand down. But stay ready."

Finally, the young man folded the knife and dropped it into his jacket pocket. That's when Creed noticed the faded denim jacket was too small on the guy. The sleeves came inches above his wrists and pulled tight across his back.

Creed looked over at Norwich and her deputy, but both turned their attention to the man stumbling his way closer.

"And who exactly is Sully?" Norwich asked. Her bangs stuck to the sweat of her forehead. The rest of her steel-gray hair was pulled back into a ponytail sticking out the back of her Santa Rosa Sheriff ball cap. Lean and nimble even after a heart attack six months ago, Norwich had a calm but authoritarian stature and approach. "Is he the owner of this property?"

"He's one of the old-timers. He has a nice set-up."

And he hadn't answered her question.

Norwich exchanged a glance with Creed, that made him almost expect an eyeroll. But she kept her face expressionless, as much for her deputy as for the young man. Both were focused on Sully, while Creed watched the spot where the dog named Gunner had gone silent.

As its owner got closer, Creed held back a smile, recognizing the swish of grass as a tail wagging. He could see the hunched back slowly rising. A black snout poked between the green and red of a holly bush. But again, the dog waited, the grasses waving and twirling, the closer the owner got.

The man named Sully stopped and placed his hands on his knees. He wheezed and gasped for breath. Feather-white hair stuck to his scalp in a band of sweat where a hat or cap had recently been. His skin reminded Creed of worn leather, brown and creased with lines in his forehead and at the corners of his eyes. Bushy eyebrows were more gray than white.

Creed wasn't good at guessing anyone's age, but the man was older than Creed expected. When his head bobbed up with the rest of his body, his chest still heaved. He looked over at them, and his eyes didn't quite track like they should, which probably accounted for that awkward run.

"Gunner," he said. "Come on over here."

The dog obeyed, and they finally got a good look at the animal. A mixture of brown, Gunner surprisingly stood a foot shorter than Bolo.

Creed guessed it was a terrier mix with short floppy ears and a wiry coat that stood up on its head like the dog had just gotten out of bed. There was one other surprise. Gunner was a girl.

She definitely attracted Bolo's attention. The Ridgeback approached with purpose, his nose twitching and sniffing without a signal from Creed. Only now, Creed realized what drew Bolo's interest. It wasn't the dog. It was the bone Gunner proudly displayed, clenched in her teeth.

Sully noticed, too. "She found that this morning," he told them. The man was still trying to catch his breath. Another wheeze came from his throat, and his chest moved underneath the threadbare shirt. "Been parading around with it. What's going on here?"

Bolo had led them to the young guy with the knife, but now his nose worked overtime. He moved tentatively, sniffing the other dog, no longer interested in his initial target. He leaned so close he triggered a growl from Gunner.

"Are we going to have a problem here, Mr. Creed?" Norwich asked.

Creed readied himself, but he didn't interrupt. He hoped he didn't need to. A few more sniffs, and Bolo turned back around, then sat at Creed's feet. He waved his nose toward the bone in Gunner's mouth. At the same time, he tapped the ground with his paw.

"Mr. Sully, where did your dog find that bone?" Creed asked.

"Somewhere out in the woods. Looks to me like a bear."

"I don't think it's a bear." Creed looked back at Norwich and gestured to Bolo sitting at his feet. "Bolo doesn't alert to animal bones."

He watched her do a double take, looking from the bone to Bolo, then finding Creed's eyes. She understood.

"So, what exactly is he saying?" the deputy asked. It hadn't quite registered with him, and he stared at his boss, waiting for an explanation.

Creed answered for her. "Bolo tracks missing people, but he's also a cadaver dog."

4

Washington, D.C.

FBI agent Maggie O'Dell turned the corner and immediately felt the cold slap her in the face. More snow was on the way. But there was something else in the air. A disgusting smell rode the wind. People on the street had their scarves pulled up or their hands over their noses. As usual, steam escaped from the grates in the sidewalk, but that wasn't where the odor was coming from.

She showed her badge to the officer standing guard at the first barrier to the crime scene.

"Is that a sewage leak?" she asked him as she lifted the yellow tape and slipped underneath.

"Dumpster." He gestured back behind him. "City maintenance dozer plowed into it. Knocked it so hard it tipped over on its side." He rolled his eyes and added, "Last week, one of them picked up a homeless tent with someone still in it."

"I heard about that."

"O'Dell." Julia Racine waved at her.

The detective already looked perturbed and impatient. And it was only ten in the morning. But that was Racine. Maggie knew much of her abrasive behavior was for show. Even her stance—legs set at shoulders-width, arms crossed—telegraphed her tough-as-nails reputation. She was finishing up with a young man who looked like he was enduring a reprimand. He would have been taller than Racine if his narrow shoulders weren't slouched up almost to his ears trying to defend himself from the cold and snow.

"Special Agent O'Dell, this is Detective Sheldon," Racine introduced them.

He nodded at Maggie, then to Racine, he said, "I'll get that taken care of right away." And he left in the direction Maggie had just come from.

"Does the Dumpster have anything to do with the crime?" Maggie asked. The smell only seemed to get worse.

"The asshat who dumped it found the body."

"Asshat?" Maggie raised an eyebrow.

"Yeah, I know. It's disgusting how much my language has been sanitized. That's what happens, O'Dell, when you give in and live with someone's munchkin. You were smart to dump your doctor."

Racine was referring to Dr. Benjamin Platt, although he and Maggie had never been in an actual relationship. Ben had a daughter once upon a time and wanted someone who wanted to have kids. That wasn't Maggie. Racine's significant other had a daughter. Maggie couldn't remember the girl's name, but knew she was still in elementary school.

"So, she's a good influence," Maggie said.

"She's a horrible influence." Racine glanced around before she continued. "You know how hard it already is as a woman to be taken seriously in this job. Now, she has me saying things like 'rats' and 'OMG.' It's just not right."

"I think you'll survive."

"I heard there's a new guy in your life."

Maggie and Racine weren't friends. But they'd worked enough cases together over the years, and they had a history. In Racine's mind, that made her think they were. Maggie, however, preferred to keep her private life private.

When she didn't answer, Racine continued like a response wasn't necessary. "Sounds like you're trading in your doctor for a dog handler." She gave Maggie a sidelong glance, then added, "Not a bad idea." Racine being Racine weighing in with her unsolicited opinion didn't stop there. "I heard he's hot."

Maggie wanted to ask where the information was coming from, but to do that would only make Racine believe the topic was open for discussion. It was not. Certainly not with Racine.

"Are you lead on this case?" Maggie asked, attempting to steer Racine back to business.

"Yes. And it's getting stupid-crazy fast. That's why my boss is anxious to offload it."

Maggie guessed "stupid-crazy" was one of the new alternate phrases. "Victim was homeless?"

"Not homeless, O'Dell. Unhoused or unsheltered are the politically correct terms. How is that any better? As far as we can tell, he was living on the street. My officers are still talking to people. And these people are the worst at sharing information.

"Even when they do talk, we have to be careful. They're very good liars. Seriously, the CIA should be recruiting from the streets. Guy can be knifed in the tent right next to them, and they claim they haven't seen or heard a thing.

"To be fair, some of them are so zoned out, stoned or drunk they might not have seen a thing. They aren't even plugged in to reality. And those who do still know what's what, they frickin' don't want to get involved."

Maggie restrained a smile. It was weird listening to Racine without her using the f-word.

"Chances are, they wouldn't have even reported it," the detective continued. "Took the Dumpster crasher to notice. Probably why he plowed into it in the first place. He's young. A little shocked. Not used to seeing dead guys."

"You said on the phone this is number two?"

"Ten days ago. Three blocks away. Similar MO."

"Victim was also homeless?"

Racine nodded. "I know the holidays bring out the homicidal maniacs, but I sure as hell didn't expect a serial killer."

"What do you know about the killer? Anything caught on video from ten days ago?" Maggie's eyes darted under the awnings of the small businesses dotted along the street. At the end of the block was a three-story brick building. She made a mental note to check for surveillance cameras.

"Preliminary search didn't tag anyone suspicious or out of the ordinary. In fact, I was starting to think he might be homeless, too. Possibly mentally ill. Maybe it was revenge for something trivial. Happens, you know. They have belongings and can be very possessive of their stuff."

"Weapon?"

"Weapons. Neither one has been recovered. Last week's victim had blunt trauma to the back of his head. M.E. said it looked like a ball-peen hammer. But it wasn't the cause of death. May have been used to incapacitate him. There were no defensive wounds. He was stabbed. Double-edged blade. Three to five inches."

"That one happened at night, too?"

"Early morning. M.E. doesn't think he died immediately, so if we back up from approximate time of death, we're looking at midnight to three or four in the morning."

"No one noticed him bleeding on the street?"

"Actually, he was inside his tent. Makeshift tent. Basically, a blue tarp draped over a cardboard box. It wasn't until he crawled partially out that someone saw him. Called 911."

"And today's victim?"

"We think he was sleeping against the lamppost, close to the sidewalk grate to keep warm. About five feet away from the Dumpster. Looks like the same MO. Hit on the back of the head. Then stabbed."

Maggie scanned the area. Cars parked on this side of the street would have given a limited view of anyone asleep on the sidewalk. Two- and three-story brick buildings were broken up by a few businesses. A nail shop, deli and grocer, a coffee shop interspersed, all with several concrete steps up to the front doors. Some with canvas awnings. None had entrance doors at ground level. Not that any of them would have been open at the time of the murders.

"Tell me about the victims," Maggie said.

"Both male. This one looks to be in his thirties. Last one was older. Maybe forties. No ID on him. Prints didn't register. No hits from NamUS."

NamUs was a national database for missing, unidentified and unclaimed cases from across the United States.

Racine pointed to an area where a CSU team was still working and said, "This morning's guy was found tucked in over there. Like I said. Not far from the Dumpster."

But the body was gone. Maggie wished Racine had called her sooner. Examining the crime scene with the body would have been helpful.

"Is there a shelter nearby?"

"Where've you been O'Dell? Shelters can't keep up. Besides, a lot of these people don't like rules to begin with, so getting clean, sober or finding Jesus is not on their to-do lists. The city keeps moving them off the streets. They just show up somewhere else. Don't even get me started."

Maggie decided she needed to get it off her chest. "Why didn't you call me before they moved the body?"

"Hey, I've got orders to clean things up and clean them up quick. I'm not sure if the powers-that-be were more upset about another homeless body or the overturned Dumpster. When I mentioned calling in the Feds on account of the similarities, I could literally hear my boss' sigh of relief."

"My team's going to want all the evidence you collected along with today's."

"Not a problem. Glad to hand over whatever you need. So, can I tell him you're on board?"

"One other condition."

"Name it."

"You learn something new. You call me immediately."

"No problem."

"I'm serious, Racine. I should have been here before the body left the crime scene."

"You're right. My bad." She put up her hands in surrender, and Maggie couldn't help wondering if this was a newly learned behavior that came with the language clean up.

"Detective Racine." One of her officers called out. He was in hazmat coveralls and standing in the middle of the garbage pile. "We might have found something."

Neither Racine nor Maggie hesitated.

As they got closer, Maggie could see the plastic bag he held in his gloved hands. It opened enough to show a piece of fabric. The blood looked fresh. The bulge at the bottom suggested there were other items in the bag.

"Now, this is interesting. Did he really think we wouldn't go through the Dumpster?" Racine asked.

"Maybe not today," the officer told her. "It was pretty full. Coffee shop owner said pickup is normally before noon. If it got dumped before we got here, it'd be a nightmare to track down and go through."

"Do you think the killer knew that?" Racine asked Maggie with an intense look that expected the profiler to be worth the early morning visit to her crime scene.

Maggie glanced at her, but her eyes stayed on the bag dangling from the officer's hand. "He may have known and took advantage of the disposal. Or…"

"Or what?"

"Or he simply didn't care." Maggie's gut instinct told her it was the latter.

"Either way," Racine said, "it looks like that young asshat who crashed into the Dumpster may have given us a lucky break."

5

Santa Rosa County, Florida

"No way! That's a human bone?" Deputy Greer seemed a bit freaked out, and Creed wondered how long he'd been in law enforcement.

"Gunner, drop that." The man named Sully bent over his dog and pointed to the ground.

She relinquished the bone as he dug deep into the pocket of his baggy pants and brought something that looked like the corner of a dried out sandwich. Whatever it was, Gunner reluctantly made the trade. Sully picked up the bone with no hesitancy and handed it to Norwich.

From her daypack, the sheriff yanked out a pair of latex gloves. She pulled them on and dug in the pack again until she found an evidence bag. In the meantime, Creed started to retrieve Bolo's reward toy. The dog may not have found what his handler had asked for, but he did alert to a scent he'd been trained to find.

Before Creed fingered the toy, he noticed Bolo had repositioned himself to face Hogan. His nose twitched, pointed up, and sniffed directly in the man's direction. Hogan had his back to the dog and focused on the exchange of the bone from Sully to Norwich. But Bolo was no longer interested in the bone. Instead, he inched forward until his nose almost touched the hem of Hogan's jacket.

The final snort got everyone's attention, especially Hogan's. He wheeled around, almost losing his balance. But Bolo was finished. He patted the ground at Hogan's feet, then look over his shoulder to Creed, making sure his handler noticed.

Just as Hogan started to dig in his pocket for the knife again, Norwich stopped him, putting up her gloved hand. "Hold on." Then to Creed, she said, "Looks like your dog is still trying to tell us something."

"I didn't do nothing wrong."

"Hush up," Sully told the younger man, and it was clear this was finally someone Hogan would listen to.

Before Creed responded, Norwich addressed the two men now casually without letting on that they were squatting on private property.

"Mr. Creed and his scent dog are here helping us find a missing teenager. A witness claims the boy ran behind the Red Roof Inn and into the woods early this morning."

She paused, as if sealing the evidence bag required her full attention. But Creed knew Norwich was studying the men's reactions. Hogan's eyes darted to the old man, but he had been acting strangely since they arrived. Sully, to his credit, didn't flinch.

Norwich continued, "His parents are awfully worried about him. He's only fifteen. Kind of small. Maybe five three, five four. Dark hair. Blue eyes. His name's Caleb Monroe."

"I didn't see no runaway boy this morning," Sully offered.

"Are there other staying out here? In the woods?" she asked, again casually, no recriminations or accusations.

Sully shrugged. "Sometimes. It's hard to find a quiet place where people won't bother you. Gunner and me try not to bother anybody in return." The dog looked up expectantly at the sound of her name. Sully waited, not backing down and holding eye contact with the sheriff. "Are we in trouble, Sheriff?"

"Some of this land is private property," she told him and paused. Sully only nodded. "Right now, I'm only looking for the boy." Then Norwich lifted the evidence bag. "And you'll need to show me where your dog found this bone."

"Sure, sure. I can do that." He fingered his chin, already trying to remember.

Hogan fidgeted, and the deputy stood stock-still, his weapon holstered but his hands on his waist as if he might need to be ready to draw again.

During this whole exchange, Bolo hadn't moved. When Creed glanced down at him, the dog tapped his paw again and wagged his snout in Hogan's direction. He looked up at Creed. Another tap as if to say, *Why aren't you getting this?*

"Sheriff," Creed said. "Do you know what Caleb was wearing the last time anyone saw him?"

Norwich glanced over. She noticed Bolo, his nose back up, sniffing and all but pointing. Then she took a hard look at Hogan.

"That jacket seems a bit small for you."

6

"I didn't steal it!" Hogan tugged at the jacket, pulling it together over his chest, trying unsuccessfully to make the sides come together.

"But it's not yours?" Norwich asked.

He teetered on the balls of his feet, and Creed thought he might run. He looked even younger now with this fresh panic. His eyes darted between Bolo and Deputy Greer, who had his weapon unholstered again.

"I found it," Hogan said too loudly and pointed. "It was right there on the mattress. Nobody else was around. I didn't see no teenager. And I found the jacket tossed in the middle of that mattress. Somebody threw it away. People throw away really good stuff."

"Slow down, Hogan. Sheriff," Sully stepped forward. "I can vouch for this young man." Despite the gravelly, deep voice and the eyes that didn't quite focus, the old man sounded like a gentleman diplomat, if you discounted the worn-out cargo pants and the stained T-shirt. "I can tell you, as long as I've known him, he's never taken anything that hasn't been left behind."

Left behind. It was an interesting phrase.

Creed glanced at his dog. Bolo seemed content.

As Norwich questioned the two men, Creed couldn't shake the feeling that something wasn't right. He'd asked Bolo to find Caleb Monroe using a sweatshirt the family had given Sheriff Norwich. They started the search from the entrance to the woods behind The Red Roof Inn's parking lot. Someone at the Waffle House next door claimed to see a teenager matching Caleb's description walk across the lot and into the woods.

He tried to remember how far they'd walked before Bolo caught the scent and took off. It wasn't in the parking lot. Not at the edge of the woods. But Bolo led them directly to Hogan. Well, not Hogan, but the jacket he was wearing. Caleb's jacket.

Now Hogan was repeating himself and over explaining why he'd put it on.

"People throw away some really good stuff," he told Norwich.

Creed tuned out their conversation. He didn't care if Hogan was lying or not. Instead, he tried to figure out why Bolo led them to the jacket and stopped. If Caleb took the jacket off and left it on the mattress, where did Caleb go from here?

Creed scanned the woods, then his attention came back to the mattress. Trash spilled out around it. In fact, the mattress itself appeared to be lopsided and seesawing on top of whatever was underneath.

Suddenly, a cold shiver slid down Creed's back. He turned and examined his dog.

Trust your dog. It was a phrase he drilled into his handlers.

Was it the jacket Bolo had originally alerted to? Or was it the mattress? Had Creed missed it? Was it possible that Caleb Monroe's body was the lump underneath?

He tamped down his suspicion and tried to keep his pulse from ticking up. Bolo was watching him, concerned that his handler was starting to smell like panic. Or was he simply waiting for him to turn over the mattress?

"Sheriff," Creed said, interrupting a conversation that had gotten drowned out by his argument with himself.

Norwich looked over and immediately was concerned. "What is it?"

"Probably nothing," he told her, his hand automatically flattening at his side to tell Bolo everything was fine and to relax. "I'd feel a lot better if we had a look under this mattress."

The color drained from the sheriff's face, and instinctively, everyone else stepped back.

"Deputy Greer," Norwich instructed. "Can you carefully flip that mattress over?"

Creed moved to assist, but the deputy quickly stopped him, purposely stepping in front of Creed as if to make a point. "I've got this."

"Wait!" Hogan became agitated again. "You think that kid is hiding underneath there?"

The others ignored him, all focused on the dirty, ripped mattress, but Creed kept an eye on him. Hogan was either still flying high, knew more than he was telling, or maybe just a little slow. Creed glanced at Bolo. He hadn't moved. If anything, the dog looked bored.

Deputy Greer stalled, pulling on latex gloves, then planted his feet and squared his shoulders. He looked like he was preparing to deadlift a loaded barbell from his gym floor. The flimsy mattress would be an awkward grab, but not heavy. Creed wondered how many dead bodies the deputy had seen. He wanted to reach around the guy and simply flip the damned thing over just to stop his churning stomach.

"Deputy Greer." Norwich was getting impatient, too.

He gripped the edge and flung it, upending a cloud of leaves and dirt and garbage. Something small and alive scurried out from the debris pile and into the grass. Bolo's and Gunner's ears pitched, but neither dog pursued.

A musty scent filled the air, mixed with a rancid tang. Creed drew in a sigh of relief almost at the same time as Norwich. One thing was certain. The smell didn't include human decomp.

The garbage dump consisted of fast-food wrappers, bulging plastic bags, bottles, cans and foam takeout containers scrambled together with mounds of decaying leaves and brush. No dead body.

Hogan's bunched up shoulders finally relaxed. Deputy Greer wiped sweat off his forehead with the back of his gloved hand. Norwich nodded to the men.

Creed was relieved his dog had done a good job. But something still bothered him. How did Caleb Monroe come down into these woods, discard his jacket on this mattress, then disappear without leaving a scent?

7

Washington, D.C.

Snow began to fall, and Maggie pulled her ball cap down tighter. Her eyes tracked along the buildings as she walked, searching for surveillance cameras.

The collar on her FBI jacket was already turned up, but wet flakes still slid down her neck. It was only December, and she was tired of the cold. It felt like she couldn't warm up ever since getting caught in an early October snowstorm back in the middle of Nebraska.

Other than instilling a bone-deep chill, that blizzard had revealed a lot of things for her personally. Her friend, Gwen Patterson, often said a crisis pushed people to show their true selves. It churned up and sifted out what was trivial, then brought to the top all that was real—what mattered most. A sort of push-come-to-shove analogy.

For Maggie, that storm and what was lost in it, forced her to admit some things to herself. It wasn't until she'd almost lost Ryder Creed that she realized how very much she needed him. That was a hard pill to swallow considering she'd spent the last ten years convincing herself she didn't need anyone else.

Two months later, she still wasn't comfortable with that admission.

"You FBI?" a woman's voice called out from behind Maggie.

When she turned around, it took her a minute to find the woman. She had tucked herself alongside the concrete stairs to a small coffee shop. An awning over the entrance protected her from the snow. It looked like she was wearing every piece of clothing she owned. Her small face scrunched between a pink scarf and a knit cap.

"Yes, I am," Maggie told her.

"You don't look FBI."

"Sometimes that helps."

The woman didn't smile at Maggie's attempt at humor, but she nodded like she understood exactly what Maggie meant.

Since she made no effort to move, Maggie backtracked until she was a few feet in front of her.

"You working with those other cops? Cause all they wanna do is move us out. They don't care where we go as long as we're not in their way. They don't even care about Danny. They just dragged him out of here in that bag like he was nothing."

"Did you know Danny?"

The woman's eyes flicked to the side, and she pursed her lips together. Mentioning his name may have been a slip of the tongue. If Maggie remembered correctly, Racine's team didn't even have a name connected to the victim, yet.

"I don't know anything about nothing," she said, shaking her head and crossing her arms over her bundled chest.

Despite the slip, she'd called out to Maggie. Maybe she just needed prompting.

"It's really cold out here. You want to get a cup of coffee?" Maggie gestured to the door on the left and three stairs up from them. Morning rush was over. From what Maggie could see, there were plenty of empty tables.

"They don't allow us in there."

"I doubt they'll say anything if you're with an FBI agent."

The woman looked up and held Maggie's eyes, studying her as if searching for a trap.

"I can't leave my things." She pointed to a battered canvas tote and a plastic garbage bag tied up in a way to leave a handle at the top.

"Bring them along." Maggie moved to the front of the stairs, leaving the railing side for the woman to join her. She was tempted to help carry her things, but stopped herself. She didn't want to look pushy or worse—anxious about whatever information she had.

When the woman stood, she was barely five-foot tall, but she knew how to leverage the bags over her slumped shoulder and under her arm. She followed, one step then two, stopping to look up and examine Maggie again. Her head swiveled back to the street, checking if she'd missed a setup. Even as Maggie held the door open for her, she came through slowly, eyes now darting to the employees, expecting someone to shout and tell her to leave.

The man behind the counter simply nodded when he realized the two were together. Maggie chose a table in the corner where no one was in earshot. And there was extra space for the woman to deposit her bags and keep them close.

Maggie shrugged out of her jacket and sat down. The woman didn't remove a single piece of clothing, but she pulled down the scarf beneath her chin.

"I'm Maggie, by the way. What's your name?"

"Years ago, they called me Vanessa. Now I go by Nessie."

"I'll get us a couple cups of coffee. How do you like yours?"

"Hot would be nice."

Maggie smiled and waited. Then she realized she was serious. That was her only request. All Nessie cared about was that the coffee be hot.

8

Maggie kept Nessie in her peripheral vision while she ordered. The woman watched out the window but glanced at the door. Was she worried someone might see her with an FBI agent? Maybe she was having second thoughts and considered bolting.

Maggie brought a tray with the coffees, along with a plate of freshly baked doughnuts and assorted pastries.

"I wasn't sure what you'd like," she explained, "So, I got a few of each."

She saw something flicker across the woman's face that surprised her. Something childlike. The tight line of her mouth eased and almost curved up. She clapped her mittened-hands together before she caught herself. Though she still hadn't taken off any of her outer wear, she now carefully pulled off the thick mittens. She set them aside, her eyes not leaving the freshly baked goods, as if she expected them to vanish as easily as they appeared.

Then she sat back and inhaled. Finally, she looked up at Maggie.

"You're bribing me to talk about Danny." But there wasn't a trace of suspicion or accusation in her voice. Instead, she gave an admirable nod to Maggie's tactics.

"Actually, I haven't had breakfast," Maggie admitted and helped herself to a cake doughnut with chocolate frosting. Then she pushed the plate closer to Nessie.

The woman wrapped her fingers around the ceramic mug, enjoying its warmth before she brought it to her lips for a careful sip. Tentatively, she set the mug aside and took up a fork from the tray to lift her choice from the plate, putting it onto a napkin. Maggie wasn't sure if Nessie was being prim and proper for her sake or to prove she was still capable.

"I only knew him from Lydia's Kitchen."

"Lydia's Kitchen?"

"They serve hot meals once a day during the week."

"You said his name was Danny?"

"Mm huh," she mumbled around a small bite of glazed crueler, closing her eyes and taking her time.

"Do you know his last name?"

"Don't know anybody's last name. Only noticed Danny a couple of weeks ago because he made such a fuss. He's a strange one."

"What do you mean, a fuss?"

"He got loud. A bit cankerous. Made a scene at Lydia's. Accused Lewis of giving him less than the rest of us." She shook her head. The pompon on top of her knit cap bobbed. "Lewis is the most honest man I know in D.C. It wasn't right. Danny making such a fuss. So many of these young ones are flying high on things I can't even pronounce."

"Was there an argument between Lewis and Danny?"

"Oh, no. Lydia and Lewis are kind and generous to a fault. They let Danny rant and then he went and sat down and ate his food. Don't get me wrong, they would have called the cops if Danny didn't back off. They run one of the safest places around. They can't help it that their meatloaf tastes like crap."

"Do you remember what day this happened?"

"Well, it wasn't the weekend, because the kitchen's not open. Maybe last Thursday or Friday?"

"They don't serve meals on the weekends?"

"Nope." She popped a piece of the pastry in her mouth and washed it down with the coffee.

"Do you think it's possible the person who did this is someone in the homeless community?"

"I don't think he's homeless, if that's what you're asking."

"Why do you say that?"

"Just my gut instinct. I wasn't always homeless. I used to be somebody. When I was at State, they all knew I was good at figuring people out. Pretenders, imitators, charmers, and cons…it was pretty hard to fool me." She paused to take another bite, but raised her finger to indicate she had something more to add. "It's not necessarily a stellar personality trait, by the way, especially when your boss is one of the pretenders."

She made a good point. Maggie's past boss could easily fit that category. She held back her reaction to Nessie's claim that she worked at the State Department. Racine said the homeless weren't reliable witnesses.

"They lie," was what Racine had told Maggie. "Drugs. Alcohol. Messes with them. Sometimes they don't know what's real, what's not."

Still, Maggie was interested in what this woman had to say. Maybe the victim's name wasn't even Danny, but it was more than they had to go on an hour ago.

"He seems to blend in," Maggie said.

Nessie shook her head. "Doesn't mean he's one of us. Just that he has a bone to pick. Wants to get rid of us. On a mission or something."

"From what I know, there's nothing ritualistic left behind."

"FBI. I should have known. Profiler, right?" Before Maggie could answer, Nessie stuck her tongue out and blew her a raspberry. "Pfft! Your vast knowledge is causing your tunnel vision."

"How can you be so sure he's not a part of the homeless community?"

"It doesn't make sense. For one thing, why would he whack Carlo? Danny, sure. But everybody liked Carlo. He didn't deserve that."

"Wait a minute. You knew the other man who was killed?"

"We all knew Carlo. He's been on the street longer than most of us."

"Did you tell the police any of this?"

Nessie sent the pompom swinging again as she shook her head. "Police don't do us any good. They just want us off the street." She took another bite.

"Then why are you telling me?"

"I like the way you talked to that policewoman. She thought she was in charge until you came along." Nessie raised an eyebrow at Maggie as she said, "Pretty obvious that you're the one in charge."

9

Peter Gregory had been watching the woman in the FBI ball cap and jacket. He'd never had the FBI join his crime scenes before. He wasn't sure whether to be thrilled or disappointed. Or terrified.

It usually got boring after they took the body away. What did he expect? He chose throwaway victims for a reason. There was little follow-up. Cops didn't waste much time on dead people nobody missed. In fact, this morning, everyone looked more upset about the garbage spilled all over the street.

Although finding his throwaway bag in the Dumpster was something he didn't expect. It was a good thing he was so careful.

Nothing to see in there.

He'd made sure of that. Ended up being anti-climactic. All their thrills would quickly dissipate.

Even the FBI woman had already gotten bored and taken a coffee break. She was so desperate to escape the cold, she bribed one of the street people to join her.

The FBI? He had to admit he was intrigued. What did that mean?

He pulled out his pocket-sized notebook. His new gloves were bulkier than the ones he'd just thrown away, but these were nice and toasty. Without taking them off, he jotted down a couple of details he found interesting. Then he underlined the top one. Usually he avoided D.C.'s souvenir shops, but he bet he could buy an FBI ball cap in one of them.

He tucked the notebook away. This new jacket was warmer, too. The last one drove him crazy with too many pockets, most of them with zippers and some pockets with hidden pockets inside. The only thing he hadn't replaced yet was his shoes. He glanced up at the coffee shop windows as he walked by.

Around the corner, and up the street, was his favorite secondhand store. Miriam's Thrift Shop had the best selections and still gave out handwritten receipts from a pad, perforated at the top, where they tore it off and handed it to you. He didn't know such a thing still existed. He'd asked about it once, pretending to make small talk with the old woman named Miriam who owned the store. She told him their donated inventory changed too much to entertain computerizing it. Then she added, "I've been doing it this way for thirty years, and I'm not fixing something that's not broken."

It was one of the genuinely honest things anyone had said to him in a long time. It was Gregory's experience that people lied more often than they needed to. And in a city known for its professional liars, he appreciated the woman telling it like it was.

The winter gear was mostly picked through. He'd bought extra jackets and gloves three weeks ago. His locker at the YMCA was stocked. It helped that the two places were so close.

He bought things one at a time. Always cash, crumpled and saggy dollar bills and an assortment of coins, so it looked like he had to scrape just to buy whatever he chose that day. He went on different days and at a variety of times, so the store clerks didn't recognize how often he came in.

He kept his presence on the down low, but he took time to check out the clerks and even the regular customers. Today, a balding guy named Randy was working close to the sneakers. He wore a sweater vest, purple-framed glasses, and scuffed loafers.

Gregory picked at a few pairs before selecting the ones he already knew he wanted. He was about to head to the checkout stand when Randy decided to be helpful.

"Those are a bit too big for you. We have some more in the back if you want me to check."

"No, these are good. They're for a buddy."

"Oh sure. Have a great day then." And Randy headed off in the other direction.

Would Randy remember him? Would he remember the shoes? He'd obviously paid enough attention to notice they were too big for Gregory.

He wandered around the busy store. It was better that it was crowded. No time for guys like Randy to pay him much attention. Especially when some of those coming in were just getting out of the cold. Miriam's regular bargain hunters didn't necessarily appreciate mingling with street people.

Gregory grabbed a couple pairs of thick socks to roll into the toes of his new shoes. These were a size smaller than the ones he'd tossed in the Dumpster. That FBI woman looked excited when they found his tossed bag.

He smiled at the thought of CSU techs casting the shoe print, searching retailers and hoping to find the killer by tracking down his footprint and footwear. How long would it take them to figure out he'd worn the slightly used thrift store shoes for less than three hours? Shoes that weren't really his. That didn't even come close to the size of his foot.

Big flakes fell covering the sidewalks as he walked the three blocks to the parking garage. The adrenaline was already dissipating. By the time he slipped behind the wheel of his Mercedes, he was cold and hungry. He hadn't eaten since last night. He'd go back to the house, take a hot shower, then order his favorite takeout. And if he was lucky, he'd sleep, spent and exhausted for a few hours before the reel in his brain began all over again.

10

Santa Rosa County, Florida

"So, this is as far as the scent goes?" Norwich asked when she took Creed aside. She left Deputy Greer to bag Caleb's jacket. The other two men watched and waited. Gunner had fallen asleep in the grass, and Bolo seemed fascinated by her snoring.

"Yes," Creed finally answered.

"That's a bit odd, isn't it?"

Creed and his handler, Jason Seaver, had worked scent dogs for enough cases with Sheriff Norwich that she knew how things worked.

"It is. I don't have an answer."

She glanced back at Bolo. Now he was dozing in a patch of sunlight alongside Gunner.

"Could the boy have gone back up the way he came into the woods?"

"That's a possibility. When did your eyewitness say this happened?"

"The boy's been gone two nights. An anonymous caller claimed to see him late last night."

"Doesn't make sense he'd leave his jacket."

"There is something else." She hesitated. "I haven't mentioned this, because I know you prefer to know less about the victim."

"It makes it easier. If I make assumptions, I might mislead my dog."

"Sure, sure. I understand. And I respect that. But I could use a fresh perspective on where we go from here."

Creed nodded. "Okay."

"This boy's home life is not great. Over the past year, my deputies have been called to the family's house twice. Once was a domestic dispute with his mother and father. Another was between Caleb and his father. There are two younger children. I've been told that Caleb has run away before. Not officially, but I can't help wondering if there have been other times."

"Who told you he's run away before?"

"The father. The mother didn't deny it."

"What do they say this time?"

"They disagree. Quite a bit, actually. Mrs. Monroe claims Caleb didn't come home and hasn't answered her phone calls or texts. She said that's very unusual, and she's worried he might be hurt and unable to answer. Mr. Monroe says the boy's been hanging around some bad influencers. Got a tattoo. Won't listen anymore. Gets angry about not getting his way. Claims he stomped off to cool off."

"Did he give you any names of the bad influencers?"

"Couldn't come up with a single one."

"Can a fifteen-year-old get a tattoo without a parent's consent?"

"No, but that doesn't stop them."

"What was the tattoo?"

She pursed her lips to think. Realized she didn't know and said, "That's a good question. I'll make sure it gets added to the description. One thing I will say, they both were a little odd when I asked for a piece of Caleb's clothing. I swear the mother went white as a ghost. Almost like she believed that somehow meant we were looking for a dead body. Shortly after that, we got the tip about someone seeing Caleb. I'm sure she was relieved to hear that."

"You think he ran away?"

"I think it's a strong possibility."

"We could do a fresh search and start from the family's house."

She reached out and patted his arm. "I was hoping you'd say something like that."

"As long as you understand, his scent is going to be all over that neighborhood. Chances are, the dog will only lead us to the places Caleb's been to over the last week. We still might not find him."

She nodded, and her expression told him she hadn't thought of that.

"You and your dogs make it seem like magic sometimes. I need to remind myself how many times—like today—that we don't find what we're looking for. Well, not exactly anyway. Your dog did find Caleb's scent. But no Caleb."

She twisted her wrist to check her watch. "I need Mr. Sully to take me to where his dog found that bone. I'm afraid if I don't do it now, he'll disappear into the landscape. And if that bone is human, I'll be asking you and one of your dogs to do that search as well."

"Jason and I can split up searches." Creed was already thinking that Jason's dog, Scout, might be a better choice if they needed to start in a residential area. Scout had better manners than Bolo.

He missed Grace. Creed and the Jack Russell had worked together so well she knew what to look for before Creed even asked. She'd gotten injured two months ago, taking a brutal kick to the side. Dr. Avelyn, their veterinarian, said Grace was ready to return to duty, but Creed was stalling. She'd told him that almost a week ago. Grace was getting impatient. Even Hannah looked impatient with him.

He didn't want to think about putting Grace at risk again. Obviously, it was his hang-up, not Grace's.

To keep his mind off the subject, he said to the sheriff, "I didn't know homeless people were living out here."

"Not many. But there are a few. When they booted them out from under the I-110 bridge, they scattered. Out here they're mostly peaceful.

We haven't had too many incidents or complaints…yet. But if a property owner asks that we remove them, we do so."

"Sully seems like a nice man. But Hogan is definitely on drugs, right?"

"His pupils are so constricted you can barely see them. Pinpoint pupils can be a sign of opioids."

"You're not going to arrest either of them, are you?"

"No. Not today anyway. I used to think I was doing them a favor. Giving them a warm place to sleep and three square meals. But if they wanted that, they'd be staying in one of the shelters."

"Do you know if Caleb's been using drugs?"

"Good question." She glanced over her shoulder at Hogan. "I'm gonna be pissed if this is some new meeting place that I haven't heard about. Clearly, drugs are accessible." Then she looked back at Creed. "You sure you're not interested in becoming a law enforcement officer? We could sure use someone with your eye for detail. Lord knows, I could use some help." She jerked her chin in the direction of Deputy Greer.

"Sorry, Sheriff. I don't think I'd have the patience."

"Yeah, I don't blame you. You're smart working with dogs. They get along better than people." She smiled and pointed to Bolo and Gunner. Side by side, both dogs were sleeping in the grass.

11

As Norwich questioned Hogan about Caleb and where exactly he'd found the boy's jacket, Creed stayed close to Bolo and Gunner and the man named Sully. He pulled a bottle of water and a collapsible bowl from his daypack. After he filled the bowl, he offered it to Gunner. Bolo sat up but waited his turn even when Creed rinsed the empty bowl, then refilled it.

He reached into his pack again and pulled out two more bottles, this one for himself and the second bottle he handed to Sully.

The man was still surprised by the gesture to his dog. He hesitantly took the bottle and mumbled a "thanks." Creed simply nodded and drank his own. Out of the corner of his eye he saw Sully lick his lips, slowly twist the cap and sip. When he noticed Creed had downed more than half of his, Sully tipped it back and gulped.

Normally, Creed wouldn't feed Bolo out here. Not unless they were starting a new search. Usually, he'd wait until they got back to his Jeep. He made an exception and dug a plastic Ziploc out of his pack. Bolo was drooling water when he noticed and accepted the treat. Just as casually as he had done with the water, he held out a piece of the homemade dog treat to Sully.

"My business partner makes these," Creed explained. "They're protein bars for the dogs, but she uses human grade ingredients."

When the man hesitated, Creed took a bite of one. Again, Sully stared, then nodded and took the offering. He broke it and handed a salivating Gunner one piece while he popped the other into his mouth.

Sully chewed and swallowed, trying to pretend it was no big deal, but clearly, he wasn't sure how to respond to Creed's generosity. "Your partner," he finally said, "she's a pretty good baker."

"You should taste her cornbread."

"My wife used to make skillet cornbread with black-eyed peas and collard greens. Mmm...I could have eaten that all day long."

"Used to?"

"She's been gone a good long while." He looked off in the direction he'd come from, and suddenly his entire body seemed to slouch with sadness. "She taught me how to make a wicked good bowl of rice and beans. Grateful for that these days."

"There's a place in Pensacola called the Segway House. My partner helps run it. They have some pretty good meals."

"Yeah, most of those places don't allow dogs. They make you sign up for stuff. Or they put you in a room with no windows. Me and Gunner are doing just fine. Aren't we, girl?"

She was looking up at him, but also watching Creed and the bag of treats.

"You know what? I've got another bag in my Jeep. Go ahead and take these. For Gunner."

Sully hesitated, but a glance down at his dog was enough to put his pride away. He took the bag. "Thank you. Tell your partner, thanks, too." He gestured to Bolo and asked, "So, where did you get a dog that knows how to find people? And bones?"

"My partner who made the protein bars. She and I rescue dogs from shelters. Sometimes people abandon their dogs at the end of our long driveway. We train them for scent detection."

"Where'd you learn to do that?"

"Mostly in the military. I was a K9 handler in the Marines."

Sully raised an eyebrow. "I'd never figure you for a jarhead."

Creed smiled at the man's surprise. "What branch were you with?"

The man raised both bushy eyebrows now. "What makes you think I'm a vet?"

"I haven't been called jarhead in a long time. Plus, you named your dog Gunner."

Now Sully wagged his head as if he appreciated that Creed had bothered to put the puzzle pieces together. Through his beard, Creed thought he saw an uptick of a smile.

"U.S. Navy. But that was long before you were even born."

"Mr. Sully," Norwich interrupted them. She was finished with Hogan. "Mind taking me to where your dog found that bone?"

"I can show you the vicinity."

"Mr. Creed, I'll be in touch when I know more about that next search. Thank you for your help." She bent over and petted Bolo along the ridge of his back. "Thank you, too, Bolo."

Creed watched the three of them disappear into the woods. When he turned around, it startled him how much he didn't recognize. Overhead, clouds had moved in and now blocked the sun. While racing after Bolo down the ridge and trying to keep up with his dog, they had zigged and zagged through the woods. He hadn't paid enough attention to how many times they had changed directions. Trees surrounded him. He couldn't even see the ridge.

The recent stab wound had healed, but he had to admit—if only to himself—that his mind and body were still playing catch-up. Some days, a mental fog appeared out of nowhere. It was more unsettling than the physical aches. Those he could power through…mostly.

He pulled his cell phone from his pocket and thumbed it on. Only one bar, but a slew of text messages. Before he could take a look at any of them, a familiar ringtone joined the chirping birds above him.

He smiled as he answered, "Hey, Maggie."

"So, are you and Grace enjoying a therapeutic walk on the beach?"

"Hardly," he laughed. "Bolo and I are in the middle of the woods."

Maggie loved the beach and grabbed any chance she had to dig her toes in the sand when she got down to the area. She'd told him once that just the sight of Pensacola's emerald, green water and sugar white sand had the power to drain the tension from her body. Creed lived at the edge of Blackwater River State Forrest, miles from the beach.

"Bolo?" she asked, the question laced with concern. For some reason, she felt personally responsible for his and Grace's injuries. "I thought you said she was doing great?"

He winced. He *had* said that. *Exactly* that.

"She is doing great. I guess I'm being a little overprotective. But there's a lot of debris and trash here where we were searching, so I'm glad I didn't bring her."

"There's snow here."

"Snow?"

"And it's cold."

"I don't miss that."

He was grateful she was letting him off the hook. It was exhausting trying to explain himself to Hannah.

He wanted to tell her to get out of the cold and come down early, but he hesitated. He didn't want to push it. Besides, the reception was patchy. He held back the phone and saw one bar flitting every time he attempted to move.

"I'm probably going to lose you," he told her.

"Actually, I just wanted to hear your voice. You and Bolo be careful. I'll talk to you—"

And there it went. No service. He waited. It didn't return.

He stashed the phone back in his pocket as he turned and inspected his surroundings one more time. He hated that he still didn't know what direction he needed to head back. Then he looked at Bolo.

"Take us back to START, buddy."

12

Linden Estates
Santa Rosa County, Florida

Taylor Donahue hated waiting. She was convinced her mother-in-law knew that and made her wait on purpose. Maybe the woman wasn't that calculating. Maybe Taylor needed to cut her some slack. But then Dora walked into the room carrying a tray, what looked like tea for two.

What the hell? This was supposed to be a quick stop to pick up her son. But tea? A tall pitcher of it, filled to the brim. Ice tinkling against the sides. Two glasses. Only two. Not three. So, Will wouldn't be joining them for this little refreshment. Taylor wondered if his grandmother had even told him she was here.

Taylor immediately felt her spine straighten, her muscles tense. What in the world did Dora think they needed to talk about now? Talk? Chat? They weren't friends. Hardly even friendly. It took every bone in Taylor's body to be polite to the woman. But she always reminded herself this was Will's grandmother. Mike's mother. Michael. Dora insisted her son be addressed by his given name, but she had no problem reducing William to Willie.

Stop it, Taylor, she told herself. It was the holidays. A time for good cheer, right?

Of course, she could take time for a glass a tea. Taylor stopped from licking her lips while thinking vodka would be more appropriate.

She shook away the thought. It'd be fine. Everything was fine. She needed to relax. The first of next year, Will was coming to live with her. That was the important thing. She needed to concentrate on that.

They'd been living apart for much too long, and both mother and son were excited. They were mere weeks away. And in-between was Christmas! Will would be spending Christmas day plus the following three days with her. She didn't even mind that she couldn't pick him up until after ten in the morning, because Dora insisted he be there for their family's traditional Christmas breakfast. Taylor didn't question or even mind that she hadn't been included or invited.

No, she needed to stay calm. She hadn't done anything wrong.

So, stop acting like it.

She quickly admonished her impatience, and at the same time, she prepared for the lecture.

Dora poured as she said, "Willie is gathering his things. I thought it would give us a chance to chat."

"Is there a problem with the Christmas schedule?" As soon as Taylor said it, she wanted to kick herself. Why invite a problem by suggesting it?

"No, no. Christmas is all set." She offered Taylor her best fake smile. "I think you know what this is about."

Her mind reeled. She was careful to never badmouth Dora around Will. In fact, she thought things were going well. Obviously, Dora wasn't going to give her a hint. "Actually, I don't know."

Dora sat back, crossed her legs. The gesture required her to shift in the chair and rearrange her knit top. Her designer clothing didn't hide the bulge around her middle. Despite being a bit overweight, there was nothing soft about this woman. She conducted herself with a confidence Taylor would never have. It was a confidence born of the entitlement her money brought.

"We've always been very clear about Willie needing stability," Dora began. "Lately, you probably noticed that he's been lying more and more."

"Lying?"

"I'd hate to see it become a habit."

"What exactly has he lied about?"

"You haven't noticed? The stories he makes up? It's gotten worse."

"He has an overactive imagination."

Dora raised her perfectly manicured eyebrows, then shrugged and said, "He never *used* to lie like this." This time, her eyes stayed on Taylor as if testing her, making sure Taylor knew what she meant. The "used to" referred to before Taylor came back into his life.

"Will is creative. He makes up stories and imaginary characters for his comic books."

"Yes, his clever little cartoons and doodles."

Dora confirmed what Taylor already knew. She didn't appreciate or approve of Will's creativity. He drew constantly on anything available, but they were hardly doodles. His multi-color illustrations were works of art. Sometimes he told full stories frame by frame. But Dora had made other references that indicated Will's creative endeavors were a waste of time.

There were previous conversations about getting Will into a sport where he might be able to excel.

"Excel," not enjoy.

A glance around this living room reinforced what Dora considered appropriate extracurricular activities. On side tables and up the open staircase wall, there were framed photos of her son, Michael—Will's father—as a boy and teenager in football and baseball uniforms. On top of the fireplace mantle, a small shrine of more photos included trophies. Relegated to a hallway side table were a handful that dared to include the rest of the family members.

Every time Taylor sat down in this room, she was reminded how much her son resembled his father, right down to the left-side cowlick that spiked his hair and the lopsided smile, a curve of the lips. Never any teeth. In fact, a couple of the photos of Mike as a boy could easily be mistaken for Will.

Shortly after his seventh birthday this summer, Will had a growth spurt that suddenly made him tall for his age. But there was more—a rebel spirit, a wit and intelligence that also made him seem older and wiser. He saw things, felt things, intuitively knew things. Taylor figured it was one of the reasons he constantly needed to draw and sketch. His mind and imagination worked in ways she'd never understand. But she wouldn't change that for anything.

The rebel spirit she did understand. She knew he got that part from her, despite their temporary separation.

"The lies are a problem," Dora said. "I can't help thinking it's his way of trying to get attention."

"Attention?"

"You promised you wouldn't lapse back into your…shall we say, slutty habits."

Taylor immediately felt a flush begin at her neck. She shouldn't be surprised that Dora's perfectly lip-sticked mouth could utter that word. What was worse, Dora felt she had the right to use it.

The man who had talked Taylor into giving up temporary custody of her son had also convinced Dora and her husband that Taylor was a slut, who drank too much and slept around. At one time in her life, there was a morsel of truth to that scenario. These days, she worked long hours as a nurse. If allowed, she would spend all her free time with her son. But she wasn't allowed.

"I've been dating the same man for several months."

"Some would say he's more a boy than a man. Barely over the drinking age, I believe."

"Man enough to go to war and have half his arm blown off."

Dora waved a hand at her. It was a gesture Taylor couldn't decide was dismissive or a concession. Either way, she seemed to say it didn't matter.

"Jason Seaver is a good man," Taylor continued. "He's strong, smart and brave. He's an excellent role model for Will."

"A young boy shouldn't be exposed to his mother sleeping with a man she's not married to. It's just not good for a boy."

"Will hasn't been exposed to it. And how would you know about my relationship with Jason? Are you having me followed?"

"You live above Howard Johnson's Marina. People see him coming and going. Are you saying he never spends the night? Perhaps I see now where Willie gets his lying ways."

"Jason has never spent the night when I have Will."

"What about when he comes to live with you full-time? Are you expecting me to believe your behavior will change in several weeks?" Dora took a sip of tea, deliberately stretching out the pause and waiting for a response.

This was ridiculous. Whatever Taylor answered would be used against her.

"When you *left* Willie with me, you gave me the right to decide what I viewed as right and wrong for him. Until the court decides otherwise, I continue to have that right."

Taylor stared at her. Could she really insist she stop seeing Jason? He was one of the most decent men she'd ever dated. She had given in to every rule Dora and the court-appointed minions had demanded. But this…this felt like harassment. She was less than a month from regaining custody.

Or was that part of the plan? Had it been Dora's intention the entire time? To wait until the last weeks and throw in a delay?

"What exactly are you saying, Dora?"

Another shrug, like none of this was a big deal. "I think it would be a good idea for you to reevaluate your priorities."

"You're demanding I stop seeing Jason."

"Would it hurt to give Willie your full attention? Or do you really need the sex?"

Taylor blinked. It felt like a slap across the face. She swallowed the first words that came to mind. How could they even be having this conversation?

"Mom, you're here!"

Will came around a corner. He was stuffing items into his backpack even as he made his way across the room.

Before Taylor could respond to either of them, Dora caught her eyes and added, "Just something to think about. You know, before the end of the year and the next court hearing."

13

"What were you and Nanna arguing about?" Will asked.

"Arguing?" Taylor looked up at the rearview mirror and met his eyes. "We were just talking."

His hair was tousled, the cowlick even more pronounced. His T-shirt was wrinkled. He looked like he'd just crawled out of bed. But he had his seatbelt buckled and his backpack secured beside him. Already settled in, he was digging out a notebook and pen.

This fall after his growth spurt, Will had put up a fuss about still having to sit in the backseat of vehicles. He didn't want to be "treated like a baby" anymore. Besides, he told her, Nanna let him sit up front…sometimes.

Now Taylor wondered if that was one of the lies Dora was referring to. Letting him sit upfront didn't seem like something Dora would allow.

"What were you talking about?"

"Nothing you need to be concerned about," she told him, when she really wanted to ask how much he'd heard. Then she added. "Just grown-up stuff." She had used this excuse before, and it usually satisfied him. Today, it seemed to do the same.

His head swiveled to the construction site and the equipment at the end of the block. There were always new homes going up out here. Bigger and grander, with two-story entrances in front and enclosed swimming pools in the back.

Bulldozers had stripped down a fresh line of trees from the forest that backed up to the development. They seemed intent on pushing deeper and deeper into the woods. It was as if they wanted to get farther away from the neighborhood on the other side of the highway. That community, called Woodriver, was much older than this one. It was a well-established working-class neighborhood with small houses interspersed with double-wide trailers. Taylor couldn't help thinking the contrast couldn't be starker.

She glanced in the rearview mirror again, and now Will's eyes and attention were tilted down. He was already drawing. His hand took broad strokes with the pen.

Though he seemed mature about so many things, she had to remind herself he was only seven. After everything she'd put him through, she didn't want him to worry there might be yet another delay in his coming to live with her full-time. A knot began in her stomach, just imagining his disappointment.

This was all her fault. She couldn't believe she'd surrendered custody of her son. To be fair, she wasn't the same person back then. When she returned from Afghanistan, all she longed for was a piece of normal, only to discover she was pregnant. Maybe it wouldn't have been so bad if she and Mike could have carved out a life together. But his tour of duty hadn't ended yet. They got married at a courthouse, promising they'd do a real wedding when he returned. Two months later, he was dead.

Mike wasn't the love of her life. The grief wasn't what did her in. She wished it was. No, it was the unexpected nightmares that sent her into the night running through the dark streets, pounding the asphalt to take the place of the sound of helicopters bringing more wounded.

In her nightmares, she couldn't stop their bleeding. She worked all night trying to find the pieces to put them back together again. Back then, she woke to sweaty sheets that she mistook for pools of blood until she turned the lights on.

As a nurse, she recognized PTSD, but she hadn't come up with a way to treat herself. Instead, she resorted to how they'd handle the daily trauma in Afghanistan. She'd learned to cope like the rest of her team. Vodka.

It wasn't such a problem that she couldn't quit, and she did quit while she was pregnant. A beautiful baby boy should have brought enough joy to silence the nightmares. Unfortunately, PTSD didn't work that way. Will just reminded her of how very broken she was.

Taylor blinked and shook her head. Driving over the I-10 bridge, she took in the sparkling waters of Escambia Bay. That was one thing she loved about this place. She couldn't go far without seeing water. Large bodies of water. Living on Pensacola Beach had helped maintain her sanity throughout this.

The small apartment above Howard's marina shop felt more like home than anywhere she had lived in the past ten years. She counted it as good fortune that she had snagged the place. She could run every day on along the Gulf of Mexico, listening to the waves and feeling the spray of salt water. And she felt safe. Howard made sure of that.

No, she wouldn't let Dora's snide remark make her second-guess her choice and the decisions she was making for herself and for Will.

A rustling from the backseat made her check the rearview mirror.

"Did you forget something, Buddy?"

Will dug in his backpack, emptying items onto the seat.

"I think I forgot my markers."

"We can stop and buy some."

"These aren't the regular kind. Miss Rosa usually helps me pack my bag."

He didn't seem upset. Just frustrated. Already, he was stuffing everything back inside, but doing it haphazardly. She packed for him when it was time to leave her apartment. She didn't mind. He was seven. But she didn't realize this was something Dora had left for the housekeeper to do.

Now she wondered if Miss Rosa was the one who reminded him to comb his hair and make sure he chose a shirt that wasn't wrinkled.

"Miss Rosa wasn't there today to help you?" she asked.

"No."

"Is she on vacation?"

"I think she's dead."

"Will! That's not funny. And it's not a nice thing to say."

"I saw her fall down the stairs last week, and she hasn't been back since."

"I'm sure she's probably taking time off to recover."

"Her body looked all weird." He pantomimed, flinging his arms out and twisting his body. "She didn't get back up. She didn't even move."

"Did the ambulance come?"

Will shrugged and went back to drawing. "I don't know," he said. "Nanna made me go to my room. It looks out over the backyard, so I couldn't see."

"Did you ask Nanna about her?"

"She just said Miss Rosa wouldn't be coming back." Another shrug. "Hey, are we gonna see Jason? I did some drawings I want to show him."

"I don't know, Will. Maybe. We'll see." She wasn't sure what she was going to do about Jason. She wondered about the housekeeper. Would he make up such a story?

"I'm doing a whole new series with him as the superhero. It's so cool. His mechanical arm can lift cars and shoot death rays. I wanna show him the first drawings."

"That's great, Will. I'm sure he'll be excited to see the pictures."

"Not pictures, Mom. They're drawings, and when I add color, they'll be illustrations."

Then it occurred to Taylor. "Did you show them to Nanna?"

"Yeah, but she doesn't always like my stuff."

And now Taylor understood the reason Dora might not want Jason around. Could it be that simple? She didn't want another man replacing her son in her grandson's life.

14

Florida Panhandle

Creed had texted Hannah earlier, so he knew she was in the kennel when he arrived. He let Bolo into the fenced yard to stretch his legs, but the dog headed for the electronic dog door, ready for a meal and rest.

He barely stepped into the warehouse-sized facility when he heard the skittering of nails trying to gain traction on the floor. The Jack Russell terrier raced at him across the wide expanse. Other dogs followed in her wake. Grace slid into his legs. Her backend wiggled so fiercely her tail almost thumped against her head.

"Hey, Grace! Hey guys." He dropped to his knees and elbows and gave her his face.

As the others arrived and surrounded him, Creed gave up and plopped down on the floor, allowing them to greet him each in their own way. A couple of the big dogs head-butted him from behind. A tongue slobbered in his ear. Noses pushed at his elbow and shoulder. Even Bolo had come over to join the fuss.

Creed's lap was full, but Grace still managed to hold her own in the center, paws on his chest, reaching up and giving his bristled jaw a tongue-bath.

"You'd think you were gone for a week," Hannah said from the other side of the kennel, where she continued to fill water bowls. "And don't believe that excited nonsense from that one," Hannah pointed at Grace as she came closer to the pile of dogs and man. "That girl has been miserable since you left."

It had been a longer day than he expected. After leaving Norwich, he had grabbed lunch, then run errands.

"Dr. Avelyn gave her a thorough check-up again," Hannah told him. "Rye, that girl is ready to get back to work."

He let her continue licking his chin as his hands reached out to the other dogs, his fingers finding and scratching ears and hind quarters. He made no effort to restrain them or remind them to settle down.

Fact was, this was his favorite place to be. These dogs were his family. Some of them had been through hell before they arrived here. A few of them had gone through hell alongside Creed. None more than Grace. They had saved each other in more ways than he could count. It was no wonder Grace displayed separation anxiety when away from him.

Not a good thing. For either of them.

He knew it didn't help matters that he was being overprotective.

This was the first time Hannah had weighed in on the topic. Sometimes he just needed Hannah's reassurance. When it came to the dogs, she usually held back. Let him fuss and worry and plan even when it might be excessive. How many times had she come looking for him in his loft apartment only to find him down below, here in the kennel, fast asleep on a dog bed next to a sick dog or a new, frightened one? And never once did she question what others might consider over-the-top behavior.

"She's healed and strong, Rye. But you need to be okay with it. If you're still worried, you know that girl will pick up on it."

He nodded. He noticed Grace had sat back on her haunches as the other dogs started settling around him, a few of them heading back to their routines. But even though Grace was giving him a reprieve, she knew they were talking about her. Of course, she knew.

Hannah glanced from him to Grace, then her eyes returned with a smile. It was as if Grace had just reaffirmed Hannah's statement that, of course, she could "pick up" on Creed's worry.

"Did you find that teenager?" Hannah asked, changing the subject.

"No, we didn't." Creed readjusted himself and scooted over so he could lean against one of the support beams. With fewer dogs, he could stretch out his long legs. Grace climbed back onto his lap.

"Bolo picked up his scent, but all we found was his jacket. On a homeless guy."

"I thought you were searching the woods behind the Red Roof Inn off of Avalon."

"We were."

"And you ran into a homeless guy? In the woods?"

"A couple of them, actually. Looks like a few camps back there."

Hannah shook her head. The problem was a familiar one. Years ago, she helped start the Segway House in downtown Pensacola. It was a community outreach and shelter for teenage runaways, homeless veterans, and domestic abuse victims. But there was never enough room or money. The annual fundraiser took up a chunk of Hannah's time. Creed didn't know how she did it all, plus run their K9 scent business.

"What did he say about having that boy's jacket?" she asked.

"Told us he found it on a discarded mattress. The same mattress Bolo found him on top of."

Again, Hannah didn't look surprised.

"Oh, and one of the guys—an older man named Sully—had a dog. A dog with a bone."

She smiled at that until he added, "Bolo alerted to the bone."

Then her lips went from a smile to an "O."

"You think it's human?"

"Bolo seemed convinced. I guess Norwich will find out soon enough."

"Sounds like you boys had an adventurous day."

Grace snuggled down into his lap. He'd take her with him for a swim later. Work out some of the kinks in his back. It was good for her, too, and she loved it. And he did have to admit, lately, she did look stronger.

Hannah went back into the kitchen area. Poured a travel mug of coffee and brought it over to him.

"Thanks," he told her. Grace's head weighted his right arm, so he drank with his left hand.

A door opened behind him. All the dogs that had greeted him now raced around him. Bolo and Chance jumped over Creed's outstretched legs. Hannah gestured to the new person, then started to pour another mug of coffee.

"That's quite impressive," Creed said over his shoulder without looking back. "Not many veterinarians get that kind of welcome."

"It would be entirely different if they were over at the clinic coming to see me." Dr. Avelyn Parker took her time greeting each dog.

They were excited to see her, but they were happy and excited, not anxious. She was on their turf, inside their home. Here, she never wore her white lab coat. She was dressed in blue jeans, a sweatshirt and hiking boots. Her hair was tied back in a ponytail.

Years ago, they hired the vet on retainer when it made more sense for her to come to their facility instead of them constantly loading up and taking dogs to her clinic in Milton. She still owned a portion of that clinic, though much of her time was spent with their dogs. Especially after Creed built a clinic and surgical center to Dr. Avelyn's specifications.

Hannah brought her a mug of coffee, too. Dr. Avelyn thanked her, then sat cross-legged on the floor opposite Creed. Hannah sat in an empty spot on the closest dog sofa. The two dogs, already occupying the ends, moved in to cuddle next to her. Down on the floor, Molly, a yellow Labrador plopped her head on Hannah's foot.

"You're here late," Creed told the veterinarian.

"I needed to finish some paperwork."

He glanced at Hannah. She looked like she already knew what this was about. Dr. Avelyn caught his eyes, as if knowing exactly that he was feeling somehow left out.

She told him, "Hannah said I might be able to catch the two of you together tonight. There's something I need to talk to you both about."

15

"Is everything okay with the dogs?" Creed wanted to know.

"Oh sure. There fine. I wanted to ask about quarantining some dogs in the new area of the clinic. Possibly in the next few days. I know it's not quite finished, so I'll understand if you don't want to rush it."

They had taken a separate unit and started renovations. The space would allow them to quarantine a few dogs at a time before they added them to the kennel. All of their dogs came to them after being in a shelter or after being abandoned. Grace had been dumped at the end of their long driveway.

"How many dogs are we talking about?" Creed asked.

"About a dozen."

"A dozen all at once?"

"If we're lucky. I was thinking we might be able to push out into the storage area temporarily. I can move a couple of the racks. That room is huge." She looked from Creed to Hannah. "I don't mind doing the work myself."

"No," Creed told her.

"No?"

"No, you're not going to do it yourself. Jason and I will help. It shouldn't take that long. Let's get a list of everything we'll need for them."

Dr. Avelyn stared down into her coffee mug and went quiet. Creed glanced at Hannah again, hoping to see some explanation written on her face. When Dr. Avelyn looked up, she was smiling. Creed breathed a sigh of relief.

"You didn't even ask where these dogs were coming from or why they need urgent shelter." She looked down again and just shook her head. Now Creed could see the tear at the corner of her eye.

"I figure it must be from a disaster site." Creed shrugged. But now he realized it might be something more personal.

He knew she was a member of an emergency response organization that sent veterinarians after mudslides or earthquakes to take care of working dogs and any other animals affected by the disaster. They were trained in protocol for decontamination as well as treating on-site injuries, dehydration and hypothermia.

"It's something like that," she said. "One of our members served in the Army as a veterinarian in Afghanistan. He's been working stateside with a couple of former K9 handlers. They've been trying to locate and rescue the war dogs left behind. We're hoping to get them back home. But it's turning out to be quite the challenge."

Creed felt a sudden knot twisting in his gut. As a military handler, he and others had their own personal stories of pushing for policy change, and legislation for how retired dogs were treated. After much lobbying, the dogs had finally been given concessions like the K9 soldier having a higher rank than its handler, so the handler's number one priority was the dog. Robbie's Law allowed for handlers to adopt their K9 after the dogs retired. But the military still wouldn't pay for transport back to the states.

Still, all of that was better than what had been done in the past when dogs were simply left behind. And yet, here they were, again. All those concessions, all those "changes" had they been tossed out?

"We heard the rumors," Hannah said, watching Creed out of the corner of her eye. "But the Pentagon claims they never left any dogs behind. Do you have any idea what happened?"

"In the days before the fall, we were told all the military dogs would be on flights routed through Europe. They said they'd let us know when they were arriving in the US, and that we should be ready to receive them. We'd need to process and quarantine them."

A couple of dogs wedged themselves against Dr. Avelyn on each side, and her fingers absently petted them.

"Did they tell you how many?"

She shook her head. "Originally, no. We were working in real time, and we were only one of the groups receiving dogs." She crossed her legs, readjusting to make herself comfortable when clearly the subject made her uncomfortable. "When we didn't hear anything, Van Berg—the Army vet who was leading our team on this—hounded his contact.

"Even from a distance, we could see the evacuations were spiraling out of control. Next thing we hear is that a bunch of the dogs weren't allowed on the planes. An animal rescue organization was trying to arrange charter flights. But they were told the area was too chaotic, and they wouldn't even be permitted to land, let alone take off.

"Remember, all this is happening in real time. In a matter of hours. Frantic hours. Frantic even before the suicide bomber. Translators who were promised safe passage with their families were having a tough time getting on flights. And some of them were also told they weren't allowed to bring their family pets. From what I understand, the panic and chaos at the airport made it terrifying.

"Then Van Berg gets a call." Dr. Avelyn's eyes dropped to the dogs and where her hands were caressing them. "His contact told him they wouldn't need us. At all. The dogs had to be released at the airport or on the streets. They had to abandon them."

There was silence. Even the dogs seemed to sense the need to be quiet. Creed's immediate reaction? He wanted to pound his fist through a wall.

Finally, Hannah asked, "Hasn't the Pentagon insisted those dogs released at the airport were not military dogs? I've heard them say they were under the care of the animal rescue organization that you mentioned. Or that perhaps, they were left by families not able to board with them."

"All I know is that they told us to be prepared to receive, process, and quarantine dogs. Then suddenly, they told us the dogs were no longer coming. That they had no choice but to release them at the airport. They refused to explain why they abandoned them. Then, after a few weeks, they refused to admit any dogs were even released or abandoned."

She took a deep breath and stretched her arms as if willing the tension from her shoulders. "Now, it's been over a year. We've stayed in touch with that animal rescue organization. Their staff and our own sources in Kabul have been tracking, locating, and finding dogs. And they've actually been finding K9s that served alongside our troops. One of the handlers in our group recognized her dog from a photo."

"So, the Pentagon's been lying," Creed said. "Imagine that."

"Initially, their defense was that these dogs weren't military dogs. They were contract working dogs."

"Seriously? Like that would make a difference?" Creed shook his head. He knew the military couldn't keep up training as many dogs as they needed, so they had begun contracting the work. Those contracted dogs worked alongside handlers no differently than the ones trained by the military. This was ridiculous. And cruel. But he wasn't surprised.

"It's not playing well after military handlers are recognizing their dogs from those captured off the streets back in Kabul."

"And now?" Hannah asked. "Are you finally bringing them home?"

"Hopefully. It's taking forever to secure permission. And we're still having to depend on people we're not sure we can trust. Of course, we're not getting any help from D.C. They couldn't even get the remaining translators out. Honestly, I think they want to push the whole debacle out of sight and out of mind.

"And things are so screwed up in Afghanistan. After the takeover, the rescue organization was told they wouldn't be allowed to have female staff. The head of the organization is a woman. Somehow, she managed to get them to make an exception. But for how long? The Taliban keeps putting new requirements and handing over more paperwork. They don't really care to facilitate the survival of these dogs, let alone exporting them."

"The dogs were never a welcomed sight," Creed said. "They taught their kids to throw rocks at them. Villages were afraid when we brought along a dog, almost as if they believed the dogs had mystical powers. We called our dogs truth detectors, because one dog on site could get people to confess easier than a brigade of armed soldiers.

"But the Taliban knew we had an emotional attachment to the dogs. And they used that against us. They targeted them. If they could take down a dog, we'd do anything to rescue it. And sometimes that included making mistakes.

"Now here they are again. Able to use one last vulnerability against us. Able to send us to our knees all over again."

16

Creed and Hannah made their way across the yard to the main house. He opened the back door, releasing an amazing aroma. The familiar scents from Hannah's kitchen helped soothe his lingering tension.

"Something smells good," he said, holding the door open for her.

"I don't know how much of an appetite we'll have after talking about those poor dogs." She caught his eyes as she crossed in front of him. "You okay?"

"Sure." But there was no putting off Hannah. She knew him too well. "Makes me angry, if anything."

She nodded and continued into the kitchen as if that was exactly what she expected to hear.

"It's just you and me for dinner," she told him. "Jason and Brodie have poker night at the Segway House."

"That's right. I forgot about that." He greeted Hannah's dogs, Lady and Hunter, but they were more excited to see Grace. "How do you think that's going?"

"Poker night?"

"Yeah. Every time I ask Brodie all she says is that she's learning a lot. But she says that about so many things."

"Truthfully, I think she's having a ball. She trusts Jason's friends, and I think she feels safe at the Segway House. The one person who has a problem with it is Taylor."

"Taylor? Did Jason tell you that?"

"Uh huh. She's been working some nights at the hospital so she can get extra time off for Christmas to be with her little boy. But poker night lands on her only nights off."

"I'm sure they'll work it out. He's crazy about her."

"Speaking of Christmas, the boys are asking when we can put up the tree."

Hannah's boys were still young enough to believe in Santa. In years past, they'd have the tree up and decorated the day after Thanksgiving.

"You're worried about Brodie?" Creed asked her.

"Aren't you?"

It was just over a year ago that Creed found his sister. After sixteen years, he'd almost given up.

Brodie had disappeared from a rest area during a family road trip. She was eleven at the time. Creed was fourteen. Hannah called it a miracle when Brodie was found in an old, abandoned farmhouse. It was nicknamed the Christmas house because its previous occupant had been committed to a nursing home just before Christmas. The family hadn't bothered to take down the decorations. Instead, they simply abandoned the house.

"Has she ever talked to you about it?" Hannah asked.

He shook his head. He didn't like to think about what his sister had gone through. And he certainly didn't want to remind her. She had been working with a therapist, but their sessions were becoming less frequent.

"She seems to be doing really well." But he looked to Hannah for reassurance.

She waited too long to agree, then said, "Maybe I'll ask Jason."

"Jason?"

Hannah raised an eyebrow at him. "You didn't notice? Those two have been thick as thieves since y'all got back from Nebraska. I think worrying about and looking for you brought them a lot closer."

Maybe he'd been too concerned about Grace's injuries, and Maggie's revelation that she loved him.

"How close are we talking?" He matched her raised eyebrow, and she immediately waved a hand at him.

"I don't mean like that. You're right when you said Jason is crazy about Taylor."

But Creed had noticed the way Brodie sometimes looked at Jason when Jason wasn't watching. He would never claim to be an expert on women—far from it—but he thought he recognized that look.

"Also, speaking of the Segway House," Hannah had moved on, "your tuxedo arrived."

As a dog handler, Creed had trained himself to control his emotions, but he now allowed an audible groan.

"Stop that!" she laughed at him. "You're always the most handsome man at the ball. I love how all the other women are so jealous of me. Plus, I only ask you to do this once a year."

"You're right."

"It's for a great cause."

"I know."

"You sure Maggie's not coming?"

"For the ball?"

"Yes! It's a chance to get all fancied up." She looked up from the chopping board. "You didn't even ask her?"

"I'm pretty sure it's not her kind of thing. Besides, it's already a challenge for her to take off an entire week and come down here for Christmas."

"You sound like maybe you're expecting her to back out."

"I just know it's a big deal. It's a lot to ask."

"Did you ask? I thought it was her idea."

"It was."

"But?"

Creed wasn't sure how Hannah could sense things about him that he wasn't able to identify himself. His relationship with Maggie O'Dell had been complicated from the first time they worked together. Since then, over the course of about two and a half years, they had saved each other's lives, exchanged secrets, confided vulnerabilities and learned to trust each other. And all of this happened before they admitted that they loved each other.

Creed knew that admission came at a tremendous cost to Maggie. It made a huge difference to her. But for himself, he didn't think it changed much. Not in the way he thought about her or how he treated her. And unfortunately, confessing their love for each other certainly didn't change their circumstances.

Their jobs, their homes, their lives were rooted in separate places. Places that were sacred to them. Places they'd worked hard to create for themselves. And those places were about a thousand miles away from each other. Admitting they loved each other didn't change that. He didn't expect it to. He didn't expect Maggie to pack up and leave Quantico, her home, her brother, and her friends. He wouldn't ask her to do something he wasn't willing to do.

This place, this acreage with the training facility and kennel and the dogs. He and Hannah had worked hard to build what was much more than a business. It wasn't something he saw himself ever leaving.

Just then, he realized Hannah was still waiting for a response, looking at him with her hands on her hips.

He shrugged. "I just know it's a big deal. And besides, I already have a date for the ball with the most beautiful and powerful woman that's going to be there."

She smiled and rolled her eyes at him as she filled a bowl with lettuce and freshly chopped vegetables. He could tell she knew there was more, but she wouldn't push.

The fundraiser reminded Creed of Sully and Gunner again. And he was anxious to change the subject off of him and Maggie.

"Hannah, does the Segway House allow dogs?"

"I don't see why not. Jason and Brodie took Scout and Hank with them. I know for a fact those two dogs will be under the poker table."

"Yeah, everybody knows them. Knows they're connected to you. But if someone who's homeless and has a dog comes in for a meal or needs a place to stay, would they let the dog come on in? Would they let the dog stay in a room with them?"

She stopped to think about it. "I don't recall anyone staying with a dog. But I helped write the rules. You know I wouldn't have put something in that said no dogs allowed."

"But if dogs aren't mentioned in the rules, is it possible some of the employees and volunteers don't allow them?"

"I guess it's possible. Are you saying someone with a dog was turned away?"

"This guy named Sully told me most places won't let him bring in his dog. I'd hate to think he couldn't go get a hot meal just because he couldn't bring his dog inside."

Creed realized he wasn't just thinking of Sully and Gunner. In the back of his mind, he knew he'd never leave his dogs.

No, it was more than that.

If anything, the conversation with Dr. Avelyn simply reaffirmed his priorities. His dogs would always come first. All their dogs had been abandoned. Creed had rescued them. They depended on him to be there. To make things right. To make sure they were never hurt or abandoned ever again. He would put himself in the line of fire before he'd ever let anyone hurt one of his dogs. He'd already done that a few times.

17

Segway House
Pensacola, Florida

Brodie Creed watched the men over the tops of her playing cards. She held them with one hand and ate French fries with the other. Only recently had she discovered how good they were dipped in Ranch dressing. She had no idea French fries could taste better than they already were.

The men took forever, deciding whether to hold or fold or take another card. Brodie didn't mind. The best part of playing poker was watching and listening to them. It took her a few times playing with them before she realized the cards were only a prop. What they really wanted to do was get together and talk. Men were complicated.

Actually, Brodie believed *people* were complicated. Nobody said what they meant. She tried as hard as possible to understand sarcasm, but still didn't get it. And then there were certain topics that couldn't even be discussed.

She and Jason talked about anything and everything, but she had learned that his relationship with Taylor Donahue was off limits. So even though she noticed him checking his phone every five minutes and scowling at it, she couldn't ask. She didn't really need to. Only Taylor seemed to trigger those creases in Jason's brow.

"Is everything okay?" she asked him when they first arrived because he'd immediately checked his phone.

"No worries," he told her as he texted a short message, then slid the phone into his back pocket.

But it didn't end there. The checking the phone, the furrowed brow continued throughout the evening.

Now, Brodie glanced down at Hank curled up at her feet. She preferred the company of dogs and her cat named Kitten. They weren't complicated. Most of the time, she could figure them out. Sometimes the big dog snored when he was fast asleep. Now, despite his eyes being closed, she knew he was not asleep. They were safe here, but Hank was always on alert, ready to pounce into action to protect her.

The poker room at the Segway House was small. Still, Jason insisted she have the seat at the table that put her back to the wall, knowing that's where she'd feel most comfortable. He sat across from her with his back to the room's entrance. Benny and Colfax sat across from each other. Both men were veterans, like Jason. All of them carried obvious wounds they'd brought back from their tours of duties.

Brodie was used to Jason's mechanical arm. When she first met him almost a year ago, the fingers were still black jointed metal that looked like something from a sci-fi movie. His most recent update included a coating that resembled skin. It even felt like skin. Though he still didn't have fingerprints, the addition of micro-sensors—added to the neuro-translator ones he already had—gave him a higher level of sensation. In other words, he could feel what he touched.

According to Jason, the only reason he was able to get all these amazing updates was because of a deal Ryder made with some guy from DARPA. Brodie wished Ryder could get a deal for Benny and Colfax, though both men seemed resolved and content. Benny had a souped-up truck with hydraulics for his wheelchair and special equipment so he could drive with his hands. Both Benny's legs were amputated above his knees.

As far as Brodie knew, Colfax came back whole. But one side of his face looked like a jigsaw puzzle with some of the pieces put in the wrong spots and melted into place.

Benny tossed two cards on the table and asked for "two better ones" from Colfax, who was the dealer tonight. To Jason, Benny said, "So Romeo, what are you getting your girlfriend for Christmas?"

"I haven't decided yet," Jason said, but when he looked up from his cards, he glanced over at Brodie before his eyes landed on Benny.

Benny didn't even notice. He focused on the new cards, and Brodie could tell he was pleased. These guys were awful at telegraphing their cards.

Brodie, on the other hand, had spent sixteen years learning to equate any emotional expression with pain and punishment. It was safer to hide her true emotions. She had gotten so good at it, she now struggled to show her feelings. Lately, she caught herself slipping. Even now, she tried not to look interested in what Jason was thinking about giving Taylor. She hoped Benny would continue to press him. She wanted to know the answer, too.

She'd already bought her gift for Jason. With Hannah's help, she'd tracked down a first edition of *To Kill a Mockingbird* signed by Harper Lee. It was incredibly expensive, and Brodie would never have been able to afford it. But somehow Hannah's grandmother, who had owned a bookstore many years ago, knew the book collector. All Brodie knew was that trades had been made, and the price for the special edition came down significantly.

The book was Jason's favorite. He had a dog-eared paperback on his bookshelf that he'd read so many times pages were falling out. Even his dog Scout was named after Scout Finch. Brodie hoped he'd like it. Hannah said he would love it.

"What do you have, Brodie?" Benny asked.

She'd lost herself in thought, and they were waiting for her. All of their playing cards were displayed on the table. Benny smiled, and she realized his full house—three aces and a pair of fours—had distracted him from digging further into Jason's gift for Taylor. Colfax had a pair of kings. Jason had three twos.

She put hers down and listened to their groans. It was a straight flush: five, six, seven, eight and nine and all hearts. Jason grinned at her from across the table even as he joined Benny and Colfax's chorus of groans. She could tell he was proud of her.

Brodie couldn't help but smile. Another slip, and she still couldn't help wondering what it would cost her to feel joy and happiness. That's when she noticed Jason picked up his cell phone again. He winced before he tucked it away. How could being in a relationship cause so much anxiety?

"Excuse me a minute." Jason got up from the table and headed out the door.

"Are we dealing you in?" Colfax called before he disappeared.

"Sure. Yeah. Of course."

The shuffling of cards amplified in the silence. Brodie's eyes shifted from one man to the other. They exchanged a glance, but avoided looking her way.

"What?" she asked. "I'm not made of porcelain. I can handle it." She'd just read that line in a book and thought it was perfect for how they all still tiptoed around her.

"She usually leaves him alone when he's just with us," Benny finally said, swinging a finger to indicate himself and Colfax like he expected her to fill in the blank.

"This has something to do with me?"

"Of course." Colfax started dealing the cards. "You and Jason spend a lot of time together."

"We work together." Brodie was still baffled.

"And have meals together and live—what is it—about 100 feet away from each other?"

"And," Benny joined in. "You're really easy on the eyes."

Again, Brodie looked from one man to the other, trying to decide if they were serious. Then she shook her head and smiled. “Right.”

They were messing with her. Sometimes she was slow at getting their humor, but she’d seen them do the same thing with Jason.

No way Taylor felt threatened by her. Just the idea was silly.

18

Walter's Canteen
Pensacola Beach, Florida

Taylor shoved her cell phone to the edge of the table. She needed to stop. She glanced at Will sitting across from her, his eyes glued to the three hotdog surfers fighting the December waves. She grabbed the phone again. This time she shut it off, then reached over and dropped it into the tote bag she'd left on the extra chair between them.

She did need to stop it. Why did it drive her so crazy? She and Jason were not officially in a relationship. He hadn't done anything wrong. Instead, he'd gone overboard trying to do everything expected. And yet, it bugged her.

No, that was too mild.

Fact was, it pissed her off that he preferred playing poker with his buddies when he could have been here having dinner with her and Will.

He claimed he didn't prefer playing poker. It was a commitment he'd made to spend time once a week with these men. She understood that it was more therapy than some drunken excuse for them to get away from their significant others. Benny and Colfax didn't have wives or girlfriends. The Segway House didn't even allow alcohol.

Damn it! She was becoming one of those women she despised. If she was being honest with herself, she'd have to admit that it wasn't about the weekly poker game. It hadn't been a problem before. Not until recently, when the guys started including Brodie.

Jason never hid the inclusion. On the contrary, he seemed pleased that it was helping her get out and socialize. Put aside her fears. Give her a sense of self-confidence. Yada, yada...oh, she was tired of hearing about it.

Maybe she was being insensitive. She knew some of the tragedy Brodie had suffered. She had been taken as an eleven-year-old and held captive for years. What was it? Fifteen or sixteen?

To be fair, Brodie never played the victim-card. The first time she met her, Taylor knew nothing of her past. And what she saw was a tall, willowy, young woman with a natural beauty and gorgeous eyes that listened intently. What was worse, she was one of those women who didn't know she was pretty. Or care how she looked or dressed. How could anyone compete with that?

Jason didn't see it. Not yet.

But Taylor had noticed the way Brodie looked at him.

Taylor shook her head. She really needed to stop thinking about it. Jason was a nice distraction, but she needed to focus on Will. He was what mattered most.

He had his sketch pad out and his head down. One hand held his marker, the other blindly fetched popcorn shrimp, bringing them to his mouth without taking his focus off his drawing.

"Can I see?" she asked.

"Not yet." He switched up markers. But the other hand continued with the shrimp.

"How about we go shopping tomorrow and get you those new sneakers you've been wanting?"

This earned her a look up. "I thought I had to wait for Christmas."

"Maybe you're getting other presents." She pointed to his worn, dusty pair under the table. "You need new ones."

He smiled—a wide, happy smile—then went back to sketching. No other trace of suspicion that his mother could be overcompensating because something might screw up their Christmas.

She sat back. Forced herself to take a deep breath, then let her eyes wander out across the water. The emerald waves sparkled in the last rays of sunset. There were very few diners on the patio. Too chilly for most. But Will loved it out here and never forgot his jacket so they could have their once-a-week dinner watching the sun go down. Walter always saved them this table. "The best view in the house," he told Will.

Walter Bailey, the owner, was a retired Navy commander. He wore jumpsuits—sometimes tan, green, blue, even red—reminiscent of the ones he probably wore as a Navy pilot. His full head of hair was more white than gray. That, along with a slow, saunter and arthritic-bent fingers were the only signs of his age. He had a laugh that was full of life, deep-throated and genuine. When he called her "a lady," it was out of respect, an old-world gentleman. She was glad that he and Will had become instant friends.

This was a good place for her and Will to start their new life together. She didn't care if Dora didn't approve of her too-small apartment above a marina shop. Harold was another good man. Another veteran. Taylor had run from military men when she came back to the States. In an effort to rid her mind and stop her nightmares, she thought it would help to be surrounded by people who didn't share the same experiences. Only recently did she realize her mistake. Those shared experiences and talking about them were what she needed.

Just in the last six months she'd created a community of friends—all men, all veterans—and she'd never felt so mentally healthy. Being able to talk about the nightmares, listen to stories more horrible than her own…that was what she needed to feel whole again.

Dora lost her son. Mike had said his mother didn't want him going to Afghanistan. She'd even gone as far as to say she hadn't paid for him to be a doctor, only to have him go off and get shot at. As a result, she didn't like Taylor "exposing Will to so many military men."

As a mother, Taylor actually understood this. At one time, she may have even agreed with Dora. But Walter, Harold, Jason, Benny and Colfax were some of the best men she'd ever met. And she wanted her son to know them.

"How are my two favorite customers doing?" Walter Bailey weaved his way through the tables.

Will looked up and grinned at him.

"More shrimp?" he asked the boy.

"No, I'm good." He glanced at his mom, then added, "I'm good, sir."

"Did you save room for key lime pie? Freshly made this morning."

"Can we, mom?"

She was trying to get him to slow down on the sugar. "How about one piece and two forks?"

"And coffee for the little lady?"

"Yes, please. Can you join us, Walter?"

"I'd love to. I'll have Rita bring the pie and coffees," he stopped and gestured to Will, "and a milk?"

Will nodded.

"I have something to finish," he told them. "Then I'll join you. I'm anxious to see that latest creation." He chin-pointed to Will's sketch pad, garnering yet another grin.

"I like him," Will said when Walter was out of earshot. He started working on his drawing again, but suddenly, his head bobbed up as he remembered something. "Do you know what happened to my real grandpa?"

Taylor's father had died from a heart attack when she was in college. She had told him this, so he was referring to Mike's real father. In their short time together, Mike had never talked about him. Or at least she couldn't remember.

"Have you asked your nanna?"

"She said it's none of my concern. But Miss Rosa knew him. She worked for him a long time ago. She said I look a lot like him. She told me he liked to paint, and that's probably where I got my…I think she called it inherent talent." He sounded out the word inherent, breaking it into three words.

"Are there any paintings of his on the walls?"

He shook his head. He'd obviously asked.

"Miss Rosa said he was murdered."

"Oh, Will, I'm sure you must have misunderstood."

"Do you know what happened to him?"

She felt bad she had no answer. Usually, Will's questions about his father were easy. But she knew nothing about his grandfather.

How could she tell her son that his father didn't talk much about his family? That he'd joined the mobile surgical unit partly to get away from them. And worse, that she never really knew his father very well.

They were never a couple. They were together only a few times, and it was only sex. A stress relief for both of them. No emotions or love attached. In Afghanistan, they worked in close quarters. They drank a whole lot of vodka together to forget the images of the wounded men that they'd spent their days piecing together.

So much tension and urgency. So much frustration because all they could do was staunch the bleeding before releasing their patients to an airlift that could get them to a proper hospital.

The fact that she had gotten pregnant surprised both of them. She remembered Mike saying that maybe it was a sign. Maybe they were meant to have a normal life: a home and family after all the blood and death they'd experienced.

Will was waiting for an answer. She wondered why he was so curious about his real grandfather. And at the same time, she felt a pang of guilt for not being able to provide him with one.

"I'll see what I can find out," she promised.

"Okay."

Satisfied, he capped the last marker and set it aside. Then he lifted the sketch pad for her to see. Taylor did a quick glance out at the water and back to the pad. Three abstract figures rode their surfboards over the waves that were wild and brilliant. Somehow, he had managed to even capture their movement. The sky behind them was ablaze with the setting sun.

"Oh, Will! It's absolutely gorgeous."

Dora was wrong. Her son was definitely not a doodler.

19

Santa Rosa County, Florida

"Is Taylor mad at you?" Brodie asked Jason on the drive home.

"What? No. Why do you think that?"

She shrugged. "You've been checking your phone all night. You don't look happy about what you're reading. That's usually what you do when she's mad at you."

He didn't answer. She needed to change the subject. She wasn't supposed to ask personal stuff.

"The Geminids meteor showers should be visible for the next several nights," she said. "If it's not cloudy."

"That's cool."

More silence.

"It's from an asteroid and not a comet," she said.

He nodded. More silence. This time Brodie stayed quiet.

Then Jason said, "She's not mad at me. Maybe a little disappointed."

He dragged his fingers through his short hair and added, "Well, maybe a little mad, too. She wanted me to have dinner with her and Will tonight."

"You really like Will. So, what's the problem?"

"It's poker night."

She waited to see if he was joking. Or sarcastic. She really needed to figure out the nuances of humor.

When she took too long to respond, he said, "I rescheduled a training session last week, so we could see each other." He rubbed at his jaw and stared straight ahead. "I don't know. Sometimes it feels like I'm the one always readjusting my plans. Like her schedule is more important than mine."

Brodie wasn't sure what she was supposed to say here. Taylor was a nurse. It did seem like she never knew what her work hours were, even though she was assigned to the pediatric floor. It wasn't like she was an ER nurse and on call.

"It's like she doesn't even think about me until she wants to—" He caught himself. Kept his eyes from her. "Until she wants to see me."

That's not what he was going to say. But he had made it clear he didn't want to talk about his sex life with Brodie. He told her that when Brodie had asked too many questions on their road trip to Nebraska a couple of months ago.

Again, Jason didn't wait for a response. This time changing course, almost as if he needed to get his mind back on track. "I know she wants to get full custody of Will, so she has to work her schedule around that. I just…I don't know. I just don't want to be an afterthought. I don't want to be the last thing she makes time for. Does that sound selfish or just totally lame?"

Now he glanced over at her.

"No. I don't think it's lame or selfish." But she was curious. "Why doesn't Will live full-time with her now?"

"It's kind of complicated."

"Complicated you don't know? Or complicated you don't want to talk about it?"

"I'm not sure I know the whole story. Will's dad was killed in Afghanistan before Will was born. She doesn't talk about her parents. I'm not really sure if they're still alive. I just know she felt really alone and overwhelmed. So, when her mother-in-law offered to step in and help, Taylor let her. The rest is a bit fuzzy."

"Fuzzy" was a strange word for him to use, and immediately, Brodie realized Jason knew more. She could tell. But this much was what he was willing to tell her. She found herself wondering if Will knew the whole story of why his mother gave him up. Or what version he had been told. She felt a sudden kinship with the boy, though she'd never met him. Adults were good liars.

The woman who kidnapped Brodie convinced her that her parents didn't want Brodie anymore. Iris Malone had been very convincing, so much so, that when Brodie was finally rescued, she didn't want to see her own mother. Even now, a year later, they were still working on a fractured relationship borne entirely out of lies. She couldn't help thinking that Taylor's son could be feeling something similar. As a kid, it's a tough lesson to learn that you can't trust the adults in your life. They're the people you count on to take care of you, not hurt you. Lie to you.

"Hey," Jason said, glancing over at her.

She stopped herself from sitting up straight. Tried to look like she hadn't gone away even as she casually searched his face in the light from the Jeep's dashboard.

Jason could sense stuff about her. It probably didn't help that he had witnessed one of her worst PTSD breakdowns. In a hotel just over the Missouri border in the middle of the night. It was the first time she'd left the security of Ryder and Hannah's home. Of course, it didn't help matters that they were headed right back to Nebraska, where she had finally escaped.

"You were on fire tonight," Jason told her.

Oh good. He was talking about poker.

She didn't want to tell him that she could guess what cards the rest of them may or may not have, simply by remembering the ones they had discarded. It was easy to keep them in her head, sort them according to suit.

The longer the game went, the more cards got discarded and the easier it was to figure out what ones were left to remain in their hands. It was such a natural thing that she didn't realize everyone couldn't do the same thing.

"You're a good teacher," she told him instead and was instantly rewarded with that full, genuine grin. The one he gave her earlier. The one that made her feel close to him. "It's fun. I like listening to you guys."

And she liked spending time with Jason. Even doing kennel chores together was something she looked forward to every morning. They had grown closer during that road trip to Nebraska, in spite of how tough it was. Not just her breakdown. Ryder and Grace had gone missing. For the first time since being rescued, she had to think and worry about someone else.

She wanted to tell Jason not to worry about Taylor. She wanted to tell him that, of course, Taylor must enjoy spending time with him. He was funny and smart and kind. That everything would work out. But Brodie also knew—even though she didn't know Taylor very well—that the woman had quite a few disastrous relationships with men before. Men had killed and been killed because of her.

A part of Brodie didn't want Jason to be involved with Taylor at all. She didn't want him to get hurt. Brodie realized she didn't have actual personal experiences, but she read a lot. Women like Taylor Donahue rarely had healthy relationships. But there was one thing as far as men were concerned. Women like Taylor usually got their way.

20

Lydia's Bread and Soup Kitchen
Washington, D.C.

Maggie watched R. J. Tully roll up his shirtsleeves. He eyed the pre-plated meals they were about to serve as if he couldn't wait for their free one at the end of the evening. The food actually looked really good. She hadn't eaten since her doughnut and coffee with Nessie.

From what she knew, this organization took leftover or surplus food and turned it into meals. Quantico's new assistant lab director mentioned it. Izzy Kuszak had been a chapter leader at her college. The woman still looked like a college student, and Maggie was having a difficult time envisioning her as Keith Ganza's replacement. She'd worked with Ganza since she was a newbie. It wouldn't be the same walking into that place and not seeing his gray ponytail and ever-changing rock band T-shirt under his dingy white lab coat.

Everything in her life and surroundings were changing all at once.

"When you asked us to meet you for dinner and dress casually," Gwen said while looping the apron over her head, "I expected some new, low-key bistro."

She glanced over. Her friend, Dr. Gwen Patterson, didn't look as enthusiastic as Tully. In fact, she did not look pleased.

"Hey, I had to pull some strings to get us out here serving instead of in back cleaning up."

She handed Gwen a pair of plastic gloves. Tully was already pulling on his pair. Gwen rolled her eyes but took the gloves.

They hadn't opened the doors yet, and the regular employees and volunteers were busy preparing. Only the director knew they were with the FBI. The others thought they were just new recruits.

Maggie took Gwen and Tully into the empty dining area, comfortably out of earshot.

"This place is close to both sites." She didn't need to tell them what "sites" she meant.

She had filled them in earlier about the murders. Or at least shared the details she knew about. Racine was slow in getting her the reports, even though Maggie had called twice to remind her.

However, Racine was quick to tell her, "Not everyone moves at the speed of O'Dell."

She knew Racine's crew was strapped for resources. It was one of the reasons her boss was probably anxious to off-load this case. But it still annoyed Maggie. In Maggie's mind, their response would be much quicker if the victims weren't homeless.

Was that the reason Racine's attitude seemed a bit too nonchalant even for Racine? Or was there something more? Something personal?

"Your profile suggests he's also homeless?" Tully asked.

"I'm not sure yet. I don't have enough information. But so far, it's been his targets."

"No other connection between the victims?" Gwen's eyes were already out the window, examining the line on the sidewalk.

"Racine doesn't have identities yet. I learned more this morning talking to a woman who lives on the street than I did from the homicide department."

"So, what exactly are we looking for?" Tully wanted to know.

"I'm not sure."

"If you're not sure what we're looking for, isn't this a bit premature?" Gwen asked.

"Maybe." Maggie hated how uncertain she sounded. "But it's also early enough," she continued, "that he won't expect us to be watching. He could make a mistake. What I know is two men have been killed in a matter of ten days within blocks of each other. We need to start somewhere because I doubt that he's finished."

Tully nodded. "Okay. Is there anything at all we do know about him?"

Maggie remembered the contents of the bag. She hadn't been allowed to sort through it, but she did get a good look at the pair of shoes inside.

"He has really big feet."

21

Maggie, Gwen, and Tully split up so they wouldn't draw attention. Into their second hour, she started thinking Gwen was right. It was too early. They didn't know enough. She thought something might stand out. Maybe she believed her gut instinct would point her in the right direction.

She took a plate to a wheelchair-bound man who sat patiently at a table in the far corner. Maggie didn't even see the woman come in. The dining area filled quickly with bundled bodies waiting in line or seated at small tables. She grabbed a couple more dinners to distribute, and when she turned around, the woman in the pink scarf stood in front of her.

"Hello," Maggie said, politely but not addressing Nessie by name. She should have anticipated that they might run into each other here. Her mind spun into gear. What could she say so the woman wouldn't blow her cover?

"Can I get one of those?" Nessie asked, pointing to the plates in Maggie's hands. "Or is there some sort of order to this chaos?" She jutted her chin to the right where some people stood in corners, others in line and still others sat at tables eating.

Maggie thought the process looked organized in the beginning, but the snow seemed to bring more people than expected.

"Sure," Maggie said, handing her one of the meals. "We've got roasted chicken, mixed veggies, garden salad and apple crisp."

Nessie licked her lips just like she had earlier that morning when she first saw the pastries Maggie had brought to their table. Maggie tried not to say anything more. She couldn't risk engaging with the woman or even looking like she had met her before.

"Thank you." Nessie took the plate carefully between her mittened hands as though she were being handed something heavy and precious. She didn't move. She stood still, waiting.

Maggie realized she was holding her breath. She did a quick check to see where Gwen and Tully were. When her eyes came back and met Nessie's, the woman did something Maggie never expected. She winked at her. Then she turned and headed over to a table with two others who seemed to recognize her. They greeted her by name and started talking. Nessie didn't look in Maggie's direction again.

Almost an hour later, the crowd dispersed back out onto the snowy sidewalks, hopefully to find their way to one of the night shelters. Anytime the door opened, Maggie could feel the sharp cold. She looked for Nessie, now disappointed the woman hadn't lagged behind. Not that she knew what she would have said to her.

Tully and Gwen waited for her in the far corner, next to a window overlooking the snow-covered sidewalk. They had intended on having their free meal here before heading out.

"You mind if we go somewhere else?" she asked, looking at Tully, who she knew was probably starving. He was always starving. Even now, she had to draw his attention away from the volunteers at a corner table digging into their dinners.

She and Tully had worked as partners in the field for several years, and Maggie had gotten used to "catching a bite," as Tully put it, at roadside diners. She didn't mind him dipping his shirt cuff into gravy or various stains on his ties.

Gwen elbowed him and nodded at Maggie. "What do you think, R.J.? Burgers and beers?"

"Now you're talking," he said. "I've been wanting to check out that place a couple of blocks over."

Maggie wasn't surprised he could come up with a place so easily. They got their coats, then Tully went around back to get his car. As they waited at the door, shoulder to shoulder, Gwen leaned against her and said, "I'm glad we did this."

"Did you notice someone?"

"I noticed a bunch of people that I should have noticed a long time ago. This was a good reminder. Thank you."

"Oh. Sure."

"Unfortunately, I didn't see anyone who tripped my suspicion meter."

"You were right. It was too soon. I don't know what I was expecting."

"I think it helps to see what he's seeing."

"It certainly gives a whole different perspective."

"Exactly."

"The woman I met with this morning showed up. I suspected she might. She was the one who mentioned this place."

"Did she see you?"

"Hard to miss me. I turned around, and she was right in front of me. But she kept my cover."

Maggie scanned the opposite side of the street, almost expecting to get a glimpse of the woman. Very few people were out. The snow was falling harder now.

She hoped Nessie was some place warm. And safe.

22

Saturday, December 2
Florida Panhandle

The cell phone ring made Creed jump, startling the dogs that had been asleep around him. Instead of going to his loft after dinner with Hannah, he'd come back down to the kennel. The conversation with Dr. Avelyn had sent his nerves jangling. He couldn't relax enough to sleep. His jaw remained clamped tight from anger. But being surrounded by the dogs helped.

In the dark he saw the caller's ID, and already he felt some tension slip away.

"Hey," he said.

"Did I wake you?"

"No. I was just staring at the ceiling." Or rather, the rafters three stories up above. He didn't tell her where "here" was. He doubted she'd be surprised, but he wasn't sure if she'd think it was as endearing as Hannah did. Especially if she knew how many times he slept down in the kennel on one of the old sofas or on the floor surrounded by dogs instead of his loft apartment.

He pulled himself up enough to readjust the pillow. A dog behind him readjusted, too, shifting its weight and nestling into the crook of his neck.

Creed's legs were anchored down with dog heads and one hind end that hung over his ankles.

He glanced at his wristwatch. In the stream of moonlight coming through the top windows, he saw it was after two in the morning. Creed didn't ask why Maggie was still awake. He knew she rarely slept, let alone slept well.

"Crazy new case won't let my mind shut down," she finally said. "How was the rest of your day? You and Bolo were in the woods."

"We were tracking a missing teenage boy."

"Did you find him?"

"Only his jacket." He scratched at his jaw. There was still something odd about that. Why would a teenager go down into the woods, leave his jacket and go back up the exact way? "Bolo lost the kid's scent after the jacket."

"That doesn't sound like Bolo. Are we talking about a runaway, or is it possible he was taken against his will?"

"Differing opinions on both counts. Either way, we didn't find him. What new case is driving you crazy?"

"Couple of homeless guys have been murdered. Right on the streets. In the middle of the night. No one claims to have seen a thing."

"Doesn't D.C. have a bunch of cameras?"

"I'm hoping. Problem is nobody seems to care too much. It's like they're throwaways. Disposable. Reminds me too much of sex trafficking victims. No one ever seems to see those women…girls…and boys."

She stopped. Went silent, and Creed thought about his sister Brodie. Maybe Maggie was, too. For years while Brodie was missing, Creed tried to convince himself that hadn't happened to her. But she was destined to be trafficked if they hadn't found her when they did.

Desperate to put that out of his mind, he said, "Sheriff Norwich and I met a couple of homeless guys today."

"I thought you said you were in the woods?"

"We were. They've set up camps. This one old guy named Sully seems really ordinary. Nice guy. Even has a dog."

"I met a homeless woman today who is interesting. She told me more over a couple of donuts and coffee than the detectives who've been on the case. Be careful though, Ryder."

"Careful? What do you mean?"

"I know you. People with problems gravitate toward you. And you tend to think you need to rescue them, sort of like you rescue dogs."

"Is that a bad thing?"

"Let's see. Since I've known you, your rescuing efforts of lost and needy people have gotten you on a drug cartel's hit list, buried under a mudslide, exposed to the bird flu, and literally thrown by a tornado. Do you want me to go on?"

The smile in her voice made him smile.

"So this new case…you're not calling to cancel your Christmas trip?"

"No. Not at all. In fact, I can't wait to get out of the snow. We rarely have much, and it's piling up."

"Come down early." He couldn't believe he said it out loud this time. He worried if he sounded too eager, it might spook her. And, of course, she went quiet again. Other than working on a case, they'd never spent a week together. "I'm just saying, it sounds like you could use a walk on the beach."

"That does sound good. But what about you? How are you doing?"

"I feel okay. Mended. Or maybe still mending. You forgot to add to that list, me being knifed by a girl."

"I didn't want to totally embarrass you. So, what is it that has you staring at the ceiling?"

"Dogs."

"Is it Grace?"

"No. She really is doing good. Dr. Avelyn's going to be quarantining some K9s they're rescuing out of Afghanistan."

"The ones they left behind."

She didn't sound surprised, and it wasn't a question.

"You know about that?"

"Let's just say you can't be in D.C. and not hear stuff. I guess deep down, I hoped it wasn't true. But I've had politicians lie to me enough times to know it could be."

"Yeah, well, a military handler recognized her dog. Still over there. In a dirty cage. A mining company found him on the streets." He could feel the anger rising again. Grace lifted her head to check on him.

"I'm glad they're finding them. Bringing them home."

"Me, too."

23

Santa Rosa County, Florida

Creed slowed the Jeep down as he searched for the entrance of the Monroe family's neighborhood. The pine trees along the highway were too thick to see what was on the other side, but he knew it wasn't far from where they'd searched yesterday.

Housing developments seemed to spring up in pockets of what he used to consider forest. Though the neighborhood they were looking for was two or three decades old.

He was glad to have Jason and Scout along. His eyes kept darting up to the rearview mirror, checking on Grace. Other than being overly excited, she appeared to be physically back to her old self. Despite his best efforts, he felt the tension in his back, stiff and tight against the seat. He knew he was still healing, and maybe he expected that Grace was, too.

"Taylor's in-laws live on the opposite side," Jason interrupted Creed's thoughts. He gestured with his mechanical thumb to the opposite side of the highway.

There was a recent development with paved streets that seemed to go to nowhere. Many of the lots were empty, some in the process of construction and others still being cleared. Only a sprinkling of big houses could be seen from the highway. Backhoes and bulldozers, along with pallets of construction material, filled some of the vacant areas.

"They've really cut deep into the forest," Creed said.

It reminded him of the challenges it took to make a living space in this part of the country. Their facility, K9 CrimeScents, was only about ten miles away. It backed to the Blackwater River State Forest, and woods still surrounded the fifty-acre training facility, that was also their home.

When they bought the property, the massive colonial-style house was the only structure there. He and Hannah cleared acres of trees and shrubs to add a condo-style kennel with a loft apartment for Creed. Over the years, they added a double-wide trailer for on-site handlers. It was now Jason and Scout's home. Then came a fieldhouse with an Olympic-sized swimming pool for water training the dogs. Last, they added a medical clinic with a surgical suite.

He was proud of what they'd created, but they'd always tried to preserve as much of the nature around them as they could. Developers like this one took the easy route and simply bulldozed swatches of land until it was almost unrecognizable.

"The houses are massive," Jason told him. "The Ramseys have a screened enclosure with a pool and patio that looks like a resort. They have what must be three lots. Pick of the litter, so to speak." He glanced at Creed. "They own the land. Ramsey construction is the developer."

"So, you've been invited inside?"

"Yeah, right." Jason laughed, but it was more of a scoff than humor. "Taylor showed me the photos from some architectural magazine that featured it."

Creed only nodded and stayed quiet. He knew Taylor's mother-in-law, Dora Ramsey, had been reluctant to give up custody of Taylor's son. He'd listened to Jason talk about her battle against "the high-priced lawyers" and the judge who was a long-time friend of the family. The Ramseys had enough money and influence to get the outcome they wanted no matter what Taylor did.

Dora Ramsey had even driven Hannah to frustration. Hannah had been dealing with the woman all summer after Dora had given the Segway House a generous donation. For Hannah to complain about any donor meant the woman must be a challenge.

Finally, Creed found the entrance he was looking for. A crooked sign on a leaning post marked the neighborhood as Woodriver. Ironically, it was directly opposite of the new development's entrance. The huge archway's crisp and bold lettering announced Linden Estates.

As Creed drove through Woodriver's streets, he couldn't help thinking how different the two were. Here, the lots were small, with patches of grass for front yards. Vehicles were parked along the streets, interspersed with trashcans waiting at the end of driveways to be emptied or pulled back. It made some spots a tight squeeze.

No two houses looked alike, although most were single story. There were also some double-wide trailers with underpinnings neatly wrapped around the bottoms. Toys and bicycles spilled out onto the front yards and in the driveways.

He found the Monroe's house easily, only because two Santa Rosa County sheriff department SUVs were parked in front of the single-story clapboard. The detached garage set all the way to the back of the property, leaving plenty of driveway. And yet, the minivan looked squished between a chain-link fence and the large crew cab pickup with Monroe Landscaping printed on the door. Attached to the hitch was a trailer overloaded with assorted equipment, bags of fertilizer, and rolls of sod.

"How long has this kid been missing?" Jason asked.

"I'm not sure anyone knows exactly. But he's been gone two nights."

Sheriff Norwich stood on the small porch. She waved when she recognized Creed's Jeep. The first available space for him to park was two houses down. But he noticed in passing what looked like a flicker of relief cross her face.

She glanced back at her deputies, one coming out to join her, the other filling the front doorway. She said something to them, and they headed to their vehicle. Norwich had waited a beat longer on the porch. She flinched when the door slammed shut behind her. Then she made her way down the steps and over to greet the dog handlers.

"She doesn't look happy." Jason's eyes followed Norwich. She walked across lawns to cut a path to them.

"No, she doesn't. Stay here and keep the dogs settled," Creed told Jason. "Let me see what's going on."

He met her at the tailgate of the Jeep. Norwich kept her back to the Monroe house. Her face sagged. She looked tired, and it was still morning.

"They claimed they got a text from Caleb just before we arrived." She didn't bother to hide the sarcasm or her disbelief. "Said he was staying with a friend. They showed me the text."

Creed stood at the Jeep's hitch and faced her while, behind his sunglasses, his eyes scanned the Monroe house. Even though Norwich stayed on the curb, he was taller than her and had a perfect view of the front of the house and most of the side. A curtain rustled in a window toward the back. Someone was still watching them.

"Have you checked phone records?" Creed asked, his eyes darting between the windows and the front door. "If we knew where his phone last pinged...what tower. Maybe what area, at least..."

"That takes time," she started to gesture, then crossed her arms over her chest. Norwich knew she was being watched. "I barely had a missing teenager. At best, a runaway one. Or at the very least, one who's allegedly run away before. The parents now say he's fine. What am I going to do? Argue with them? I don't have the time or resources to play these games."

They stood silent while cars drove by and neighbors looked to see why sheriff vehicles were parked in their neighborhood.

"I don't feel good about this," Norwich confessed.

"We've got the dogs here. We could do an unofficial search," he offered.

"That's the other thing. He wants no dogs on his property."

"He said that?"

"He said that."

He pushed his sunglasses on top of his head to meet her eyes. Her face softened, and she leaned forward. "Look, this isn't worth your dogs getting hurt. I'll follow up on this. If he's not in school Monday, they'll have some explaining to do."

She pursed her lips and stopped herself from looking back over her shoulder. Her cell phone rang, and she snatched it from her pocket to look at the caller I.D.

"Hang on a minute," she told Creed. She took the call, saying very little, mostly listening. "Okay then," she finally said. "Thanks for being so quick."

She slipped the phone away and glanced in the back window of the Jeep. Then to Creed she said, "You brought Grace and Scout. I've got you all scheduled. I know you were prepared to do a missing person search. Is it difficult to switch up?"

His first reaction was to tell her, "Yes. It would be too difficult." He had already gone through all sorts of arguments with himself this morning before deciding this search—a neighborhood search for a missing teenager—would be low impact, low risk for Grace.

"Depends," he finally said. "What are we talking about, Sheriff?"

"That bone Bolo alerted to yesterday. Chipped and chewed up a bit, but it turns out it is human. A left tibia."

24

Quantico, Virginia

Maggie chose the empty cafeteria to meet with her team. She was early, commandeering her favorite table next to the window overlooking the woods. Snow covered the trees. It was still lightly falling. She missed running the trails, although she'd brought her gear.

Wishful thinking. No way she could plow through. Not being able to run out in the fresh air was almost as bad as being down underground.

There would be no competition for the table. The place was empty. Classes were finished for the year. Many of the agents scheduled time off for the holidays.

The holidays. Thanksgiving. Christmas. New Years.

None of them held much meaning for Maggie. Her father died when she was twelve. Her short marriage created no holiday traditions. Even when her mother experienced periods of sobriety, Maggie still avoided her. Her half-brother Patrick had only recently come into her life, but as a first responder, he usually worked through the holidays or was on call.

Gwen and Tully, her dogs Harvey and Jake. They were her family. And now Ryder.

She smiled at the memory of his face when she suggested that she come down and spend Christmas with him. He had tried to pretend it wasn't a big deal, but his eyes said otherwise. Despite the life and death situations they had been through together, they were still sorting out this new level of their relationship. Which seemed a bit silly. They had already become close friends. Long ago, Hannah had welcomed Maggie as though she were a part of their family. Brodie and Jason and all the dogs… She knew she would fit in.

And yet, she tried not to look too forward to the trip. Like so much of her life, any time she'd let her guard down and cared about someone, it usually resulted in disappointment. Sometimes betrayal. And whether she wanted to admit it or not, Ryder was right. It was a big deal.

Gwen claimed Maggie sabotaged relationships just to avoid getting hurt. "You do that often enough," Gwen told her, "And you miss out on a whole lot of happiness."

To which Maggie replied, "I think happiness is overrated."

"Says the woman who has only dabbled in the concept."

She watched out the window as she waited for the others. Recently, she started bringing her work up here where she could breathe. Her cramped office triggered her claustrophobia. Not because it was small, but because it was down underground—too many stories—she didn't want to count. Even getting on the elevator made her break out in a sweat.

She couldn't admit it. *Wouldn't admit it.* If she did, they'd send her to see the bureau psychologist. It was the way they dealt with vulnerabilities around here.

When the new director asked her to take this assignment, and he agreed to let her build her own team, he'd also offered her a larger office. But the office he referenced was still down underground in the Behavioral Science Unit. Eventually, she'd need to figure out a way to ask for an office somewhere else on campus.

Agent Antonio Alonzo was the first to arrive. He wore an orange oxford button-down, neatly tucked into black trousers. His shiny leather shoes obviously hadn't touched the slush outside. His eyeglass frames matched his shirt, and he brought his own designer coffee.

Alonzo was a cyber-wizard. Maggie was anxious to hear what, if anything, he'd learned in the short amount of time. He grinned when he saw her and took the seat closest to her right.

"You have a habit of giving me less and less to work with," he laughed.

"It's D.C. I thought there were cameras on every street corner."

"That might be true in some areas." He opened his laptop and started tapping. "We're dealing with places where the so-called political class doesn't hang out. So, in other words, very few cameras."

"There has to be something."

"I haven't found a captured image of either murder. A couple close, but no angle or direct view. But then, he probably knew that, right? I separated what we do have of both crime scenes from the time slots you gave me. My focus was establishing patterns, similarities, anything and everything that might overlap. Facial recognition is not helpful with scarves and hoods and dark shadows. Also, these people don't move much. They spend a lot of time hunkered down under blankets and in makeshift tents."

"It's cold out, Alonzo."

"I know. I get it. But I could barely track the victims."

"Do we have identities on either yet?"

"I tapped into the autopsy report for the first victim, and—"

"Wait. You didn't get anything from Detective Racine?"

"Not yet." He shrugged. It didn't matter to him. He could access what he needed without the formalities. Who was Maggie to argue? She'd never played well with others.

"I got the fingerprints for both victims," Alonzo said. "I've already run them through all the regular databases. No hits. Which only means neither of them were in the military, had government clearance, was listed as missing or had a criminal record.

"The only other pieces of information I have are that their names were *maybe* Danny and Carlo. I'll try facial recognition, but those programs don't always like it when the only photos I've got are dead guys."

His fingers were still tapping.

"I do have something, though."

"I'm listening."

"I put in all the information into ViCAP. Narrowed it to the last six months."

ViCAP was the Violent Crime Apprehension Program that tracked communication between law enforcement agencies.

"You got a hit on the M.O.?" Maggie asked.

"October. Homeless guy inside a tent. Hit on the head, then stabbed. Coroner's report listed a ball-peen hammer as a possible weapon."

"Racine didn't mention any of this."

"She probably didn't know. It was downtown Jacksonville, Florida."

"How many miles is that from D.C.?"

"Approximately seven hundred, if you take I-95 South. About ten hours and fifteen minutes if you don't stop for coffee and potty breaks."

"You think it's the same guy?"

Alonzo shrugged. She could tell he had more.

"I opened up the perimeters to include a longer stretch of time. Same details: ball-peen hammer, stab wounds, homeless. Got another hit. February of last year. Five-day window. Two homeless victims. New York City."

"Two victims in five days? Were we ever consulted on those two?"

"Not that I can find."

"How has no one noticed?"

"Different cities. All the victims were homeless. The murders appeared to be random. Lots of random attacks on the homeless, especially in these three cities. In New York, just two weeks before, someone shoved a homeless guy onto the subway tracks as a train was approaching."

Maggie winced. He was right. Random crime had skyrocketed in the last several years for some of these cities. What looked like a serial killer to her could easily be lost in the wash of violent crimes.

For more than a decade, she'd profiled dozens of twisted killers. Sometimes all she had were their victims—or pieces of them—to tell her what happened through the evidence left behind. But not being able to identify the victims would make their job more difficult.

"Do you have IDs for any of those victims?"

"Not for October. And only one from February." He'd brought along a file folder, and now he slid it over to her.

"Do you think there could be more?"

"You know, not every department puts their unsolved homicides in ViCAP. Also, the ball-peen hammer might not have been identified or reported in some reports. That's what got me the hits. But I'm still searching. So, you think it's the same guy?"

"Could all be a coincidence."

"Except you don't believe in coincidences." He tipped his coffee cup at her to emphasize the point before taking a sip. "You said the MPD may have found his throwaway at this last scene?"

"We're hoping it's his."

"If Kuszak pulls some DNA, I'll have a whole new run at it."

"If it's the same guy, this certainly would eliminate him being homeless."

"D.C., Jacksonville and New York City," Alonzo said. "I haven't been able to determine a pattern with those cities."

"If there is one, I'm sure you'll find it. Don't stop looking though. I have a gut feeling there are other cities."

25

The others began arriving. Their chatter echoed from across the empty cafeteria. Maggie had a chance to study them and their interactions, if only for the minutes it took to cross the huge room.

Gwen was the focus. She was the center of the pack and the obvious leader, although she never tried or liked being in charge. She had an undeniable air of authority, along with an innate compassion, that drew people to her. Dr. Gwen Patterson was a private psychologist who had been a consultant for the FBI even before Maggie arrived.

Gwen's life partner, R.J. Tully, had been Maggie's FBI partner until a few years ago. He was a seasoned agent when the two of them had been forced together. Back then, Tully's directive from their assistant director was to bring calm and rationality to a rogue Maggie O'Dell.

That seemed like ages ago. Since then, they had traveled hundreds of miles together, shared many meals while tracking some crazed killers. Even with his bum knee, that she felt partially responsible for, he was still the agent she'd want in the field with her to cover her back.

The newbie was their forensic investigator and the assistant lab director, Isabel "Izzy" Kuszak. She was also the youngest of Maggie's team. Small framed with a youthful face, she could easily pass for a teenager and usually dressed like one. Today was no different. She wore baggy cargo pants and black lace-up combat boots with her white lab coat. A neon-pink

T-shirt peeked from underneath. Her pixie-cut hair was shaved up the back with a long fringe of bangs in the front. Its silver-gray matched her gray-blue eyes.

Keith Ganza, the director of the FBI Lab had recommended Kuszak when he turned down the position Maggie had offered to him. He told her he was planning to retire soon. Maggie's mind stopped listening for a few minutes, trying to process the word "retire." One more person she trusted, gone.

She barely heard Ganza while he recited a litany of the new assistant director's qualities, finally landing on, "You know me," Ganza said, "I wouldn't say it if I didn't believe it. This kid's wicked smart." Then he added, not because he thought it would make a difference, but because he was Ganza, "She reminds me of you when you came in as a newbie."

That seemed like a lifetime ago when everything was first-time interesting and exciting. Before the skepticism and all the other hard lessons. Sometimes bad guys got away. Sometimes they pretended to even be on your side. And always they left scars.

Ganza promised Kuszak would be an invaluable asset to the team if Maggie could overlook the young woman's youth and inexperience. She wondered if he had said those same words about her years ago. Over a decade now.

Antonio Alonzo was young and brilliant as well. For as much as Kuszak looked like she threw together a strange wardrobe combination, Alonzo's looked like he carefully curated it himself.

They were a motley crew of different ages, backgrounds, experiences, and expertise. But they were each a part of her team by invitation. Except for Julia Racine. She was here simply out of necessity. After all, this was the detective's case. Otherwise, she'd never be on Maggie's team. Racine didn't play well with others. And for as long as Maggie had known the woman, she still didn't trust her.

Maggie remained standing while the others took seats around the table, setting down what they brought with them: mugs, notepads, file folders, laptops and switching off cell phones.

All of them had given up their Saturday. Alonzo and Kuszak had come from different parts of Quantico's campus. Gwen and Tully had driven from their Georgetown condo and Racine from her home.

Maggie asked Alonzo to share the information he'd already told her. She watched Racine while he went through the hits he'd gotten. She wasn't sure what she expected, what she was looking for. Maybe she wanted Racine to gasp at the reality of how much she'd missed.

But Maggie reminded herself that Racine had only had this case for less than two weeks. Until the last murder, there was no reason to connect the dots. Actually, no dots to connect. Smart killers depended on that. They stayed ahead of the game, moved around, and targeted a vulnerable population that was difficult for law enforcement to track or even identify.

Listening to Alonzo, Maggie realized how daunting their task was.

When he was finished, she looked to Racine and asked, "Do we have an identity for either of the two D.C. victims?"

Racine shook her head and looked at Kuszak, anxious to give up this responsibility. Maggie tamped down her simmering irritation. Why was she surprised Racine chose the easy way out? And yet, D.C. had both bodies.

Izzy Kuszak didn't even notice Racine's deflection. Her eyes were on her yellow notepad, her pen scratching out messages to herself. It wasn't until she noticed the silence around the table that she looked up.

"Our lab doesn't have anything belonging to the victims," Kuszak said. "Can't help you there."

Maggie felt the shift of impatience around the table. But Kuszak didn't seem to notice.

"Has D.C. provided a copy of the autopsy?" Maggie asked Kuszak, but her eyes were on Racine.

"Not yet," Kuszak told her.

Before Maggie could question Racine, she put up a hand, gesturing to give her a minute. "I brought copies for everyone." She opened a file folder and rifled through loose-leaf papers inside. She pulled out sets of stapled copies and slid them across the table to each team member.

Maggie asked Alonzo, "How did you get your information to do the victim searches?"

"Oh, I have my ways."

"Give me a break, O'Dell," Racine cut her off. "This last one just happened yesterday morning."

The young forensic investigator didn't appear bothered by Racine's flippant attitude. Instead, Kuszak examined the contents and jotted down notes.

"Both victims sustained head trauma," Racine told them. "Stan—" she stopped herself when she realized not everyone around the table would know who Stan was. "The medical examiner," she continued, "says the mark left looks like a ball-peen hammer. He doesn't believe it was a fatal blow. That came from a weapon with a double-edged blade. Neither was recovered at the scene of the crime. Unless something was found in that Dumpster throwaway?"

She looked over at Kuszak.

"No hammer. No knife," Kuszak said. "The plastic grocery bag does contain some interesting things. Latex gloves. A ticket stub and receipt. A pair of well-worn shoes, size eleven with blood stains. I've already pulled samples. It is blood. If I can get some DNA from the victim, I can tell you whether the blood is his." She was looking to Racine now for confirmation.

"That shouldn't be a problem," Racine told her.

Shouldn't be a problem, instead of *yes*. Maggie found Racine's lackadaisical attitude beyond annoying. Asking for the FBI's help didn't mean checking out completely. And if she'd truly done just that, why even bother coming here today? Racine had made it sound like her boss didn't have time for a couple of homeless people getting killed. The fact that the killer could be the same person should warrant attention. At least from Racine.

Maggie was so sick of politics. She considered how she might go around the detective, when Kuszak added, "If the blood matches the victim, then it makes sense the bag belonged to the killer. That's our agreed supposition, right?"

"Yes," Maggie told her. "And I'm hoping the shoes and their treads will tell us more about him."

"We might not need that," Kuszak said in a no-nonsense tone. "I actually have his fingerprints."

26

"How do you know they're the killer's fingerprints?" Maggie challenged the young forensic investigator. She didn't mind confidence. She wouldn't tolerate cockiness.

"First, we need to prove the blood found on the items inside that plastic bag actually belongs to the victim. If the blood is the victim's, then the fingerprints are the killer's."

R.J. Tully leaned in, his elbows on the table. He didn't bother to hide the skepticism from his face. "He probably wasn't the only one to touch that bag."

"I didn't find prints on the bag." Again, Kuszak didn't seem to mind the others around the table questioning her. "I found them on a pair of latex gloves."

"Is that even possible?" Racine asked.

"Possible. But rare," Maggie answered, not taking her eyes off Kuszak and waiting for an explanation.

"There was blood on the outside of the gloves. Some of it rubbed off. I don't have the item he wiped his hands with. When people take off latex gloves, they peel them off. They're tight enough that the fingerprint doesn't smear. Like you said, it is rare," Kuszak said, looking to Maggie. "Finding these within hours of him peeling them off helps. These were fresh. There was still perspiration."

"Fingerprint powders attach nicely to sweat," she continued, "and to the oil residues left behind. I used a magnetic fluorescent powder combined with cyanoacrylate fuming."

"Cyanoacrylate?" Tully asked.

"Superglue," Maggie answered, and Kuszak nodded at her.

"I also found an excellent thumbprint on the interior of the right glove cuff. He probably left it there when he was pulling on the gloves."

Kuszak lifted her hands to demonstrate, letting the cuffs of her lab coat sag to her elbow. The sleeves of her lab coat were too long and rolled up. That's when Maggie noticed that the shoulders hit off the mark, too. The coat was a size too big, but it didn't seem to bother Kuszak. Nor did it deter her confidence.

"When you pull on the first glove," she demonstrated the process, "your other is still barehanded. Most people don't think about that. Even if they're being careful. You leave fingerprints on the glove. On the outside, they're usually smeared. Mostly useless. But on the inside, the thumbprint was well preserved. I haven't had time to enter what I've processed into AFIS."

The Automated Fingerprint Identification System would only be helpful if the prints belonged to someone already in the system. Maggie had tracked other serial killers who had started their criminal careers committing other crimes like burglary and arson before accelerating to rape or murder. So, it was possible he was already in the system.

"Were any prints recovered at the other crime scene?" Tully asked.

Racine shook her head. She didn't even check her file.

Maggie looked over at Tully and Gwen. Tully scribbled notes on the back of what looked like a greasy takeout receipt. Gwen caught her eyes and subtly raised one eyebrow, then flashed her eyes to Kuszak.

Gwen was impressed. So was Maggie.

27

Washington D.C.

Peter Gregory studied the glossy magazine photo. Ever since he'd discovered the five-page article, he'd spent hours reading over the information and examining all the accompanying photos. Originally, he'd found it on-line then immediately hunted for a physical copy. Not a simple task these days when very few places still sold magazines.

Every time he sat and read and scrutinized, it surprised him how much emotion he did *not* feel. It was as if he was staring at a stranger, a life and home he couldn't relate to no matter how much he tried.

To be fair, it had been almost eight years since he had visited. And that was only to stand on a hilltop in the cemetery and watch them put his brother into the ground.

Oh, there had always been invitations after that. Though they came less frequently these days. However, one arrived about a month ago. It came via email to an account he rarely checked. He didn't need to pull out a copy to remember. He had the words memorized:

The holidays are coming.
It would be nice if you could join us.

The holidays.

Wasn't that sweet of her? The email came about two weeks before Thanksgiving. How kind and sentimental from a woman who was neither.

Christmas music played overhead in the diner. He'd taken a booth in the back where he could stare at his magazine, eat his sandwich, drink coffee and not be bothered.

Their last Christmas as a family, his father had given him a Jedi lightsaber and a stack of Marvel comic books. He smiled at the thought of his ten-year-old self running around the backyard in the dark waving that lightsaber. He loved his father. Still did.

His mother didn't approve of the gifts. She told his father he shouldn't encourage the boy to make up stories and enjoy so much fantasy. It would make him a liar, or worse—a dreamer like his father.

It didn't matter what she said. His father embraced what he called their creativity and inventiveness.

"You can't silence a soul." That was one of his favorite comebacks.

He and his father were the geeks of the family, direct contrasts to his mother and little brother. They'd quote lines of movies or books to each other. His father quoted Emily Dickinson to him when he suspected his son was feeling down about being different:

I'm Nobody! Who are you?
Are you nobody, too?
Then there's a pair of us—don't tell!
They'd banish us, you know.

Gregory remembered climbing into the treehouse his dad had built for his sons. Mickey rarely used it, off to football practice or baseball or whatever the season. So Gregory had it all to himself. He'd read for hours. Spiderman dancing under the flashlight beam. Sometimes he pretended he didn't hear his mother yelling for him to come in.

Holidays after his father passed were just hollow attempts, a sad ritual of going through the motions. To compensate, his mother showered them with gifts. None of them were close to anything he wanted or cared about. They were always something she believed he *should* want: an expensive leather baseball glove; a chemistry set; or collared, button-up shirts to replace his Star Wars and Marvel T-shirts.

She added more tinsel to the tree, fancier meals, and then one year she even added a stepfather.

She still didn't have a clue.

He wondered why the holidays invoked an invitation. Why was that the only time of year that anyone out of sight seemed to come to mind? Did she not think about him for the rest of the year? If it wasn't for the money, she would have lost track of him long ago.

Maybe his father had known that all along. Why else would he leave his oldest son such a fortune? Had he realized that if he was gone from their lives that his wife might need extra incentive to take care of the son she didn't understand? The son she really didn't even like.

He looked at the photo of his mother in the magazine. Stared into her eyes, and silently asked, "Is that it, dear ole mom? Are you running low on cash? Are you still after dad's money? My money?"

He glanced out into the falling snow. It was supposed to have stopped by now. Maybe his mother was right. Maybe it was time for a family celebration. If nothing else, it'd be nice to feel warmer temperatures. Distract the loop in his brain. The nightmares had been showing him new and compelling details, teasing at a truth he never imagined.

He'd spent the last several years trying to dismantle the images that haunted him by setting the record straight. By trying to kill proxies of the man who had killed his father—that transient pretending his old pickup was stalled on the side of the road.

It wasn't until the last few weeks he started to realize those homeless men were insufficient proxies. His brain was unleashing new information. Maybe the killings were the catalyst. Something had dislodged the revealing details. His subconscious began showing him more and more of who that man was. The man who bludgeoned his father on the side of the road twenty years ago.

Just as he looked back from the window, a familiar figure walked by down on the street. He watched as if mesmerized. The snow formed glitter on everything it touched. Steam rising from the sidewalk grates set it swirling. So frickin' magical, even the homeless plodding along and swaddled in thick layers made it look like a scene out of Dickens' *A Christmas Carol.*

And that reminded him of his father, too. He had taken them to a live production at the Saenger Theatre. Gregory was only seven and completely captivated by the costumes, the lights, the sounds. Every time he glanced his father's way, he saw him smiling at him and nodding, knowing his oldest son would be as delighted as he was.

Christmas, happiness, joy…they all died along with his father. And yet, he had to be bombarded with songs of yuletide cheer. With fat snowflakes that glittered and twinkled and stuck to every surface.

Yes, he needed a change of scenery. But maybe he also needed one more killing to nudge his subconscious into finally showing him the face of the man who murdered his father.

28

Santa Rosa County, Florida

"There actually are other reasons for a body to be disarticulated," Sheriff Norwich explained as she led Creed and Jason down into the woods. Grace and Scout followed along.

Creed figured she was talking to fill the silence. Both he and Jason knew from experience what could happen to a body on land, in the ground, and even under water. He was half-listening while his eyes darted around. He didn't recognize this area, and yet, it had to be close to their search from yesterday.

Norwich had given them directions to a narrow two-lane about a mile from Caleb Monroe's neighborhood. Crumbling asphalt erased the faded white lines that hadn't been updated. The road curved between the trees so many times he'd lost track of direction. Now, Creed tried to draw a map in his head with this new entrance into the woods and place it next to yesterday's.

"Bears are notorious for breaking apart a body," Norwich continued.

This time, Jason shot Creed a "what's up" look with a chin-poke toward the sheriff's back. She was in the lead and couldn't see them, so Creed shrugged at him.

Maybe she was trying to convince herself that there was no foul play involved.

"You both, of course, remember last summer? Those bodies we found in the middle of the Blackwater River State Forest. Nature has a way of reducing a body on its own without human assistance."

"And that was exactly what the killer intended," Jason said.

Norwich's head bobbed in agreement without glancing at them.

Creed didn't need a reminder about that case. His back still ached at night from the bruises of being dragged and bounced along the forest floor. The killer had attempted to burn away the crime scene evidence along with Creed.

Without warning, just like yesterday, they stumbled upon a garbage dump. Creed gestured to Jason, and they brought the dogs to a halt. Norwich had also stopped, hands on her hips as she turned and scowled at the debris piles.

Before any of them had time to respond, both dogs' heads jerked up and looked in the same direction, bodies going rigid. Then Creed could hear a vehicle's engine slowing to a stop but idling. The sound came from behind a ridge of trees at the top of an incline.

Both men looked over at Sheriff Norwich.

"I didn't know there was another road up there," she told them.

"Is it worth checking out?" Jason asked.

Norwich was considering it just as a crash of branches and shrubs gave way to something tossed over the ridge. They were close enough to see huge chunks of concrete tumbling down.

"What in the hell?" Norwich said and started marching up the incline.

Creed instinctively scooped up Grace under his arm and caught up. He pointed out to the sheriff a worn path that would take them up but keep them out of range if anything else came raining down.

Sure enough, another crack of branches and swoosh and something flew over the top of the ridge. Creed glanced over his shoulder to check on Jason and Scout. The pair had moved all the way to the opposite side. Creed caught Jason's attention and gave him a wave of approval.

Norwich's breath sounded a bit ragged, and Creed stayed close at her elbow. Just six months ago, she'd had a heart attack. Since then, she'd slimmed down a bit and seemed leaner and stronger than ever. She didn't slow down, stomping through the brush all the way to the top.

There was a clearing beyond the trees. Parked and backed to the edge of the woods was a white pickup. On the door, a company logo was splattered with mud. The tailgate was dropped open. Construction material filled the bed: broken rebar, odd pieces of drywall, paint cans and chunks of concrete.

A huge man, his jeans and T-shirt coated in gray dust, stood in the bed of the pickup as he heaved pieces through the trees and over the ridge.

"What the hell do you think you're doing?" Norwich yelled, but the man's back was turned, and he didn't hear her. He kept flinging armfuls.

Before Creed could stop her, Norwich rushed to the pickup, one hand digging for her badge, the other searching her belt for her holstered weapon.

"Hey, buddy! Hold up!" Jason yelled, coming out of the trees from the other side.

The man saw him and froze. Then he did a double take at Norwich, coming up on his side.

"What do you think you're doing?" Norwich shouted, almost breathless now. The hand that originally searched for her weapon latched on to the side of the vehicle.

"One of you owns this property?" he asked.

"I'm the sheriff of Santa Rosa County." She swung up her arm for him to see the badge.

The man looked around, surprised, but then he smiled and shook his head. "Come on. Everybody dumps here, and you're gonna bust my ass? The homeless leave their trash all over the place."

"I don't think the homeless are tossing drywall and concrete."

This time the guy shrugged, though the gesture got lost with his shoulders already almost reaching his ears. “Hey, my boss told me to dump this stuff.”

Norwich pocketed her badge and brought out a small notebook and pen. “Let me see your driver’s license.”

“What?” Finally, a look of disbelieve. “You’re kidding me, right?”

“She’s not kidding,” Creed told him.

“I’ll need to see it to write up your citation for illegal dumping.”

“Maybe I don’t have my license on me,” he said with almost a snicker, like somehow, he’d outfoxed her.

“Really?” Norwich looked up at him.

He would tower over her even if he was on the ground, but the added height of the pickup bed made him resemble a giant. The sheriff, however, was not the least bit intimidated.

“So you want me to add driving without a driver’s license to illegal dumping and failing to comply with law enforcement?”

He stood perfectly still now. His eyes darted over to Creed and Jason. There was a long pause.

“Up to you,” Norwich said. “I can always get the information from your boss.” She pointed to the logo on the side of the pickup, and the man’s shoulders sagged with the realization. Still, he made them wait.

Creed noticed even the dogs were watching quietly. Finally, the guy pulled his wallet from his back pocket and handed the license down to the sheriff.

Creed kept his eyes on the man. Norwich may have believed she succeeded, but as she concentrated on writing down the information, the man glared at her. And Creed could see his anger barely restrained as he balled up his fists then crossed his bulging arms.

Later, Creed and Jason followed Norwich back down the incline and through the brush.

"It's ridiculous that people think they can throw anything away by dumping it in the woods." Norwich was still visibly angry. "Nobody learns. Twenty-five years ago, when they built Garcon Point Bridge, the construction company dumped tons of concrete pilings and rebar into Pensacola Bay. Why? Because they could."

Creed noticed they were headed back the same way they'd come. Jason noticed, too. When he started to point it out, Creed caught his eyes and stopped him with a slight shake of his head. Without being told, Creed knew the sheriff was finished out here. If she didn't agree, he'd think of something. As soon as the pickup was out of sight—and so were they—he saw that her hand trembled slightly while she tucked her notebook into her pocket. Despite her resolve during the encounter, it had shaken her.

They returned halfway down the path when she turned to them. "Guys, I'm sorry to waste your time. Wasted your whole morning."

"Not a problem, Sheriff," Creed told her.

"I didn't expect that detour."

She looked around his shoulder and back through the trees. He wondered if she was making sure the man hadn't followed them. As sheriff, she was probably used to looking over her shoulder.

"I appreciate you both having my back," she said, almost as if reading his mind. "I need to get a little something to eat. Can I buy all of you lunch?"

Before either could respond, she gestured to the dogs and added, "The Oval Office uses fresh ground chuck."

29

Creed tried not to watch Jason wolf down his burger, though it was like a car accident on the side of the road. Messy, but hard to look away.

Jason had chosen what the Oval Office called their Myrtle Burger. It was seven ounces of beef with grilled onions and melted cheese. A beautiful creation on its own. Jason included the standard burger toppings of lettuce, tomato, pickles and mayo, so the sandwich stood at least six-inches tall.

It constantly amazed Creed how much the kid could eat. His lean, compact body seemed geared to accommodate an insatiable appetite. Creed glanced over at Norwich, who was devouring her own sandwich. She caught his eyes and darted a look over to Jason, then smiled, obviously pleased.

The owner had allowed them to bring in Scout and Grace. Creed accepted his offer of bowls of water for the dogs but turned down burgers of their own. He was careful about what his dogs ate, and both understood the protein bars they'd eaten in the Jeep would hold them over until they were fed their meals. Now they lie at their handlers' feet, tucked close and content to watch the other patrons.

Their working vests signaled that they were not to be disturbed. Creed heard the couple across the room explaining to their little girl why she couldn't run over and "pet the doggies."

With his chair backed against the wall, he kept alert as he ate. His view included a window overlooking the parking lot, so he could determine ahead of time any commotion or threat before it came in the door. It was an old habit, drilled into him during his time in Afghanistan. Back then, it didn't matter if he and Rufus were on duty or off. It seemed like every hour of every day there was some potential threat. He'd learned to assess quickly and act instantaneously. And even now, without the litany of risks, he still did it subconsciously.

He was also watching Norwich closely. Both he and Jason had been with her last summer when she suffered a heart attack. She'd spent a few days in the hospital. Had some kind of procedure. Less invasive. Stents maybe?

Whatever she'd gone through, she looked good. Her rolled up sleeves exposed lean forearms. For as long as Creed had known her, her hair had been steel gray. He guessed her age to be somewhere in her fifties. Out of all the sheriffs they worked with on a regular basis, Norwich was his favorite. She was straightforward, fair, and honest. And she respected his dogs and valued their abilities.

But Creed had to admit, he was taken back by how shook up the sheriff looked after their encounter with the construction dumper. He couldn't figure out what had happened. Was it fear he'd witnessed? Did she feel vulnerable after the heart attack? No way would he ask.

"This missing teen who's no longer missing, bothers me," Norwich said, poking a French fry in his direction. "One of his parents is lying."

"Why would they lie?" Jason asked. Then he gestured to Creed's plate. "Are you gonna eat the rest of your fries?"

"Yes, I'm gonna eat them."

"The dad's a bully," Norwich said. "Just like that guy dumping concrete into the woods. No respect for laws. They follow the ones that suit them. And definitely no respect for law enforcement."

"They probably know each other," Jason said, gesturing to the waitress for a refill of his soda.

"The garbage dumper and Monroe?"

"Yeah, I mean, he works with Ramsey Construction. Monroe does the final landscape after RC finishes their custom houses."

Creed and Norwich stared at Jason.

He shrugged. "I've seen the trucks at the same sites."

"His girlfriend's father-in-law owns Ramsey Construction," Creed told her.

"Oh. Interesting." She pointed to what was left of her food. "This was my first hamburger and fries since the heart attack." She said it matter-of-fact. "I almost forgot how good this stuff tastes." She wiped her mouth and pushed the plate to the center of the table. "I didn't touch those last fries if you'd like them," she told Jason.

"Thanks." He didn't hesitate, dumping more ketchup to drag them through.

"Your girlfriend," she said, "isn't there a custody battle going on with her and the in-laws?"

"She's getting full custody after Christmas."

Norwich's brow furrowed before she could stop it. She put her elbow on the table and her chin in her hand like the gesture might prompt her to remember something.

Jason had his head down and didn't notice. But Creed noticed. "What is it?" he asked.

"Probably nothing," she said.

Now she had Jason's full attention, too. "You heard something?"

"Just made me think of what I heard going around the courthouse."

Both men stared at her. She frowned and shook her head.

"It's probably nothing."

Except it was the second time she'd said it. Creed and Jason waited.

"Ramsey Construction," she finally said. "They were just rewarded a multi-million dollar contract to do the courthouse's remodeling." Then, as if to soften the coincidence, she added, "Heaven knows that place needs it."

Creed remembered Hannah complaining that Dora Ramsey sounded as if she expected her husband's construction company to get the contract for an addition to the Segway House. The Ramseys had given a generous donation. Maybe they were used to dealing in quid pro quo.

"Her mother-in-law has been coming down pretty hard on Taylor," Jason told them. "She's critical of every little thing. Like she's keeping score."

"She might be," Norwich said.

"For the lawyers," Jason added, nodding like it was something he'd already considered.

"Custody battles are tough." Norwich folded her hands together on the edge of the table. "Years ago, I gave up custody of my boy."

Creed stopped mid-bite. He didn't know what to say. He didn't even know Norwich had a son.

She waved a hand, as if expecting their surprise and dismissing it. "That was a long time ago. Decades. I was just starting out. This profession isn't easy on women, let alone women trying to have families."

"What happened?" Jason asked.

Norwich shrugged. "He chose his father. Blamed me for everything that happened. Even a few things that didn't happen. Kids are so easily manipulated into believing the strangest things. Their minds, their realities, are so malleable." She shook her head. "After his father died, he didn't want anything to do with me."

"How long has it been since you've talked to him?"

"A long time. Too long. But I still reach out. Every year I invite him to come spend the holidays. I don't even know if he gets my invitations. But I still send them. Just in case."

"Can I get you folks dessert?" Their waitress interrupted. She stood at the vacated table next to them, stacking dishes.

Creed didn't need to look at Jason. Dessert at the Oval Office meant pie. Made locally. Didn't matter what flavor. It was a resounding "yes" all around. With coffee. Normally, Creed would have begged off, saying he needed to get back. But he enjoyed Norwich's company. And how could he deny Jason pie?

When the waitress left, Creed waited for Norwich to continue, but she seemed relieved at the interruption. To lighten the mood, he said, "I should be watching what I eat. I need to fit into a rented tuxedo tonight."

"I'm sure you won't have any worries," Norwich smiled at him. "After all you've been through, you look great. Actually, you look like you could stand to gain a few pounds. Is this for the Segway House fundraiser?"

"Yes. And it is for a good cause."

"And because Hannah's making him," Jason laughed.

30

Pensacola Beach

Taylor chopped onion and garlic. Will sat at the counter that separated her small kitchen from the rest of her apartment. His markers scattered around the sketch pad. She added the vegetables to a skillet with melted butter. The sizzle and the scratches of the markers filled the comfortable quiet between them.

She stirred while glancing at him, and she smiled at the top of his head. That silly cowlick stuck straight up. His tongue poked out the corner of his mouth as if it helped his concentration.

She loved having him here. His energy filled the space. It radiated through her in a way she couldn't explain.

"That smells good," he told her without looking up.

"It's your nanna's recipe for homemade spaghetti sauce."

"Nanna cooks?" His head jerked up.

"Your other nanna. My mom. She loved to cook. She was a gardener, too. Raised tomatoes and onions and peppers."

"Is she dead, too?"

"No, she's not dead." Taylor shook her head but smiled. His seven-year-old mind snagged on subjects sometimes and wouldn't let them go. This week it must be dead people.

"How come I haven't met her?"

"You did. You just don't remember. You were really young."

"How come she doesn't come to visit?"

"Travel's difficult for her. She hasn't been well." It was the closest to the truth that she could offer. Since her father passed away, her mother had been in and out of rehab facilities. It was hard to keep track of which addiction she was working on at the moment, especially since she moved to California.

Taylor felt Will's eyes on her while she busied herself with the store-bought vine-ripe tomatoes. These were nothing like her mother's fresh from the garden. As a little girl, she helped pick them, washing them with a garden hose. The two of them would stop to eat tomatoes like apples, juice running down their chins. She could still hear her mother's laughter, though she hadn't heard it in years. That sound filled with so much joy.

When she glanced over, Will had gone back to his drawing, satisfied for now with her answer.

Why all of a sudden was he so interested in estranged family members? He wasn't old enough to understand her mother's challenges. Even now, she hoped he wouldn't accidentally tell Dora that his other grandmother wasn't well. Dora already had too much ammunition against Taylor.

She hadn't thought about her mother in a long time. But lately the memories were good ones. Maybe it was because of Will. The memories evoking Taylor's maternal instinct. Her mother was a good mother until she wasn't.

She taught her how to cook, and Taylor actually enjoyed it. But she hadn't done much in years. It was too easy to grab something on the way to the hospital and on the way home. Days off, she'd resorted to energy shakes and protein bars. And although she enjoyed exploring Pensacola Beach's restaurants and cafes with Will, she'd recently discovered how much she missed cooking. Like this. With someone else here to share the aromas and even the silence.

"Hey, mom. What if I just didn't go back?"

"What do you mean?"

She finished filling a pot with water and placed it on the stove before she turned to look at him.

"You know, what if I didn't go back tomorrow? Maybe just stay here. With you."

She felt a twinge in her chest, an uptick of her pulse.

"I wish you could stay with me, Will. But you have school. Remember, we talked about this. You're going to finish the year at your school, then after the new year, you'll go to the school over here."

"Okay." He shrugged like it was no big deal and went back to his drawing.

Taylor had so many questions going through her head right now. Was something going on? Was there a new reason he didn't want to go back? He'd never asked to stay before. Did it have anything to do with the housekeeper being gone?

"Is Jason having spaghetti with us?" This time when he looked up at her, she knew she couldn't deflect another of his questions.

"It's pretty late for an invitation, buddy. I almost have it ready."

"How about dessert?"

"Will, it's a long drive from where Jason lives to Pensacola Beach."

"I could text him and see."

"You have Jason's phone number?"

"Yah, but I don't bother him. Sometimes I just text and say, 'Hey.'"

She didn't remember the two of them exchanging phone numbers. What else had she missed? She noticed Will's cell phone now on the counter alongside his sketch pad. Only recently and without consulting Taylor, Dora had bought him the latest, most expensive model.

"It's Saturday, Will. He probably already has plans."

"You think he's at the ball?"

"The ball?"

"Yeah, the big shindigger."

Shindig. She tried not to laugh. He must have heard his grandmother use the word.

"Nanna said everybody whose anybody will be there."

Taylor almost told him, "no," that of course Jason wouldn't go to a fundraising ball without her. But suddenly she wondered. Would he? They never agreed they were dating each other exclusively. Though not doing so was more her guardrails than Jason's. She knew when a man was crazy about her. Deep down, she knew that even her jealousy of Brodie was misguided. Or was it? Now she wanted to know as much as Will did.

"You can text him and ask," she said, "but tell him you know it's late and tell him you understand..."

But his small fingers were already flying over the phone's keypad, not waiting for the rest of her instructions.

"Don't be disappointed, okay?" she warned.

She went back to her dinner preparations, but kept sneaking a glance. Will stared at the phone's screen. Waiting.

The last conversation—a text message conversation—that Taylor had with Jason did not end well. Actually, last night she hadn't been very nice about him choosing poker with his buddies—and Brodie—instead of joining her and Will at Walter's Canteen. Would he think she was using her son to guilt him into coming over for dessert tonight?

The phone pinged, and she watched Will's excited expression slide from his face.

"Sorry buddy," Will read the message. "Have to do chores and watch the kennel. Everybody's gone tonight."

Will looked up at her. "Probably at the ball." And he shrugged again, but this time it wasn't one of his "no big deal" shrugs.

There was another ping.

Will read the message, "How about lunch tomorrow? At Walter's?"

He was grinning when he asked her, "Can we?"

Like it or not, her son was getting attached to a man she most likely considered a nice distraction. And his grandmother considered a problem. Maybe a big enough problem to be a deal-breaker.

But Will was excited and smiling and waiting.

She hoped she wouldn't be sorry, but she told him, "Sure."

31

Florida Panhandle

Brodie filled the last of the dog bowls. The dogs were scattered around the kennel's feeding area. They were in their places, some needing a gentle reminder of where exactly that was. A few others were cordoned off separately. All were waiting and watching and drooling.

"Sorry," Jason said, finally coming around the counter to help. He slipped his cell phone into his back pocket and started gathering bowls to distribute.

"Everything okay?" she asked, wondering if Hannah or Creed had forgotten some instructions. Both of them had been so preoccupied with getting to the big event on time.

Ryder knew she didn't carry her own cell phone around. It was a sore spot between them. He'd say things like, "I just want you to be safe," but Brodie had yet to see an instance where a cell phone saved anyone. It certainly hadn't helped Ryder while he was stranded in that Nebraska blizzard.

When Jason still didn't respond, she added, "Ryder already reminded me about the new meds for Molly," she said.

He looked over his shoulder at her, clearly not having a clue what she was talking about.

She gestured to his back pocket. "Wasn't that Ryder? Or Hannah? Reminding you to remind me?"

"What? No. It was actually Taylor's son, Will."

"Oh." Brodie didn't realize that even little boys carried cell phones. She hoped Ryder didn't know that.

"He invited me to come have dessert with him and his mom."

"You should totally go. I've got this." And of course, at that moment, Chance decided he wasn't being served quickly enough. He edged passed one of the littler dogs, who growled. Like a domino effect, several others joined the chorus.

"Hey, settle down," Jason told them, then gestured to the German shepherd and the dog immediately sat down to wait his turn.

Okay, maybe she didn't quite have "this." She hadn't tackled feeding time all on her own, yet.

"I'm not going to bail on you and the dogs," Jason said. "I have obligations and responsibilities. I can't just up and run whenever Taylor wants me to."

"I thought you said Will texted you."

"Yeah, but she probably asked him to. Right?"

Now he was looking at her like she really might have an answer. Clearly, she didn't. She was the last person to have advice about romantic relationships.

She shrugged the same way Jason did whenever he didn't have an answer to her question. Then, hoping to get his mind off Taylor, she started grabbing bowls and distributing them while she asked, "Can you teach me how to do that?"

"Do what?"

"That hand signal that makes dogs sit." She avoided using Chance's name, not wanting to rile him up again.

"It's not just one thing," he told her, following her lead, picking up bowls and placing them in the appropriate spots. "It's your whole manner, your stance. The tone of your voice. A lot of the things that Ryder taught me for being a good K9 handler."

It was working. He was in his element now.

"Dogs look to us for direction. I think they even look to us to make things fair."

"So they think we're their alpha?"

"Ryder says they don't care about that. It's more about them seeing us as their ultimate resource for food and care. Especially some of these guys who've lived on the streets or were dumped out in the country where they had to forge for themselves. If there's any dominating or aggression, it's sometimes when a new dog arrives. As soon as the newcomer realizes he doesn't need to scavenge for food anymore, and he's gonna get his own bowl of food like all the others, there's no need to fuss."

"But I watch you and Ryder wave your hand or say something, and it looks like magic how the dogs react." She pointed to Chance. "You didn't even raise your voice, and he sat right down."

"You know his story, right?"

"His owner chose her abusive boyfriend over him."

"Even after he tried to save her from him."

Brodie nodded. She remembered how scary she thought the huge German shepherd was when she first met him. It didn't help matters that she was afraid of dogs at the time. Despite what he'd been through, Chance still liked women and immediately was friendly and gentle with her. Jason explained that the dog's biggest challenge was learning to trust men and realize not all of them were a threat capable of wielding a baseball bat.

Each of these dogs had a story. That was one of the ways Jason had helped her get over her fear of them. He told their stories of abandonment and heartbreaking abuses. With all of their rescues, their survival had a combination of elements she could relate to hunger, cold, fear, or pain. When she started thinking of what the dogs had gone through, she realized she no longer feared them. When they, in turn, no longer smelled her fear, they calmed down around her as well.

"We're almost finished," Brodie said, looking up at the wall clock. "I'll clean up if you want to go over to Taylor's."

"I told Will I'd meet them for lunch tomorrow."

"Okay." That seemed easy. So why did Jason still look so…anxious? That wasn't the right word. Restless?

"Let's get everyone settled," he said. "Then how about we take Hank and Scout, get a couple of lounge chairs and some refreshments and set up in the backyard for a meteor shower?"

"Really?"

"Yeah."

"I didn't think you were even listening to me."

"I always listen to you." He shot her a smile. "Asteroid debris, right? Not a comet. Sounds totally cool."

Yes, it did. She wiped a strand of hair out of her face, and she was so excited she didn't mind that she'd smeared dog food across her forehead.

32

Pensacola, Florida

Creed was grateful to Hannah for giving him an early out, releasing him like a caged animal into the wild. He was conversing, being polite, sipping champagne, and she could still see how miserable he was. How did she do that?

Hannah told him the new director had offered her a ride home, and they could use the time alone to assess the event. "Maybe," she said, "bask in the glory and relief." The two women had been working together on the fundraiser for the first time.

Creed didn't question her. Simply nodded and tried to act nonchalant as his eyes searched for the nearest exit. He'd almost made it until a blond in a sapphire blue cocktail dress tapped him on the shoulder. He didn't recognize her at first. To be fair, he was used to seeing her in an orange jumpsuit, what the Coast Guard crews simply called a "mustang."

"Wow!" The word escaped his lips before he could stop it, and rescue swimmer, Liz Bailey laughed.

"You look pretty spiffy yourself," she said. "Would you like to dance?"

"You're asking me?"

"Don't tell me the dog handler can't dance?"

It was a fundraising ball with a full orchestra, including musicians from the local symphony.

"You don't dance to this," he told her. "I believe this is what you call a waltz."

He raised his arm, elbow level with her shoulder and put up his other hand, fingers gesturing for her to do the same.

She raised an eyebrow at him before she followed his lead.

They waltzed. Creed couldn't believe how easily it all came back to him. Step forward. Move to the right. Close left foot to right foot. Step back.

When his mother taught him at fifteen, she told him to envision his feet gliding around a box. She made him do it over and over again until the movements became instinctive. Until the music took over. It definitely helped to have a dance partner who could follow so smoothly along. They moved like synchronized swimmers through waves of other dancers.

It was actually quite nice. He didn't hate it.

But now, as he escaped through the parking lot, he realized he had the top button of his shirt undone and his bowtie already in his pocket before he arrived at his Jeep. Evidently, as nice as it was, he didn't want to dance all night.

Before he left, he texted Jason and Brodie. It was late, but they weren't expecting him or Hannah until much later. He didn't want to alarm them.

By the time Creed was pulling off I-10 and coming down the ramp, his phone lit up in the dashboard holder. Jason texted back that they were in the backyard watching the meteor shower.

Join us!

Meteor shower?

As he stopped to turn onto Avalon Boulevard, he looked up at the sky. Too many pines trees. His eyes swept back to the road and caught movement on the other side of the highway. It was back behind the Red Roof Inn. Close to where he and Norwich had started their search yesterday. Creed thought he saw someone running through the parking lot. Three others followed.

No, not followed. Chased.

Then Creed saw the dog running alongside the person being chased.

He sped up, reaching the intersection to the access road. Oncoming traffic made him wait to take the left turn. He maneuvered the Jeep around both parking lots that were lined with parked vehicles. No one else was outside except clear in the back corner by the Dumpster. Light didn't reach that part of the lot. It was dark, but he remembered from yesterday how the woods came all the way to the concrete.

Creed stopped the Jeep in the middle of the empty space. He captured the activity in the headlights just as one of the men shoved Sully to the ground. Gunner snapped and barked, but Sully had the dog by the collar.

He had expected teenagers, but in the stark light, the men looked older. Old enough to be legally drunk in a public parking lot.

The biggest one had a dark beard and a shaggy head of hair. When his small, narrow eyes flashed in the headlights, they made him looked like a wild animal.

Creed pegged the ringleader as the tall, scrawny guy with a mop of blond hair. He was dressed in shorts with a long-sleeved polo shirt. He wore flip-flops. Nobody started a serious fight wearing beach thongs unless they knew they weren't throwing the punches.

The third man was the shortest of the three but broad chested, his T-shirt tight to show off his muscles.

They stopped, almost freeze-framed, when they realized the Jeep wasn't just looking for a parking spot. But they didn't seem worried enough to think he might be a cop.

Creed left the headlights on as he opened the door.

"What's going on here?" he asked, giving them an opportunity to make things right.

"We caught this old guy and his little dog stealing."

He glanced over to Sully to make sure he was okay. The old man's eyes flickered with recognition then slipped away, back to the ground. His focus was on protecting his dog.

"What did he steal?"

"What's it to you?"

He was right about the tall, scrawny one being the leader. He was also right about them being drunk. Which could make this easier…or more dangerous.

"So you decided to rough him up?" Creed asked. "It took three of you to push an old man down?"

"Pushed him down? Nah, we didn't push him down. He slipped."

They all laughed.

"So who the hell are you supposed to be?" The bearded man pointed at Creed. "Take a look at this guy. Are you like some tuxedo model or something? Or did you lose your bride?"

They laughed again

At least their attention was no longer on Sully and Gunner. That's when Creed noticed Sully wiping his mouth with the back of his hand. The knuckles came away with blood.

"Why don't you all apologize to this man and then get on your way?"

"Apologize?" The muscle man moved closer and only then did Creed see what looked like a footlong pipe hanging down from his hand. Of course, he brought a weapon, which told Creed the muscles were for show.

They came at him, spreading out, intending to surround him. Creed moved slowly, knowing they'd follow. He led them into the shadows and away from his Jeep.

In the back of his mind, he could hear Hannah warning about his bruised back and the wound in his side that was still healing. He could still feel the hitch there, a tenderness below his beltline. But that wasn't why he moved the oncoming fight to the shadows. He didn't want them to dent his Jeep or crack the windshield.

"You guys don't have anything better to do on a Saturday night?" he asked, pulling them farther away from Sully and Gunner. "What are you, the Dumpster patrol?"

"Very funny. He's a tuxedo model *and* a comedian." The ringleader walked on the balls of his feet, trying for a tough-guy's bounce, but the flipflops only made him look ridiculous.

The muscle guy was the first to lunge at Creed. He swung the pipe clear over his own head, preparing to deliver a full-force wallop. Creed caught the guy's wrist as it came down. But instead of stopping him, Creed pulled while he stepped aside. The guy's forward momentum threw him off balance and he faceplanted onto the pavement.

Creed spun around just as the bearded man's right fist caught his jaw. He ducked as the man's left fist came in right behind his right. Creed's head was down, but he slammed his elbow into the guy's kidney. The man reeled back, fists flying. Creed pulled away, still getting clipped on the chin. Encouraged, the man started dancing around him like a boxer gearing up to place his final blows.

Behind them, his scrawny friend yelled his support, "Do it! Knock him on his ass."

Creed had to admit, he never liked boxing. Hitting and getting hit in the head was the worst. But as the guy closed in again, bouncing and curling up his fists, Creed concentrated on his own balance and his own feet.

The guy had already telegraphed his technique: right, then left. When the right fist came again, Creed was ready. He leaned just out of reach, then kicked out and swept the man's legs completely out from under him. Bearded guy landed hard on his back. The thud made his friend wince.

"Who the hell are you?" the flip-flop guy asked. His eyes were wide now, and he stayed back rather than attempting to help his buddies.

Creed glanced behind him. The muscle-head might have broken his nose. He sat with his hands cupping his face and blood dripping through his fingers. The bearded guy still hadn't moved. He stayed flat on his back. He started coughing, trying to catch his breath.

From the corner of his eye, Creed could see a couple of customers coming out of the Waffle House to see what was going on.

To the ringleader, Creed said, "You might want to help your friends." It looked like they both slipped and fell."

He left them to go help Sully.

33

"I wasn't stealing a thing," Sully said before Creed had a chance to ask if he was okay.

"I know you didn't."

"Sometimes people toss takeout containers from the waffle place. Full meals. Gunner gets hungry, you know."

"Is she okay? They didn't hurt her, did they?"

"No, no, she's okay. A little scared is all." His eyes darted over Creed's shoulder, checking on the bullies, and Creed knew it wasn't just Gunner who was a little scared. "She thinks she's a lot bigger dog. She thinks she's the size of your search dog."

"Actually, I have a smaller one I use, too. Grace is about Gunner's size. A Jack Russell terrier. But she thinks she's bigger, too. She got hurt a couple months ago on a job, so I've been letting her heal."

"We protect them, don't we? They're our children."

"Yes, they are." Creed sat down on the curb beside him.

"Don't know what I'd do without this girl." He pulled the dog closer. "You got any real children?"

"No. How about you?"

"A daughter. Beautiful, young woman." He shook his head. "She don't want anything to do with me."

Creed kept quiet. Waited for more.

"She doesn't understand. Thinks she knows everything. When my wife passed, she said she lost a mother and a father 'cause I was…oh, you know. Not myself, I guess. She got herself a husband, a good job. Probably a baby by now. She never did understand what I lost. I didn't just lose a wife, you know. I lost my best friend. My partner. My whole life, really." When he rubbed a hand over his face this time, his thumb and forefinger swiped at the eyes, too.

"I've got a place where you two can sleep if you want," Creed offered without giving it a second thought. "Get something to eat, too."

"Aw no. Thanks though. Got to get back. You know, get back to my stuff or somebody'll snatch it up. We respect each other's things, but if you're gone for long, it's up for grabs. Besides, it looks like your evening got interrupted. Some fine lady must be waiting for you." He gestured to the tuxedo.

"I escorted my partner to an event downtown. She was one of the hosts. Remember, I told you about her? We own a K9 business together." He left out the part about the fundraiser. It felt wrong to talk about people in ballroom dresses and tuxedoes with jewelry and luxury cars, collecting money for people like Sully, without bothering to get to know them. "She knows I'm not a fancy event guy, so she let me go home early."

"That's a good woman."

"Yes, she is."

"A keeper."

"It's not like that."

"No?"

"We're each other's family. More like brother and sister. Maybe closer. She knows me better than anybody else."

Sully nodded. "That was my Caroline."

The old man started searching for and grabbing a backpack that looked pathetically limp and empty. Creed wanted to drive him home, but home was through those dark woods behind them. He couldn't insult the man.

"I owe you one, Jarhead." Sully smiled at him as he found his hat and plopped it on his head.

Creed glanced around. The three men were gone. The parking lot was a little emptier.

"They only had hors d'oeuvres," he told Sully. "Miniature bites on toothpicks. I don't know about you, but I'm starving" He thumbed back to the Waffle House. "How about you join me for a late dinner?"

"Oh no, they won't let me have Gunner in there. And I won't leave her outside by herself."

"Yeah, you're right. Some places make a fuss even when I have a K9 working vest on one of mine. How about we eat in my Jeep? Gunner can eat in the back. I have a blanket and a water bowl."

"I don't know." Sully looked around, as if wanting to escape. He couldn't afford a meal. He'd already accepted one favor. Two might be too much.

"Waffles on me tonight," Creed offered. He had to try.

"No, I can't let you do that." He looked at the ground and shook his head.

This was harder to figure out than taking down those three bullies. But Creed understood. Sully was a man used to reciprocating, paying his way. No matter his circumstances. In his place, Creed suspected he'd be the same way.

"Okay, how about this? I buy you and Gunner dinner and you make me lunch sometime at your…camp."

"I make you lunch?"

"Yeah, I actually wouldn't mind having some wicked good rice and beans."

Sully's head bobbed, but Creed couldn't tell if it was in agreement. The brim of his hat kept his face shadowed. When his eyes came back to meet Creed's, he was smiling.

"You got yourself a deal." He stood, using his hands to push himself up off the ground, then he slung the backpack over his shoulder.

"By the way, you could use some boxing lessons," Sully told him, pointing at Creed's jaw.

"He just got lucky." He fingered the tender spot.

"Got more than lucky with me." The old man checked the corner of his mouth again. "I guess we both need a brush up."

"Three against one is never fair."

"Except that loud-mouth blond kid didn't really count."

"True. I expected him to trip over those flip-flops."

"Hey, you need to teach me that leg sweep thing. That some kind of ninja karate move?"

"Nope. It's really all about balance. I'll show you."

They walked shoulder-to-shoulder to Creed's Jeep, like soldiers surviving the latest battle. Gunner kept close to Sully's side, brushing against his pant leg.

"I need to tell you something." Sully's tone was serious. He stopped and waited for Creed. "I owe you this."

"You don't owe me anything."

"No, I do. That boy…that teenager you and the sheriff were looking for. There was a young fella about two or three weeks ago. Hard to measure time anymore. He didn't tell me his name. But it could have been your teenager. Had a big ole black eye where his daddy walloped him good. I'm not a prude about disciplining children, though I never laid a hand on my girl. He had bruises in other places, too. He stayed with me and Gunner for a couple of nights. And then left. I figured he went back home."

"Did you tell the sheriff?"

"No, I didn't."

"You saw the photo. Do you think it was Caleb?"

"That picture the sheriff had of a young boy all cleaned up, hair combed neat. No bruises. But yeah, I think it might have been him."

"I'll need to tell the sheriff. You know that, right?"

Sully nodded. They stood there under a lamppost in the parking lot. Then he gestured at Creed's rolled up sleeves and said, "So you own a tux?"

"No, it's a rental."

But now, in the light, he saw what Sully had noticed. Blood stained the cuff of his sleeve. A seam had ripped open on the trousers. Somewhere he'd lost the cummerbund.

"I think you might own that one," Sully told him.

"Yeah, I bet you're right."

This time, they both laughed.

Creed was sure Hannah would not be amused. Nor would Maggie if he still had bruises when she arrived for Christmas. But for right now, he and Sully deserved a couple of Waffle House's All-Star Specials. And Gunner could have whatever she wanted.

34

Newburgh Heights, Virginia

Maggie turned the corner into her cul-de-sac and saw lights blazing at the end. For a second, her heart skipped a few beats. It wasn't that long ago that she'd come home to find her house on fire. Tonight, thankfully, it was simply electricity. Her brother, Patrick had decorated the front of the house and the front yard with Christmas lights.

She checked her watch. He had texted her about thirty minutes ago, saying he was picking up pizza. It was one of the few nights they were both home for dinner. He hadn't mentioned the decorations. Just that he had a surprise.

Another ping came over her phone as she pulled into the garage.

Beer's already in the drift.

She smiled. Despite the cold, both of them still enjoyed sitting out on the back patio watching the dogs play in the snow. After she'd gotten back from the Nebraska blizzard, she'd added an outdoor propane heater to ward off the chill. However, Patrick, having grown up in the cold, snowy Midwest, utilized the refrigerator temps and started shoving bottles of beer into a snowdrift that ran alongside the retaining wall. It made a nifty ice bucket.

She unlocked all the security locks and paused the alarm system as she entered the house. As soon as she walked into the entrance, she could smell the scent of fresh pine and cinnamon. Her boys greeted her. Harvey looked like he had been asleep. Jake could hardly stand waiting for her to go through her lockup ritual. His entire back end wagged, his long tail a battering ram against the wall. She bent down for a lick-kiss on her cheeks.

"Looks like you guys had some excitement today."

From the entrance, she could see the fresh-cut Christmas tree in the living room. It almost reached the nine-foot ceiling. As she made her way through the kitchen to the back door, she saw Patrick's note on the counter.

We're decorating that tree tomorrow.
No excuses.

His enthusiasm made her smile.

She rarely bothered getting a tree and had never decorated the outside of the house. Both of them worked such crazy hours, it seemed like a waste of time. But again, Patrick had grown up with tinsel and baubles and lights attached to every eave of the house.

Their childhoods had been so different. Biologically, they shared a father who Patrick had never met and who Maggie could never forget. He died when Maggie was twelve; a firefighter running into a burning house and not making it back out. That his son wanted to do the same thing did not sit well with her.

They had only found out about each other recently, and there were too many missed years to make up. Maggie had bought this two-story brick Tudor on a wooded acre in a quiet, private neighborhood. It was her sanctuary. She had been able to buy it with money her father had left for her in a trust. It made sense that she shared it with Patrick. And although he refused co-ownership, he accepted her offer to be roommates.

She still felt a pang of guilt for leaving him during Christmas. Even if he did have to work, usually he'd come home to the dogs. Maggie was taking both of them with her this time. She couldn't imagine spending the holiday without them. They were her one constant in her life. She already spent too much time away from them on assignments that took her across the country.

Patrick assured her it was okay. He'd accepted an invitation from a couple of co-workers. And they had agreed they'd celebrate New Year's Eve together, enjoy a feast, exchange gifts, and binge watch college football bowl games.

She checked out the window, eyes darting along the backyard fence line. The landscape lights added ambience but also lit the dark corners enough to see any intruders: wildlife or human. Satisfied, she opened the door and let Harvey and Jake bound out into the snow. She grabbed a coat with a hood from the coatrack in the corner and followed the dogs out.

Fat, wet flakes glistened, falling against the yellow lights. Layers of white weighted down the branches of the huge pine trees that stood like sentries guarding the yards' borders. She couldn't see her neighbors on either side, and the back of the property overlooked a natural preserve with a creek running parallel.

They had arranged two patio chairs under the metal awning which protected them from the snow. Maggie had only a dusting to brush off. And close at hand was the drift Patrick had purposely left when he cleared the patio. Purposely left for them to insert their longneck bottled beer. Only the caps peeked out.

Patrick had shoveled paths for the dogs, but they plowed through the snowdrifts as if they didn't notice. She sat back and watched them. Jake performed hotdog leaps to bite at the snowflakes. Harvey snuffled his nose in and out of drifts tracking some backyard creature.

It was so quiet she could hear Harvey's snorts. So quiet she could hear the snow falling.

This place had become her sanctuary. Her retreat from the evils of the world that she dealt with on a regular basis. This was where she could breathe…and think…and relax.

"The pizza has arrived!" Patrick announced as he came out the back door. He brought out a tray with plates already filled: slices of gooey pizza and piles of salad.

She helped him set up everything on a small table between them. He slid two beers out of the snowdrift and popped the tops.

"The decorations out front are amazing," she told him, and he grinned back.

They shared their adventures for the week. She told him about the killer stalking homeless victims. Patrick told her about a tragic house fire that had left a family with nothing. But he and another firefighter had managed to find and rescue the family's cat and golden retriever.

"The cat was freaked out, and the dog wouldn't leave the cat," he told her. "Fortunately, it's pretty difficult to scratch through our jackets and gloves. And face shields."

Maggie had barely taken a bite of pizza when her cell phone vibrated in her pocket. She had to unzip her coat to pull it out. She didn't recognize the number.

"Sorry, I have to get this."

He waved "no problem" while devouring half a slice.

"This is Maggie O'Dell."

"He's on the prowl again."

"Who is this?"

"Your snitch," came a whisper.

"Nessie?"

"I trailed him." She was still trying to whisper, but her excitement made it a stuttered attempt. "All the way from the YMCA. He probably changes his clothes there. Tries to make himself look like one of us."

"Nessie, listen. You shouldn't be following anyone. It's dangerous."

"Oh, I know how to blend in."

Maggie tried to think of what she could say to the woman to stop her. She should have never encouraged her. This was crazy. Maybe Nessie was, too. Racine tried to warn her about the homeless. That they lie. And some don't recognize the lies as untruths. Now the woman was out on the streets of D.C., following a man from the YMCA.

"Nessie, I know you're trying to help, but what makes you think this man is a killer?"

"Well, he sure as hell doesn't look like a carpenter in that long black coat."

"A carpenter?"

"Danny was hit on the head. I heard Carlo was, too. I saw this guy come out of the YMCA looking all shabby."

"Nessie—"

"Didn't think anybody was watching him. Saw him stuff a hammer into his pocket."

"Wait a minute. A hammer? Are you sure?"

"Nothing wrong with my eyesight. He walks funny, too. Like he's not comfortable in those big, long shoes."

"Where are you? Right now."

"You remember the coffee shop? God, that pastry just melts in your mouth. It's like biting into a cloud."

"Is that where you are?"

"That's where I'm calling from. They remembered me and you from the other day. They're letting me use their phone in the back room. It smells like baked goods even back here."

"Nessie, listen."

"Don't worry. They don't know what I'm doing. Hmm…there's a window that looks out over the alley."

"The man you were trailing. Where is he now?"

"Up the street a bit. Not far from where he took out Danny."

"Look, Nessie, stay at the coffee shop. Order coffee and a donut. Tell them I'm on my way, and I'll pay for it. Okay? Just stay put."

"But he probably won't stay put."

"I don't want you to get hurt. Just stay in the shop."

"Pfft...I handled Russian oligarchs. This guy doesn't scare me."

"I'm on my way. I'll meet you at the coffee shop. Don't leave."

"Whoa, speak of the devil. There he is! Gotta go. Looks like he's headed up through the alley."

"Nessie don't leave. Nessie?"

Maggie stared at the phone's screen.

"What's going on?" Patrick asked.

"I think I made a mistake. A very big mistake."

35

Washington, D.C.

Before the slippery drive to the District, Maggie called Racine. To her credit, the detective didn't lecture her about the inaccuracy of the homeless. Instead, she simply told Maggie she was on her way.

"Don't spook him," Maggie warned. "If there's suddenly an onslaught of uniforms in the area, he'll leave. We'll never catch him."

"I'm not a rookie, O'Dell."

Maggie thought Racine had been sloppy on this case since the start, but now wasn't the time to harp on it. Racine may have been sloppy, but Maggie may have endangered an innocent homeless woman. She had a bad feeling about this.

It took an excruciating amount of time to get back into the city. Saturday night. Of course, she had to park several blocks away. This time she'd come prepared with boots, the hooded coat and warm gloves. She'd left behind everything that said FBI, except her badge and her weapon. The holster fit snug against her side, the shoulder harness almost too tight across her back.

Road crews had piled chunks of ice and snow along curbs and in-between vehicles parked on the streets. It was messy and slow going. She was almost at the coffee shop, not that it mattered. Nessie was gone.

Maggie stomped by the shop, trying to glance into the windows. The interior set too high off the ground for her to see inside. She stopped. Walked back to the other side. The coffee shop was wedged between businesses. There was no alley, or at least, no access from the front. It must run along the back of the shops.

She hurried to the end of the block, still trying to reach Racine on her cell phone. It kept going to voice message. She checked and double-checked. No messages *from* Racine, either. Finally, she shoved the phone deep into her pocket, angry at herself for not setting up some kind of communication system with Racine.

It was the detective's city. Her streets. Her case. Her team. Maggie should have just let her handle this. Except for Nessie.

How could she have made such a stupid mistake?

She should have never gotten the poor woman involved. And now, she needed to at least make sure she was safe.

The narrow alley ran deep and dark. There were very few windows back here and most were also dark. A couple provided dim splashes of yellow and orange light. It wasn't enough.

Maggie leaned against the brick wall and let her eyes adjust. Two or three Dumpsters. Their bulk could hide anything or anyone. Her eyes skimmed above. Wrought iron fire escapes spiraled up the walls to the second and third floors. She listened, trying to tune out the sounds of traffic. There was nothing here.

As she walked away from the alley, she noticed a police cruiser. Its lights flashed, but the siren was off. She followed, nudging between people and crossing intersections against the light. When the cruiser turned a corner, she hurried not to lose it.

Then suddenly the sirens blasted, and Maggie launched into a sprint.

She couldn't see the cruiser, but followed the sound. Her boots crunched ice and snow and clanged over metal sidewalk grates. She could see her breath as she pushed through clusters of people. Her pulse raced. Her heartbeat pounded at her temple.

Something was very wrong.

Don't be too late.

She didn't remember unzipping her coat or unsnapping her holster. But her hand already tightened on the butt of her gun.

On the other side of the street, she saw someone also running. Only the figure was racing the other direction. Away from the sounds of the siren. Maggie skidded to a stop. She stepped between parked cars to get a better look. Sure enough, the person had slowed but hurried in the other direction. He was tall and wearing a long, black coat that flapped behind him like wings.

From the other direction, she could hear voices. Cops yelling to stay back. She turned to see a crowd spilling into the nearest intersection. In the distance, more sirens screamed across the cold night air.

She looked back to the other side of the street.

He was gone.

She ran across, putting her hand out to slow traffic and still getting grazed by an irritated bumper. On this side, there were no shops opened at this time of night. Entrances and the stairs leading up to them were dark.

Where had he gone?

She rushed to the end of the block. More people were moving along the sidewalks, almost as if drawn by the sirens. The hood of her coat had blown back and strands of damp hair clung to her forehead and whipped in her face. Dread gnawed at her as she dug for her badge and held it up to push her way forward.

More police cars were arriving. Officers started barricading the streets and cording off the sidewalks. She shoved her way to the nearest one and showed him her badge.

"What's happened?"

He checked her badge and waved her on to another officer. By now, her gut was twisting in knots. Someone was on the ground. Paramedics spilled from their vehicles. Too many headlights. Too many shadows.

She held up her badge to the next officer who strung yellow crime scene tape from one lamppost to another.

"I'm with Detective Racine. What's going on here?"

He stopped and stared at her. Then finally he pulled up the tape for her to duck under and pointed. "You best talk to Detective Sheldon."

She barely recognized the detective. This time, he wore a heavy parka and a red ball cap. He stood next to a uniformed officer who was yelling into his shoulder mike, "We've got a victim and an officer down. Where's that ambulance?"

Maggie stood on tiptoes, trying to see the chaos beyond the police cruiser that parked diagonally in the middle of the street. Its flashing strobe lights made it impossible to see. Suddenly, she caught a glimpse of pink, a long slash of it against the white snow. A pink scarf. And her knees went weak.

As she made her way to Detective Sheldon, the knot in her stomach churned together a mixture of panic and anger. She got closer but still couldn't see what was happening on the ground. Only a crowd of backs with an assortment of alphabets on their jackets.

"Detective Sheldon," she called out before she reached him. She waited until he glanced back at her. "I met you the other morning."

"Right, Agent O'Dell. I remember."

"Where's Detective Racine?" she demanded. "I need to talk to her."

The officer who had been on the radio, twisted around to get a look at her. He exchanged a glance with Sheldon, who finally said, "Detective Racine is the officer down."

36

This was crazy. Too close. How did that happen?

Gregory had tried not to run. Especially against the flow. It was hard to steady his pace. He was still panting by the time he got back to his car. Teeth chattering. Stocking feet soaked and numb. His whole body shivered from the cold.

In a panic, he shed his coat and shoes. Balled them up and stuffed them into the trash bag, just like he always did. Ditched them in the first Dumpster when he was sure no one was looking. But he couldn't make it back to his stash, leaving him in his socks and only a sweatshirt. Leaving him no alternative but to get back to his car as soon as possible and escape.

Not good. Very bad. Very bad, indeed.

Usually, it was so simple. Nobody ever noticed. Usually, he had plenty of time. And tonight the old woman had made it easy on him. Following him. Sneaking around corners. Pretending.

Did she really think he hadn't noticed her?

But he was so caught up in their little game of cat and mouse that Gregory had missed seeing the detective.

Where did she come from? A parked car? A shadowed entrance?

How the hell had he missed her?

Sirens screeched, and he wanted to put his hands to his ears. The sound scraped against his nerves. From the parking garage, he could see the flashing lights reflecting off the shop windows.

Too close.

He had parked too close.

Too cocky.

Just wait. Calm down.

He turned on the ignition. Blasted the heat vents.

No one had seen him. No one had followed.

Then he noticed the blood on the steering wheel, and a fresh panic seeped over him.

No, no, no!

He was always so careful not to bring any of the blood with him. Now it was all over the car.

His head swiveled. His eyes darted around the garage. Noises echoed. Vehicles leaving. Vehicles coming in.

He needed to leave. Now.

Don't screech tires.

Calm down.

Don't draw attention.

Breathe. Through your nose, not your mouth.

He dug a towel out of the duffle bag in the passenger seat. He wiped down the steering wheel and his hands.

In the rearview mirror, he examined his face and neck for any specks or splatters. He met his eyes in the reflection and hardly recognized the frenzied look staring back at him.

"You're going to be okay," he said out loud.

Before he looked away, he caught a glimpse of an image. A small boy slouched down, tucked against the door in the backseat.

He spun around.

There was no one.

He lifted himself enough to get a look at the space between the backseat and the floor. But there was no one.

The unraveling. It was starting again. He could feel it. Thread by thread. Everything he had carefully constructed coming apart at the seams.

First came the hallucinations. Then the paranoia. The killing was supposed to help. It was supposed to staunch the leak.

Don't look in the mirror. Don't do it. He's not really there.

His hand slipped into the duffle bag, searching until he found the prescription container. Just once, he'd like to control these meltdowns without pills. Still, he twisted off the lid, popped two tablets in his mouth and dry-swallowed.

Then he closed his eyes. He tried to shut out the sounds of sirens. Counted to sixty. Listened to his heartbeat. Steadied his breaths. Then counted again.

When he opened his eyes, he pulled in a long, deep gulp of oxygen, like a swimmer coming up for air. He put the car in gear and drove. Out of the parking garage. Onto the street. And away from the chaos.

He stopped at every red light. Every single stop sign. Flipped on his turn signal long before he turned. Kept to the right. Attention focused. Back rigid. Fingers gripping.

One turn, then another. One deep breath, then another. And another. He drove until he knew no one had followed. Still, he didn't feel safe until he parked two blocks away, let himself into the house and locked the door behind him. Only a lamp on the side table in the entrance lit his path.

He had leftovers. He'd make himself eat. It would settle him down. Maybe help clear his head.

Then what? He hadn't planned to leave until the next day. But of course, he had the option to bump that up. Maybe he could get some sleep.

A sound spun him around in the dark living room.

A key in the lock. Metal against metal.

The doorknob.

There was no mistaken. Someone was coming in the front door.

No, no, no!

This couldn't be happening. Was he hallucinating?

Footsteps on the hardwood floor.

His hand dived into the duffle bag. Fingers searched, then clawed around a handle. By the time he pulled it out, a figure came around the corner. The man didn't see Gregory until he lunged at him, his arm already up and swinging. The hammer made contact with a satisfying thud, and the man crumpled to the floor.

In the light from the hallway, Gregory recognized the face from photos around the house. On the mantle in the living room, atop the dresser in the master bedroom.

The man had made the decision for him. Gregory would wipe down surfaces, gather his belongings, eat his leftovers, and leave.

He looked down at the man. "You really shouldn't have come home so early."

Then he hit him again, just in case once hadn't been enough.

37

Sunday, December 3
Florida Panhandle

"How is this your fault?" Creed asked.

"I'm not sure. But it feels like it is."

He didn't like that Maggie sounded so…defeated.

"I got impatient with Racine," she said. "I thought she was being sloppy. But I was totally careless. I missed how dangerous this guy is."

"Aren't all killers dangerous?"

"Yes, but some aren't necessarily very smart. I thought he was targeting the homeless because it was easy for him. How much effort does it take to club someone while he's asleep on the sidewalk? Then stab that person while he's unconscious."

"So convenience might not be his only reason for choosing them."

"Maybe not. I didn't give him enough credit. I didn't take him seriously enough. He left behind evidence in the Dumpster like a disorganized killer. Even his choice of weapons made me believe he was grabbing items that were handy or that he worked with on a regular basis. Now I realize a ball-peen hammer to the skull is efficient. It only takes one swing. And he doesn't just cut up his victims or stab them repeatedly. He knows exactly where to slide the knife in to do the most damage. To make it fatal."

Creed listened to her frustrated sigh.

"Nessie would be dead if Racine hadn't interrupted."

"Are they going to be okay?"

"I hope so. I don't know. I left the hospital. Too much chaos. I didn't want to be in the way. They were still working on them and not giving out much information, no matter who was asking. One of the detectives told me Nessie has a head injury. Of course she does. Probably a hammer. Racine…she ended up getting stabbed. I have no idea how bad it is."

"What happens next?"

"I'll check back every hour. See how they're doing."

"What happens next…for you?"

"I'm not sure. I guess I brace for the storm."

"The storm?"

"They'll need someone to blame. They always do."

"And you think it'll be you?"

"Yes."

Her answer came too quickly. No hesitation.

"I'm not sure I can even disagree," she added.

"I don't believe that's true. I've worked with you plenty of times now. Maggie, you sacrifice everything for a case: your physical self, your well-being. Body, mind, and soul. You aren't responsible for everything that goes wrong. Nessie and Racine made their own choices."

She was quiet. Too quiet.

"You know the best thing that you can do right now? Actually, two things." He waited her out. Made her ask. He needed her to interact, get her mind back on track.

"Is this going to be a Hannah-ism?"

At least he could hear a bit of a smile in her voice.

"Probably."

"She'd say I needed to get some rest. That everything looks better in the morning."

"That sounds about right. But that's only part of it. The other is that you need to get this guy. The Maggie O'Dell I know won't be satisfied until she does."

More silence.

"Do you need to be there on the streets to catch him?"

"Obviously, I didn't do a very good job of that tonight."

"No, I mean, do you physically need to be there?"

"I'm not sure that it'll matter. If Alonzo is right about this guy, he doesn't stay in one place for long. After tonight, I'd be surprised if he didn't move on. What are you getting at?"

"I've seen you work with your team while you've been hundreds of miles away from them. Maybe you can do that this time. Hear me out for a minute. We have a substantial computer system to run our security programs and cameras. Hannah and Dr. Avelyn have all the digital bells and whistles to run our business. What they don't have, they can get. Come down early. We have more than enough space for you to have all the peace and quiet you need. Pack up Harvey and Jake and come on down."

It would only be a week or ten days early. He was prepared to tell her to at least think about it. He certainly didn't expect it when she said, "Okay."

"Okay?"

"Yes. Okay. I guess I should clear it with a few people."

This time, both of them went quiet.

"Maybe you should clear it with Hannah," she finally said.

"Are you kidding? She's been bugging me to get you here earlier. I saved you from a fundraising ball."

"A ball?"

"Yeah, with gowns and tuxedoes and a full orchestra."

He looked down at the mess he'd made out of this one. Jason and Brodie had laughed at him when he finally joined their backyard stargazing party. Neither was surprised by his detour. To be fair, he played down his parking lot brawl quite a bit when he explained the bloody tux. Still, he was glad Maggie couldn't see the mess right now. She worried about him too much. And this was about her.

"I bet you looked handsome in a tux." The smile returned to her voice. "How was the food?"

"Stingy portions on a toothpick. I had to stop at Waffle House afterwards."

"Did they have the fancy shrimp?"

"Yeah, but they were tiny. Definitely not from Joe Patti's."

More silence. This time he'd wait her out.

"Hey, Ryder?"

"Yeah?"

"Thanks."

38

Florida Panhandle

Creed hated being tethered to his cell phone, but today he couldn't afford to miss any calls. He didn't know what to do about Maggie other than give her time and space. She knew she could call and talk to him if and when she needed. So he put an earbub in and the phone in his pocket while he worked. All the callers he wanted to hear from had designated ring tones, allowing him to ignore any others.

He and Jason had spent the morning dismantling the shelves that Dr. Avelyn had emptied inside the medical clinic. It did open up the area. They could now easily accommodate big enough kennels and crates that would be comfortable for the dogs coming in from Afghanistan.

Brodie worked quietly beside him after Jason left for lunch with Taylor and her son. She fussed with bedding and precisely attached each of the water bowls so they wouldn't tip over with a restless dog. There was a buzzing sound coming from the other side of one wall, and she hunted it down, asking if they could relocate the culprit: a small refrigerator. Creed was impressed with her eye for detail, especially when it came to comfort.

"They're being rescued just in time for Christmas," she said. "That's kinda cool."

He stopped himself from saying, *just like you last year*. It was stupid, but he found himself tiptoeing around the subject. She still struggled with

PTSD. Of course she did. Recently, he realized he couldn't be left in enclosed places for long without panic crawling inside his brain. But what Brodie had gone through? He'd understand completely if she wanted to skip Christmas entirely.

"Yeah, it is cool," he told her.

"It bothers you?"

"Christmas?"

"No, Afghanistan. It's still with you."

He simply stared at her. Here he was worried about her, and she could see right through him.

"Yeah. It still bothers me. Not often."

"Sort of creeps up on you." A statement, not a question. Of course, she knew what it was like.

In the first months after she arrived to live with him and Hannah, Creed had asked her how she was doing way too many times. Right now, he wanted to ask if Christmas would be like that for her?

As if she could read his mind, she asked, "What are you getting Maggie for Christmas?"

"I have no clue. Any ideas?"

"Does she read?"

"Yeah, but not like we do."

That was one thing the two of them still shared, and he counted on it. If he couldn't ask how she was doing, he could always ask what she was reading. It was their grandmother who got them hooked, specially choosing books she knew each of them would enjoy and giving them as gifts for holidays and birthdays. As kids, they'd read into the late night until their mom made them go to sleep. Creed had every single copy on his bookcase.

"She doesn't wear jewelry," Brodie told him.

"I already discounted that as too easy. I do know she loves her backyard."

"Have you ever been there?"

He shook his head. Started to say something when Brodie put up her hand to stop him. "I know. It's complicated."

They both smiled.

"Let me think about it," she offered, and Creed liked that she made it sound like a project they could work on together.

She went off to hunt for more beds and blankets, and he headed outside. He needed to finish constructing a fence for the temporary yard at the back of the clinic. It was something he'd been meaning to do for some time, so recuperating dogs could get fresh air and stretch their legs without the attention of all the dogs over in the kennel's yards.

Dr. Avelyn had called before dawn. Creed thought it might be Maggie, restless and needing to talk. Then he heard the veterinarian's excited voice say, "We have a flight coming in tonight. Is it even possible to be ready? We're expecting eighteen, maybe twenty-two."

Still groggy and searching for the time, he didn't hesitate and told her, "We'll make it happen."

Now, as he assessed what was left on their "to-do" list, he was impressed at how much they could accomplish when they all worked together. He realized having that many new dogs coming in at one time would be chaotic at first. Each dog would have different needs other than being quarantined. Dr. Avelyn had warned some of them could be dehydrated and malnourished. Others anxious and skittish. Creed reminded her that all their dogs had come to them with some level of disfunction.

Hannah had rented a cargo van. Jason had dropped her off to pick it up on his way to the beach. She was meeting Dr. Avelyn at her clinic in Milton to load travel carriers and supplies. The clinic had a mobile unit the vet would also bring prepared with additional crates.

Transporting twenty dogs, even though it was less than forty miles, would be a challenge. By the time they got to Pensacola's airport, the dogs would have already traveled 8,000 miles, about fifteen to sixteen hours in the air. Not an extraordinary feat for trained war dogs, but those that had been living on the street? Hiding and fending for themselves? Of course, they would be exhausted, anxious, and scared.

Dr. Avelyn had shared some of the atrocities the left behind dogs had faced in the days following the fall of Kabul. He didn't want to think about them. The Taliban had always viewed the animals as special demons that possessed powers they didn't understand. The villagers believed the dogs had magical capabilities that allowed them to see through lies as well as walls. At least a half dozen times, Creed had to shield Rufus from children throwing rocks, being instructed and encouraged to "hit the dog."

No, it shouldn't have been a surprise to anyone that dogs abandoned to these people would suffer horrible consequences. It made him physically ill, imagining what it was like. Any day of the week, he'd be willing to take the hits, even being pummeled by rocks and bottles or bullets. Anything to protect these defenseless dogs who did nothing wrong. K9s who worked tirelessly along with their handlers doing only what they were trained to do.

Late in the afternoon, Dr. Avelyn had called Hannah to tell them the flight was delayed

"Not a problem," Hannah had insisted.

She said it gave them time to sit down and have a decent meal together.

The second delay made them all a bit antsy.

Brodie and Jason decided to finish kennel chores that they originally thought could wait until after the new dogs were all settled. That left Creed and Hannah alone in the kitchen with yet another cup of coffee for both.

"I have a bad feeling about this," Hannah finally said after a long silence between them.

They stared at each other from across the table. He knew that she could see in his eyes that the feeling was mutual.

"We know they were allowed to leave Kabul. Right?" he asked.

“I think that’s all we know. You’d think this flight warranted national security risks. Dr. Avelyn couldn’t even find out how many stops or where those might be. You don’t think the government would nix this, would they?”

“They don’t like to be proven wrong. Remember, they’re still claiming they didn’t leave any dogs behind. Is there anyone we know we could ask for help with this?”

“Not on the foreign affairs side of things,” Hannah sipped her coffee as she gave it more thought. Then she shook her head. “Believe me, I’ve already been racking my brain since Dr. Avelyn told us about this.”

“Then I guess we have to wait and see.”

“And you know waiting is not my strong suit.”

“Mine either.”

39

Washington, D.C.

Maggie had spent most of her Sunday chasing down leads and digging for details. Alonzo had been in his data center office at Quantico since early morning and Kuszak at her lab. Both worked without Maggie's prompting. All of them were running on adrenaline to find something about this killer.

Maggie returned to the hospital, hoping to catch Detective Sheldon. The doctors would update Racine's law enforcement partner. They'd made it clear that Maggie was too far on the fringes of friends or families to be included. If she wanted to find out what condition Racine and Nessie were in, she'd need to get the information from the detective who was now in charge of the case.

She bought a can of Diet Pepsi for herself and a tall, designer coffee from a kiosk in the lobby. With lid and stopper secured in place, she made her way to the ICU lounge.

Sheldon was nowhere to be seen, but she recognized a woman sitting in the far corner, tapping on her phone.

"Rachel?"

The woman looked up, eyes swollen, skin pale. She barely resembled the photo that accompanied her weekly newspaper column.

"We've never met," Maggie explained, her hands full so she couldn't even offer one. "I was working on this case with Julia. I'm Maggie O'Dell."

"Oh, of course. She's mentioned you."

"Would you like a coffee?"

"Starbucks! You're a lifesaver."

Maggie ignored the irony. She was the one who'd almost caused Racine to lose her life.

"You mind if I sit with you for a while?"

"No, please do. They're changing out some things in her room. I figured it was a good time to get out of there for a few minutes."

"How is she doing?"

"Heavily medicated right now. The knife punctured her spleen. The doctor said surgery went well."

"She's a fighter."

"She is. And she'll be mad as hell when the doctor tells her she needs to rest and heal for three to four months."

"I'm so sorry this happened."

"Julia warned me it comes with the territory. But there's really no way to prepare yourself for it." Rachel shook her head. Took a sip of the coffee. "Sometimes I think she believes she's made of steel."

Maggie wanted to say, *we all do in the beginning.* She'd lost track of the scars on her own body until Ryder Creed came along and wanted to know the story behind each. She didn't mind under his gentle, exploring touch. He had enough of his own scars that it made for an interesting trade of war stories. But for people who didn't put their bodies at such risk, people like Rachel and her daughter, this would be a nightmare they hoped to never experience.

She wanted to tell Rachel that it was her fault Racine was even on the street last night. Confession might be good for the soul, but it sucked at solving anything. And it would bring no comfort to Rachel.

"The woman she was trying to save. Will she be okay?" Rachel asked. "I heard she got hit in the head."

"I'm not sure. I know she's still unconscious." Maggie had been trying to check in for updates on Nessie, but again, doctors weren't releasing much information. "What I can tell you is Julia saved her life. We'll get this guy. I promise you."

Rachel gave her a half smile. "Now you sound like Julia."

Maggie's phone started vibrating in her jacket pocket. She pulled it out, took one look and said, "I have to take this."

"Go ahead."

"If there's anything I can do for you or Julia, please just call me." She dug out a business card from behind her badge wallet. Across the back, she'd scrawled her personal cell phone number.

Rachel nodded. "Thanks. And thanks for the coffee."

Back in the hallway, Maggie finally answered Alonzo.

"Please tell me you found something," she said in place of a greeting.

"Actually, Kuszak did. Remember the throwaway bag?"

"Yes. A pair of large shoes that led to nowhere. Latex gloves with fingerprints that identified no one. And some trash receipts. Was there something we missed?"

"The trash receipts. Kuszak got to thinking that wad looked a lot like when she cleans out her car. You know, you toss things you no longer need. There was a printed copy of an Amtrak eTicket. What you'd use for boarding."

"Didn't you already check out the name on the ticket?" Maggie started to pace the hallway.

"I did. And I got nowhere. But…Kuszak recognized that it was a ticket for the Auto Train."

"I have no idea what that is."

"Neither did I, but Kuszak did. She has family members who've taken it in the last six months."

"So it's not Amtrak."

"Oh yes, it's Amtrak, but it's a special train where you can take your vehicle along with you. You check it in, sort of like you would luggage. They place a magnetic number on your car so you can easily identify it at your destination site. But they also put the vehicle's VIN number into their computer system with that corresponding number."

"And the VIN number connected you to the name of the vehicle's owner?"

"Bingo! Black 2018 Mercedes-Benz C300 four-door sedan registered to Peter Gregory of Miami, Florida."

"Miami? He lives in Miami?"

"It's an office address. An investment group that owns, operates and manages vacation homes. Sort of like Airbnb. These are all elite luxury places. He's listed as one of five owner executives."

"Does the train go all the way to Miami?"

"It does. More interesting though, it also goes to Jacksonville. And New York City."

"Really?" She stopped in her tracks. The other murders. Is this how he traveled? "So what do you know about Gregory?"

"Not a lot so far. He seems like an ordinary guy. Thirty years old. Pays his taxes on time. No priors with the law. Not even a traffic ticket. I'm still searching. I'm betting he's never been fingerprinted."

Maggie let out a frustrated sigh and moved further down the hallway to stay out of the way of hospital workers.

"But here's the thing," Alonzo said. "Most criminals have a weak spot, right? I think this Mercedes might be his. I happened to access Amtrak's computer system."

He paused, as if waiting for a reprimand. Maggie knew Alonzo was a wizard when it came to "accessing" cyberspaces that perhaps he had no business accessing. She had played against the rules too often to lecture anyone else.

Satisfied by her silence, he continued, "He obviously used aliases when he booked his Amtrak tickets. I couldn't find Peter Gregory or the name on the eTicket we found. I'm not exactly sure how it works, but it doesn't look like vehicle registrations are checked to match the ticket holder's name. Probably would take too long. Entering the VIN number looks to be strictly for backup. Who knows? I thought by tracking the Mercedes VIN number I could see what other trips it's taken."

"And you found Jacksonville and New York City."

"Yes, and the timelines easily match to the homicides."

"That only places him in those cities. Without fingerprints or some evidence—"

"Hold on, I know all that. While I was tracking the VIN number, I accidentally discovered something else. It's on its way to Jacksonville. Right now."

"The Mercedes?"

"Yes."

"You've got to be kidding?"

"Left this morning at seven. Amtrak doesn't allow you to send a car on its own."

She stopped at the end of the hallway, where a window looked out over the parking lot.

"He's running," she said it in almost a whisper. "After last night, he's getting the hell out of D.C. How can I get on that train?"

"It only makes one stop, but it's not for boarding or departing. So even if we could get you on, you might spook him, because there's no way to get on that train at that point without raising a whole lot of red flags and special treatment."

He let her digest all that, then he added, "Actually, I think I have a better idea. I already put in for the warrant. You'll still need to pack a bag and catch a flight."

40

Santa Rosa County, Florida

Taylor could feel the tension. The trip back to Dora's house was harder than usual. She knew Will was feeling it, too. The more time they spent together, the more she wanted.

He was extra quiet in the backseat. Usually he had his head down, fingers sketching, only stopping to dig in his backpack for a different marker or colored pencil. Tonight, every time Taylor looked in the rearview mirror, Will stared out his window.

She didn't dare ask what he was thinking about. She knew what he was thinking about. Telling him it would be only a few more weeks did not help…not today. Not tomorrow.

And what was worse? Her son was getting attached to Jason. He was fascinated by Jason's mechanical arm. Today at lunch, he asked if he could touch it, then bombarded Jason with dozens of questions.

"Does it give you superhuman strength? Can you feel hot and cold? Have you tried climbing a wall with it? Is that why your arms are so muscular?"

And Jason answered every single question, even after she told them both to stop talking about it and eat their lunch. Then they started talking about what to eat to build strong muscles.

She wanted to hug Jason for that one. She continuously harped on Will about eating better. Eating more. Dora had him trained to be polite, but did she feed him? He looked too thin. Maybe being a nurse on the pediatric floor clouded her judgment. She reminded herself that after this summer's growth spurt, Will was tall for his age. Maybe the rest of his body just needed time to catch up.

He'd chowed down his lunch, mirroring Jason, even sopping up the remnants with a last bite of biscuit in the same sweeping motion. Jason could be a good influence on her son. He was also the one thing that could blow up her entire custody arrangement.

She thought about asking Will not to tell Dora that they had spent the afternoon with Jason. How could she ask her son to lie without explaining? How could she explain without getting him worried? Besides, Dora already claimed Will lied too much.

No, she wasn't going to ask her son to lie to his grandmother. Dora couldn't be serious about keeping them apart for longer. She couldn't get away with it. And yet, Taylor knew she absolutely could get away with it.

The woman thrived on rubbing elbows with people of influence. She'd made it a hobby. No, more than a hobby. She'd made it a profession to worm her way into organizations and clubs and onto lists with donations and through her husband's contracts. She dropped names of judges and council members and CEOs and talked about them like they were longtime personal friends.

Many of them had been to Dora's house for her elaborate parties. Some were investors and members of the golf course and country club that her husband was building. His construction company seemed to have a hand in dozens of developments and new projects in the Pensacola area.

She remembered Mike once telling her that if his mother wanted something badly enough, she could make it happen no matter how long it took. At the time, Taylor thought it sounded like a trait to be admired. But she knew that wasn't what Mike had meant.

He became a doctor because it was what his mother wanted. But she did not want him to go to Afghanistan and had tried every measure within her reach to prevent it. It was one of the reasons he was okay with going. He said it felt like the first thing he'd done in his life that hadn't been orchestrated by his mother. Ironically, it had gotten him killed.

Part of Taylor's problem was that she didn't know how to talk to Dora. She'd always been treated like competition by other women. Evidently, she had gotten into the habit of reciprocating because she viewed them as competition as well. Wasn't that exactly what she was doing with Brodie?

To be honest, she'd never had close women friends. Still didn't. She couldn't even imagine going out with other mothers and talking about kids and kids' stuff. Over six months working at the hospital, and she hadn't once gone out for drinks with any of the other nurses she worked with. But she was amazingly comfortable throwing back a few drinks and exchanging war stories with Jason's buddies.

Men, she understood. Or maybe she only thought she did because she knew how to manipulate them. Still, she'd never been in love. Didn't want to get too attached. Never had her heart broken. She made sure of that. Surrounding herself with men gave her a sense of security and a sense of confidence.

Of course, surrounding herself with men was also the exact kind of thing Dora would use against her. Even if it was only being seen in a public restaurant in the company of a group of men.

She turned onto the two-lane highway. They were almost there. In her head, Taylor repeated the mantra: *Only a few more weeks. We can do this.*

Another glance in the rearview mirror. Will hadn't moved. His eyes stared out the window, the rest of his body so still. So quiet.

She'd been in war zones. Helped piece together young soldiers. Steeled herself against the things she saw. She'd turned her back and walked away from relationships. She'd buried a husband she hardly knew. But this…

This kid was going to break her heart.

41

Washington, D.C.

Maggie had rushed home, packed an overnight bag and barely had enough time to eat with Patrick and the dogs before she raced off to the airport.

"You're not getting out of decorating that tree with me," her brother told her, eyes serious, before launching into a tired smile.

"Of course, we'll do it when I get back," she promised. "I won't be gone more than a day or two."

She hoped she sounded convincing because her mind hadn't stopped churning over the information Alonzo and Kuszak kept uncovering. Their texts—brief and coded—were coming fast and furious. Their generation's communication tool for immediacy was annoying to Maggie, but admittedly effective. And after years of working as a lone wolf in the field, digging up information all on her own, this was different. Different but good.

Now, if only she could shake the image of Nessie's small body in her ICU bed. Before Maggie had left the hospital, she'd checked in on the woman. Without her bundles of clothing, she looked even more vulnerable.

Detective Sheldon had placed guards outside both Racine's and Nessie's rooms, but hospital personnel did a good job of denying access. Her badge had only gotten a generic response from the nursing staff:

"There's been no change." And when Maggie asked to see Nessie, she'd gotten a curt, "Ten minutes. That's all."

However, her badge at Nessie's door garnered a polite nod of respect from the uniformed officer as he held the door open for her.

There wasn't a customary chair by the bed, but Maggie lifted a stool from the corner. She placed it close enough where she could see Nessie's face. Then she sat quietly by her side. She wanted to apologize to the woman. She wanted to take her hand and tell her everything would be fine. Instead, she simply sat, hoping somehow her presence was felt, and that it mattered.

Later, after she'd left the hospital, after she'd left Patrick and her boys to rush off to the airport, she ended up having plenty of time—too much time—to think. She waited in line to board the plane. Waited for take-off. Maggie hated flying, or rather she hated being 30,000 feet above control.

Thankfully, it was a non-stop, two-hour flight. That it was a night flight made it seem longer. That's when Maggie allowed the flood of images to leak from her well maintained and carefully compartmentalized mind. The mistakes and failures that haunted her. She would do everything possible to fix this one.

"Get me a photo of this guy," she'd told Alonzo earlier, before her flight took off. "Oh, and Antonio, I want to know about Nessie."

"I'll keep checking in with the hospital," he said.

"Not just that. I want to know who she is. She must have family."

"Not to be disrespectful, but if she had family who cared about her or that she cared about, would she have been on the streets?"

"Good point." Maggie was a prime example. Other than Patrick, her family was comprised of friends and dogs. Never had she once considered calling her mother when she landed in the hospital. "Just see if you can tell me who she is. I'd like to know more about her."

"You got it, boss."

She had stopped herself so many times from asking him not to call her "boss," that it was probably too late to tell him now. It still made her uncomfortable.

Despite having a non-stop flight, Maggie knew she would be cutting it close. That departure and arrival had been on time, helped tremendously. Peter Gregory had a huge head start, having left early in the morning hours before they figured out who he was. The good news? His Amtrak trip would take fourteen hours to get to Jacksonville, Florida. Otherwise, they wouldn't have been able to consider Alonzo's plan.

As soon as Maggie landed and turned her phone back on, a chorus of pings greeted her. Alonzo and Kuszak were working non-stop. There was also a new number for Wren Warren.

Alonzo had arranged for an agent from the Jacksonville field office to meet Maggie at the baggage claim. Immediately, from the top of the escalator, she spotted Agent Warren, a young black woman dressed casually for a Sunday evening.

She waited off to the side and wasn't interested in the bags moving around the luggage carousels. There was something about her that signaled "federal agent." Her shoulders squared, her head barely pivoting as her eyes roamed. Her arms hung at her sides. Her back to a wall. She carried a small duffle bag in one hand. The other looked ready…for anything.

To her credit, Agent Warren's eyes landed on Maggie before she got to the bottom of the escalator, and she met her halfway.

"Maggie O'Dell?" she asked, head cocked with a polite smile, in case she was wrong.

"Wren Warren, thanks for meeting me at such short notice."

"No problem. I'm glad to help. Antonio and I go way back."

Maggie wondered what "way back" was for a couple of twenty-something-year-olds. The only important thing to Maggie was that Alonzo trusted this young woman, and Maggie trusted Alonzo. Which in Maggie's world was a big deal.

"I brought everything Antonio asked for," Warren said, gesturing to the duffle bag in her hand. "Do you have any other baggage?"

"No. Just my carry-on." It was looped around her neck and shoulder and slung to hang high over her back. She realized now how pathetically light it felt as they started walking through the crowded baggage claim area.

"I have your rental waiting out in the parking lot," Warren told her. "They only had small SUVs available. I hope that'll be suitable?"

"Black?"

"Yes."

"That'll work fine."

"I have the electronic receiver already set up inside your vehicle." She tapped the duffle bag and said, "The actual device is in the inside pocket. It's about the size of a credit card. A little thicker. The magnet is strong, so it's best you keep it away from your real credit cards. It's fairly simple to activate. There's an ON switch. Green light flashes. Inside a tire well is still usually the best spot. Easy access and difficult for anyone to see."

They were suddenly in front of the exit doors leading to the parking lots. Warren stopped. She handed over the duffle bag along with a key fob and the parking ticket that showed the garage floor and slot number for the rental.

"If you need anything else," the agent told Maggie, "don't hesitate to call me. You have my number."

She liked Agent Warren but knew much of that was influenced by Alonzo's trust in the woman. However, Maggie liked her even more when she slipped into the SUV and discovered a small cooler on the floorboard. Inside were three cans of Diet Pepsi and what looked to be two deli sandwiches.

As she dug into the duffle bag for the GPS tracker, she also found a blue Amtrak ball cap, a fluorescent vest, bottles of water, and several protein bars. Last was a small brown paper bag containing two cake doughnuts with chocolate frosting, each carefully wrapped in wax paper.

Agent Warren had done good. Maggie was impressed that Alonzo remembered all these details. Maybe giving up her lone wolf creds would be worth it. But that was a fleeting thought. Moments later, in the dim light of the parking facility, Maggie took a flashlight and crawled around checking the rented SUV's interior, exterior, undercarriage and tire wells. She was about to put a tracking device on a suspect's vehicle. How easy would it be for anyone to do the same to her, no matter how well intentioned?

Back inside with the doors locked and the engine running, she actually hit the A/C. Maybe she'd grown a little too accustomed to the snowy cold in D.C. and Virginia.

She shrugged out of her jacket, tied her hair back into a ponytail, and pulled on the blue ball cap. She had less than two hours to get to the Amtrak station. Gregory had paid for Priority Vehicle Offloading. His Mercedes would be one of the first to leave the train. Maggie needed to get to the car before he did.

42

Monday, December 4
Pensacola, Florida

By the time Creed and the rest of their crew were ready to caravan to the airport, they were all exhausted and running on pure adrenaline. It was after midnight when the call finally came. Thunderstorms in the distance lit up the sky and threatened to delay the flight again.

In his head, Creed couldn't shake the mantra: *Nothing good happens after midnight.* As a dog handler, he hated night searches. Avoided them if possible. There were too many dangers lurking in the dark that could harm his dogs. As their guide and protector, it was his responsibility to watch out for those dangers while the dog concentrated on and worked a scent. They were partners, and even if the dog's eyesight was better in the low light, it didn't matter if the dog wasn't paying attention to what hid in the shadows.

Of course, in Afghanistan, they didn't have the option to not work at night. The night-vision goggles helped to some extent. But wearing them now still reminded Creed of crouched enemies, hiding and waiting until it was too late for handler and dog to retreat.

He needed to stop thinking about it.

Creed probably shouldn't have been surprised that Brodie had noticed how much this affected him. Despite a few social skills being stunted by her years of captivity, her observation skills had been enhanced and fine-tuned. She saw things that others looked right by.

And yes, he'd spent too much time thinking about the dogs and Afghanistan. Without much prompting, he could see the streets and hear the noises from their viewpoint. There was a saying that emotion ran down the leash, meaning a handler needed to stay calm and confident. But for Creed, the opposite was also true. Emotion ran up the leash. If a dog was in distress, it was like an electrical current running directly to his body.

The person who had trained Creed told him it was one of the things that made him such a good K9 handler. Sometimes, Creed considered it not just a vulnerability, but almost a curse. This was one of those times.

As soon as Dr. Avelyn had told them about the abandoned dogs, memories started flooding back. Some of them were so vivid he could smell the dust of Afghanistan and feel its grit on his skin. His nerves felt on alert as if he'd stepped outside the wire and hadn't made it back to safety.

It probably didn't help matters that Hannah kept reminding him how his body was still healing. Not just from what happened in Nebraska less than two months ago, but also the incident last June in Blackwater River State Forest. His bruised back still ached—it was throbbing tonight—and he wondered if it would ever be normal again.

Then he reminded himself of the men who'd attacked Sully. He was pleased he had been able to take them down in the parking lot. Truthfully, it surprised him how easy it had been. *Amateurs.*

Was that only last night?

Dr. Avelyn led them to a designated area at the Pensacola Airport. There was little activity. Most commercial flights were already in for the night. She stopped her mobile unit along the side of the building. Creed idled behind her in the rented van. Jason sat alongside him. Both of them were quiet. Tired.

In a matter of minutes, a man came out and gestured while he spoke to Dr. Avelyn. He pointed to around the corner of the building where Creed could see an aircraft as it taxied out to a runway. Only small bits and pieces of other aircraft could be seen.

In a matter of seconds, his cell phone lit up, the ringtone he'd designated for the veterinarian jolting both men in their seats.

"The flight just landed," she said. "You can sit tight here. I'll go check on things."

"Okay."

They watched her exit her vehicle, leaving Hannah sitting in the passenger seat. Brodie had volunteered to stay behind and keep all their dogs settled. It was the first time Creed had seen her actually make sure her cell phone was charged and close by.

Jason's leg bounced, a nervous tick. Creed could feel the movement from where he sat.

"Do you have to do that?"

"Do what?"

"Your leg."

"Oh, sorry."

They were all on edge.

It must have only been thirty minutes later, but it felt like an hour when Hannah called.

"Dr. Avelyn's on her way back. Rye, she's pretty upset."

"What's going on?" He hit speaker so Jason could listen.

"The flight has only three dogs."

"You mean on this flight? Is there another one following?"

"This is the only flight. She's trying to get an explanation from her contacts. Evidently, they wouldn't release the others."

"The organization? Maybe the dogs were too weak or injured to fly."

"No, Rye. They weren't allowed to leave. They wouldn't release them. Or at least, that's what we're being told."

She didn't need to tell him who "they" were. It had to be the Taliban. Dr. Avelyn had mentioned all the recent changes the animal rescue was subjected to since the Taliban took over. They restricted female workers and required the submission of dozens of documents for each animal. Not just proof of vaccinations, but ownership verification and certificates that might no longer exist.

"Sounds like they won't let the others leave the country," Hannah said.

"Bastards. They just realized how much the dogs are worth to us."

As if to emphasize his point, lightning forked across the sky. A single clap of thunder followed, then the sky burst open with a downpour.

43

Florida

Maggie kept her distance. Peter Gregory was traveling west on I-10 and hadn't stopped since he left Jacksonville.

Installing the GPS tracking device had been easier than she'd anticipated. Five Amtrak workers drove cars down ramps, emptying two levels of each train car. They did their work in a steady stream. The Priority Offloaded vehicles came first and lined up along a separate street for their owners to pick up. It was still two lanes away from where the passengers were to exit the building.

That door and kiosk to pick up the keys to the vehicles stayed slightly hidden by a long half wall that made sure passengers left the parking facility correctly. Posts and columns provided even more shadows.

Maggie had found the black Mercedes, twenty-four cars from the front of the line. It gave her plenty of time to make sure the magnetic number on the door matched Gregory's.

Only one man saw her, a tired traveler dragging his roller board suitcase. He noted her ball cap and vest and simply nodded. As soon as he disappeared out of sight, Maggie pulled the GPS device out of her pocket. She bent to the ground as if she had dropped something and tucked the magnet inside the back tire well on the passenger side of the car.

Now, as she followed about a mile behind, she kept glancing at the monitor. According to Alonzo, Gregory and his Mercedes had been to Jacksonville in October. The dates coincided with the murder of a homeless man inside a tent in the downtown area. His business offices were in Miami, and he'd taken the Amtrak Auto Train all the way down several times.

This time his ticket was for Jacksonville. They had expected him to stay in the area. Or perhaps get on I-95 and drive the rest of the way to Miami. Kuszak told her to watch when he stopped at gas stations, fast-food restaurants or rest areas. Then the lab tech gave Maggie step-by-step instructions on lifting fingerprints or bagging discarding items.

They all knew that was a long shot. It was hard enough to get decent fingerprints at a cordoned off crime scene. An interstate gas station or fast food place? Next to impossible. Maybe if and when he finally checked into a hotel.

But it didn't look like he'd do that anytime soon.

Now, Maggie stared at an approaching thunderstorm in the distance. They'd been on the road for a good two hours. Signs started to appear, signaling upcoming exits for Tallahassee. Gregory hadn't stayed in the Jacksonville area, and he wasn't heading south to Miami. Instead, he was going west. She watched as the black car icon on the monitor ignored every single exit to Tallahassee and continued on I-10.

Just at that moment, her cell phone started ringing in the holder on the dashboard. She tapped the screen to take the call.

"Where the hell is he going?" Alonzo asked. The speakerphone amplified the irritation in his voice.

"Aren't you supposed to be telling me?"

"This guy's a ghost. Major investor and executive in a business, but definitely keeps a low profile. No Linked accounts. No memberships. No home address. No credit cards."

"Unless he uses an alias."

"I can usually find those. I'm still looking."

Maggie glanced at the time. It was long past midnight. "Wherever he's going, he's not going to stop for the night."

"Of course, not. He probably slept on the train for fourteen hours. He's charged and ready to go."

She scrubbed a hand over her face, fingers stopping to dig the exhaustion out of her eyes. Alonzo was right. Gregory's trip had refreshed him, while her trip left her frayed around the edges. She had hardly slept after racing around the streets of D.C. and spending every waking hour since looking for information and details.

"You could probably stop and catch a few winks," Alonzo told her, as if reading her mind. "With the tracker we'll know where he ends up."

Just then, she noticed the car icon leaving I-10. But it was well after all the major exits for Tallahassee.

"Here we go," Alonzo said, obviously watching his own monitor.

Maggie tapped the screen to zoom in and see the exit marker. There were no icons for hotels or food. Only a lone gas station that Gregory blew right by. When Maggie finally took the exit, the car's icon had taken another turn down a winding road.

"Alonzo, there's no way I can follow him without being noticed."

"I'm looking at a satellite view. It's wooded. Not marked as a highway. Probably a back road. Yes, you need to stay away. Drive on by. Let's see what he does."

There was no other traffic. All she could see in the headlights was her own two-lane with asphalt crumbling edges and faded white lines. She didn't even slow down at the intersection where he'd turned. Dense woods prevented her from seeing any signs of his vehicle. Not even his taillights. After a safe distance, she stopped, did a three-point turn, and headed back to the gas station near the interstate ramp.

"I'm going to get gas," she told Alonzo.

"Good idea. But stay on the phone with me. Do you have the charger plugged in?"

"Yes." She smiled at his reminder. "Maybe he has a house or cabin out here."

"I don't see any signs of property lines. No roofs. No driveways. I'm checking another satellite view."

It wouldn't matter how many satellite views he brought up. There were no real-time ones here in the middle of nowhere. She listened to him in her ear as he described the area, and while she pumped gas, grateful for the twenty-four-hour automatic pumps. The clerk inside of the shop barely looked up from the glow of a television on the wall. There were no other vehicles, but she could hear the steady hum of interstate traffic.

She washed her windshield just to kill time.

"He stopped. Looks like there's a stream or a river right next to him."

"Maybe he's taking a bathroom break."

"He could do that anywhere. Why stop practically on top of a bridge?"

"Could be tossing something."

"Like a weapon. I'm locking in the coordinates."

Finished, Maggie headed back in the direction Gregory had gone. She overshot the intersection just as Alonzo told her the Mercedes had turned around and was on the move again. She slowed down but kept driving into the dark. On her own monitor, she watched the car icon take a right at the intersection. She was turning around by the time Alonzo announced that Gregory was back on the I-10. He was still headed west. So this detour wasn't his destination.

It took less than ten minutes for Maggie to travel down the gravel road and find the bridge, an ancient structure with steel railings stretching over the top. It was only about fifty feet long. The headlights gave a glimpse of the stream below, more marshland than water.

As she left the SUV, she knew the addition of her flashlight wouldn't be much help. Vines and brush grew thick all the way down the ledge to the water.

"He picked a great place to toss a weapon," she told Alonzo.

"Lots of water?"

"Loads of ground cover. Very swampy. Looks like a great place for alligators."

"Oh crap! I didn't think of that."

"Maybe Peter Gregory did."

"You definitely shouldn't be tromping around there in the dark. I can get someone to check in the daylight."

Maggie ignored him. The foliage looked freshly pushed down. Leaves had been dragged along. Shrub branches broken. The path led all the way down.

"You're right. Alligators can be found in any body of water." Alonzo kept talking. Now it sounded like he was reading from something he'd found on-line. "Swamps, ponds, ditches, creeks, rivers. Wow! Even storm drains."

"Not helpful, Antonio."

The flashlight flicked across something blue. Bright blue. She shot the stream of light across the surrounding vegetation, looking for the reflection of eyes and listening for movement.

Alonzo was still telling her about alligators in her ear.

"Stop! Okay? Just stay quiet," she told him. "Give me a few minutes."

"You're not going—"

"Quiet."

She glanced up to see how far she'd already gone down. The ledge wasn't steep, but it was slick with dew. Tucked into the shrubs and almost underneath the bridge was a blue bag. An oversized duffle or golf bag. The metal zipper glinted against the light.

She set her flashlight on the ground, leveling it against a sapling, so it didn't roll. Then she grabbed onto a piece of rebar sticking out from the bridge's underpinnings. She stretched and grabbed a corner of the bag but couldn't lift it up. It was too heavy.

Before she pulled herself back up, she caught the zipper and easily yanked it down. The smell jolted her. The glimpse inside almost made her lose her grip. She didn't need her flashlight to confirm what was inside.

Back up on the road, she waited for her pulse to slow. For her lungs to fill with fresh air.

"Damn it, O'Dell, I can hear your breathing. What's going on?"

She gulped in a couple more breaths, then said, "You know how Kuszak wanted me to pick up something he discarded?"

"You found the weapon he tossed?"

"Not the weapon. A body. He just dumped a dead body."

44

Pensacola, Florida

Peter Gregory felt refreshed and energized. Driving over Pensacola Bay with the water shimmering in the moonlight always had this effect on him ever since he was a boy. He kept the driver's window open a couple of inches just to suck in the cool sea air. Yes, he needed this. And he definitely needed to get away from the snow and cold.

The trip itself had managed to restore some mental clarity. Something about the isolation and security of his own private bedroom suite onboard the train allowed him to relax like no other place. For fourteen hours, all he had to worry about was eating and sleeping. The suite also included a private bathroom. No interruptions. No outside stimulations or irritations. The motion of the train never failed to lull him into a deep and restful sleep.

Even the five-hour drive in the dark felt liberating, including the slight detour. The heavy-duty cargo liner that he'd used to wrap the oversized sports duffle had worked perfectly. Not a hint of smell had leaked through.

The Mercedes was his one constant, not just a home on wheels, but a safe haven. Like an old friend, they'd been through a lot together. He took good care of it and the car returned the favor. He certainly didn't want it to smell with even a hint of a dead body.

Before he parked it, he took it for a deep cleaning: inside and out.

When he got to the house on the beach, the horizon started to take light. It took him three trips up and down the stairs to bring in his supplies. Each time, he stopped to stare out the wall of windows at the glistening water of the Gulf of Mexico.

He calculated that he had the house for two weeks if he wanted. This time on the digital schedule, he'd crossed out the dates, making it look like the house was occupied, not just vacant. No more surprises like what happened back in D.C. No one questioned or paid attention to where he stayed. It was one of the perks his investment funds provided.

As a result, he had no need for a long-term address for over five years. Honestly, it didn't feel like a vagabond life. Instead, it allowed him a good deal of freedom, along with a furnished luxury home whenever he wanted.

He tried to remember how long ago it'd been since he'd been in this part of Florida. Seven years? Maybe eight. He'd spent only a few days. That's all that was necessary for a funeral.

Less than an hour, and he was back on the road. The old blue pickup still ran great. It certainly fit in better on these back roads and would draw less attention. So much had changed across the bridge in Santa Rosa County. Housing developments had cut deep into the wooded areas. Concrete replaced clay. Businesses dotted along the way. At least the Waffle House and the Red Roof Inn were both still there.

Gregory checked his map and continued into unfamiliar territory. It figured that his mother would build her mansion some place entirely new. She'd want to be the first. She'd expect to set the standard.

Just as he slowed to search for street or road markers, he saw the huge brick and wrought iron sign for Linden Estates. He turned into the entrance but pulled aside and let the realization sweep over him. He didn't know whether to smile or scream. Why was he surprised? Of course, his mother named the frickin' development after her favorite son. Linden was Mickey's middle name.

He shook his head and glanced at himself in the rearview mirror, as if expecting to witness his head finally exploding. That's when he noticed a little boy. Was it another hallucination? Like the image he had seen the other night sitting in the backseat of his car.

This boy stood tucked between the trees on the other side of the highway. There wasn't much traffic, and he seemed to be hiding but trying to watch Gregory's pickup.

He turned the vehicle around as if he was leaving. But when he pulled back onto the road, he drove up on the shoulder in front of where the boy was. Gregory rolled down his window, and the boy peered out at him.

He got a closer look at his face. A jolt of recognition hit him. Gregory became speechless. He stared. His fingers clutched the steering wheel.

How was this possible?

He was looking into the face of a ghost.

45

Florida Panhandle

Creed hadn't been to bed yet. None of them had. They took turns watching over the new dogs. He'd just finished his shift and was headed to Hannah's kitchen when his phone rang in his back pocket. A generic ringtone. It wasn't Maggie's. It wasn't Dr. Avelyn's either. The veterinarian was still here somewhere. He had kept an earbud in all night, and now he tapped it without pulling out the phone.

"This is Creed."

"Sorry to bother you so early in the day."

Sheriff Norwich. She sounded almost as exhausted as he felt.

"Not a problem." Anger had kept him awake. Caffeine fueled him. No reason to stop now.

"Caleb Monroe didn't show up for school. I practically had to bully the principal to check."

"Actually, I've been meaning to call you. I ran into that man named Sully on Saturday night. He's not sure, but he wanted us to know there was a teenaged boy about three weeks ago. Ran away from a beating he took from his father. He thinks it could have been Caleb. Sully let him stay for a few nights."

"Really? Why didn't he mention it when we found the boy's jacket?"

"He said he hadn't seen him again. But I'm guessing you the know the real answer. None of these folks want law enforcement combing through their makeshift homes."

"Why did he tell you now?"

"I helped him out. I think he felt he was returning the favor."

"Is it possible they're hiding him again? Could he have been trying to tell you that in a nonchalant way?"

"I guess I never thought of that. Considering the circumstances, I think he was being straight with me."

"You don't care to tell me what those circumstances were?"

"There were some guys hassling him behind the Red Roof Inn."

"Drug dealers?"

"No. Assholes."

She surprised him with a laugh.

"Well, my people are trying to get the boy's cell phone data, but for some reason, that's taking longer than I'd like. Of course, it's difficult to press for warrants when the parents are now saying he's no longer missing. And one of them never believed he was missing."

She was quiet for a while, then added, "Something's not right. I feel it in my bones."

"We'll help any way possible, Sheriff."

"I appreciate that. I wanted to get on your schedule. Late this afternoon or first thing tomorrow morning. I'm just not sure where to start a new search."

"We can give his neighborhood a shot. It might only take us to all the places he frequented, but it also could find something your deputies might not find on a door-to-door search."

"That sounds good. Should I try to get another article of clothing? I gave them back Caleb's jacket that the homeless man was wearing."

"No, need. I have the sweatshirt they gave us. It's bagged and still in my Jeep."

"Okay. Thanks. I'll be in touch."

"No problem."

He rubbed at his bristled jaw. He definitely wasn't in search-ready condition. Which meant he needed to grab some sleep, except his stomach suddenly insisted on breakfast first.

Opening the back door to the kitchen, the scent of bacon instantly revived him. Hunter and Lady scrambled across the floor, hind ends swaying along with their tails.

Hannah had taken her boys to school, then had errands to run. Yet, she left homemade breakfast sandwiches, wrapped individually and ready to pop into the microwave. Creed knew she hadn't gotten much sleep either, but she still managed to take care of them all.

He bypassed the coffee. Put a couple of the sandwiches into the microwave. Hannah's creations included homemade biscuits with egg and bacon stuffed in-between. When the microwaved pinged, he was practically drooling.

"Hey." Brodie appeared. "I thought I heard the back door." Hank and Kitten followed. "How are they doing?"

She meant the Afghanistan dogs.

"Good," he managed around a mouthful. Swallowed then added, "The spaniel's a bit scrawny and scuffed up, but nothing we can't take care of. I think Dr. Avelyn was expecting them to be in worse shape."

Brodie went to the refrigerator and took out a breakfast sandwich for herself. He wished she'd take out three. She was still so thin. But he stopped from saying anything.

"Did you get any sleep?" he asked instead.

She shook her head.

Last night was the first time she'd spent the entire night here alone. He didn't want to make a big deal of it. A glance at her eyes didn't give him a clue. His sister had become an unwitting expert in hiding her emotions.

"I stayed up reading. Hannah kept me up-to-date."

He thought about kidding her that she finally had her phone with her, but any amount of humor had been drained and replaced with a simmering anger. His mind continued to batter him with a compilation of greatest hits from his own time in Afghanistan. He hoped some sleep would turn it off, but feared it might only turn up the volume.

They ate in comfortable silence, the dogs and Kitten lounging around their feet.

"You never talk about it," Brodie said.

"Afghanistan?"

She nodded. "Why did you go?"

There wasn't a way to tell her without her suspecting why he needed to escape. It was right after their father had committed suicide. Right after Creed had found him lying on his sofa with a football game blaring in the background. He had told her about it as simply as he could without any graphic description. Her pained expression on her face—a face she'd trained to show very little emotion—had nearly broken his heart. Though she agreed she wasn't to blame, it was obvious that she did, in fact, blame herself.

"Joining the Marines sounded like an exciting adventure." That was partially true. He forced himself to meet her eyes to show her that morsel of truth. "I can't complain. It taught me a lot. How to take care of myself. Becoming a K9 handler saved me in more ways than I can count."

They both got quiet again. Creed finished his second biscuit. Contemplated a third. As if reading his mind, Brodie went to the refrigerator, pulled out two more, and put them in the microwave.

"You're worried about the dogs that were left behind." It wasn't a question. She looked back at him and didn't wait for his response. "You never gave up on bringing me home. I'm betting you'll bring these dogs home, too."

"You think so?"

"Yup. In case you haven't heard, I've been winning a lot of my bets."

46

Pensacola, Florida

Maggie had lost almost five hours. There was no comfort in knowing that Peter Gregory's Mercedes had stopped some place in Pensacola and hadn't moved since. As Alonzo tried to figure out where, he kept saying it looked like a residential area. New construction.

"Maybe he finally felt safe enough to rest," Maggie told him, knowing that the Florida Panhandle might not be his final destination.

She wasn't willing to relinquish Gregory's trail to anyone else. But she had to hand over the body he'd left behind. For the second time, she had to trust Alonzo's judgment and bring in Wren Warren and her team. Gregory had brought this body across state lines. He was suspected of multiple murders. She needed someone on the federal level to step in. Someone who would treat this dead body as part of Maggie and her team's ongoing investigation.

Alonzo assured her that Agent Warren "was solid." Maggie had to remind herself of his words when Warren showed up on that dirt road. She looked nothing like the self-assured professional Maggie had met at the airport.

Instead, Warren wore a baggy sweatshirt, jeans that were threadbare at the knees and hiking boots. Maggie caught a glimpse of the agent's eyes under the shadow of her ball cap bill and knew immediately she hadn't dealt with something like this before.

"CSU team is right behind me," Warren had told her.

But when Maggie said she couldn't wait and needed to get back on the interstate, Warren's eyes widen and flew around the surroundings. The thunderstorms had moved to the north, but the remaining cloud cover added to the complete darkness. The headlights of their vehicles provided the only glimpse of thick foliage and tall pine trees. The symphony of night sounds didn't help. Maggie couldn't distinguish between bird calls, frogs, or maybe the hiss and slither of an alligator.

"Will you be all right?" she'd asked, trying not to embarrass the agent.

"No worries."

Maggie almost regretted her last words to the newbie when she saw they had sent her even more on edge. But the warning was necessary. "Remind your team about alligators."

That was hours ago. And by the time Maggie took the exit off I-10 and arrived in Pensacola, Alonzo and Kuszak were already getting preliminary details from Warren's CSU team.

It didn't squelch Maggie's anxiety. Nothing seemed to calm it even after she'd eaten one of the deli sandwiches out of her cooler and downed all three cans of Diet Pepsi.

Now, as she followed the last couple of miles, her eyes kept flicking to the GPS monitor. Gregory's Mercedes had not budged. Her senses were on high alert as she drove along Airport Boulevard.

She tapped her cell phone in the dashboard holder, and Alonzo answered after just two rings.

"You there yet?" he asked.

"Almost. You didn't mention that he parked the vehicle this close to the airport. How do we know he didn't take a flight this morning?"

"I checked all last-minute tickets bought, flying out of Pensacola."

"But he could have booked a flight weeks ago. And we know he uses other aliases."

Silence.

Had Gregory just taken her on a long distance road trip and bailed as easily as getting on a flight to who knows where?

"I'm working on something that ties him to Pensacola," Alonzo said.

"You mean like family?"

"Yes. Maybe."

"Which is it, Alonzo? Yes, or maybe?"

"A very strong maybe."

She was exhausted and didn't bother to hide it. She felt drained. Not to mention her shoes and pant legs were muddy from tromping around a swamp. She wanted a shower. A couple hours of sleep. The only things keeping her going were that image of Nessie and a promise to Racine's partner.

"Also, I finally found a photo of him. It's a group photo. I had to crop and zoom in," Alonzo told her. "I'll text it to you. It's about four years old, but right now, it's the best I can do."

"Are you sure it's him?"

"Considering I'm starting from zero, no. Not a hundred percent. But there are others from his management office. The caption identifies him."

Right now, a photo wasn't going to help her. She'd tried to get a look at him when he picked up the Mercedes at the Amtrak station. Shadows made it almost impossible. Nessie had described him as tall. The man Maggie saw running away in the D.C. streets looked young and agile.

"Speaking of the management company, are any of their properties here in Pensacola?"

"Already thought of that. They don't distinguish between what they own and what they just manage. In Pensacola plus Navarre, there are thirty-three."

"Thirty-three? Am I headed toward any of them?"

"No. Most of them are on the beach."

She turned the corner onto the final street. A sigh of frustration escaped before she could tamp it down. She pulled her rental to the nearest curb and stopped.

"What?" Alonzo wanted to know. "What is it?"

"A storage facility. Probably over fifty units."

"No way. It doesn't show on my satellite feed."

"Maybe it's new. My monitor shows it's somewhere inside. He parked his Mercedes in a storage unit."

She rubbed her fingers over her eyes, then leaned her head back.

All their efforts and here they were. A dead end.

47

Baptist Hospital
Pensacola, Florida

Taylor still had three more hours of her shift, and she was exhausted. She'd spent most of the night missing Will and battling with herself. After having such a great day yesterday, how was she supposed to tell Jason they should take a break? And right before Christmas?

She was almost grateful to have four long days at the hospital. She could avoid talking to him. He was good about letting her have alone time. Letting her call when she felt like talking or getting together.

The unit secretary waved her down, holding up the telephone receiver.

"Taylor, call for you." She kept her hand over the mouthpiece as she handed it to her. "Your mother-in-law."

"It's super busy today. Tell her I'll call her back."

She shook her head. "I tried that. She's pretty upset."

Her first thought was that Will must have told her about their day at the beach with Jason. Taylor took the phone. Restrained herself from rolling her eyes or even sighing.

"Dora, I'm on duty. Can't this wait until later?"

"What did you do with him?"

"Who? What are you talking about?" Before Dora could answer, Taylor felt a shiver down her spine.

"You took him! Where is he?"

"Dora, I'm at the hospital. What are you talking about?"

"Willie didn't come home from school. I know you have him."

"What do you mean, he didn't come home?" She twisted around to see the wall clock above the unit counter. He should have gotten home about an hour ago.

"I called. They said he didn't show up for school this morning."

"How is that possible? Why didn't they call?"

"Don't pretend like you don't know. Where is he? What did you do with him? I swear I'll have you arrested. If you think—"

Taylor dropped the phone on the counter. Without a word, she went to the cabinet underneath the main desk. Punched in a code and retrieved her belongings. Immediately, she checked her cell phone for messages.

"Everything okay?" the unit secretary asked.

"I have to leave."

"What do you mean, leave? You can't just leave."

"My son is missing."

She didn't wait for a reaction. She left the area and walked down the hallway without looking back. The elevator opened just as she got to it. Taylor barely saw the couple exiting as she entered and tapped the button. Before the doors squeezed closed, she could see the unit secretary gesturing to someone and pointing at her. They were a slice of motion. And then they were gone.

She arrived at her car, fumbling with the key fob, sunlight blinding her. She wasn't even sure how she had gotten all the way through the hospital and through the parking lot when she didn't remember exiting the elevator.

All she could focus on were Dora's words. "He didn't show up for school this morning."

And she remembered Will's words: "What if I don't go back?"

Could he have run away? Was that even possible?

He was only seven years old. He wasn't even allowed to ride his bicycle across the highway to play with his friends from school. The bus picked him up at the entrance to their housing development. What was that? Two blocks? Maybe three?

He'd been so happy this weekend. They laughed. Had a great time with Jason yesterday, sharing his drawings with a new superhero. He talked a mile a minute about sandpipers, the color orange and his favorite candy: Sour Patch Kids.

She shook her head, remembering it all in a flood of memories. Her wonderfully creative little boy ordinarily didn't talk much and kept his head down with his fingers moving, sketching, coloring, creating masterpieces. Many of them, she only now realized, included the color orange.

They'd both been so happy…and then so miserable on the drive back.

Oh, my sweet, Will. What did you do?

48

Pensacola Beach, Florida

During the drive to her apartment, Taylor had convinced herself that Will would be waiting at the bottom of the stairs. Or maybe the dock. She'd given him a key. Could he already be inside?

But there was no sign of Will.

Her knees felt like spaghetti as she climbed the stairs, turning to see if she'd missed him at one of the bistro tables next door at Bobbye's Oyster Bar. There was no one. Then she remembered that Howard had shuttered the place for December. Her eyes flew across the marina. Howard's deep sea fishing boat was gone.

By the time she went inside and found it empty, cockroaches began assembling in her gut. She could feel them marching along the lining. She needed to pull herself together.

Will wasn't here.

Of course, he wasn't here. How did she expect him to get here?

She'd done such a good job of convincing herself that she hadn't even considered a Plan B. What was she supposed to do now? It was worthless to try and talk to Dora when the woman had convinced herself that Taylor had taken him.

Who could she call? She couldn't wait for Howard. Walter Bailey, maybe?

On the drive home, she'd dialed Will's new cell phone. It rang only twice. Went directly to voice mail. A machine voice. He hadn't had it long enough to learn how to put in his own message.

Two rings. Did that mean it was shut off?

She called a couple more times. Same response.

The battery had run low while he was at her house over the weekend. He was a kid with a new toy. He probably didn't remember to charge it.

Oh, Will! Where are you?

She couldn't panic. She wouldn't let herself. Not yet. It wouldn't help Will. What if he was hurt?

Oh my God! What if someone had taken him?

Then her mind went where she did not want it to go.

What if Dora had done the very thing she accused Taylor of doing? What if Dora had hidden him? Taken him away?

There had to be someone she could call. She knew exactly who she *wanted* to call.

Wanted, but probably shouldn't.

She wanted to call Jason. But what if that was exactly what Dora thought she'd do, so she could use it against her? Did it matter? This was ridiculous.

Her fingers shook so badly she could barely scroll through her contacts.

He answered on the third ring.

"Hey, I was just thinking about you," he said.

"Will's gone."

"What do you mean, gone?"

"Dora said he didn't come home from school."

"Maybe he had to stay after?"

"The school told her he never showed up this morning."

"That doesn't sound right. Did any of his friends see him?"

"I don't have a clue who his friends are. Dora doesn't allow him to have friends over. I live too far away for him to have friends over when he's with me. But I should know. I should know who his friends are."

"Okay, hold on. We'll figure this out."

"Jason, she's accused me of taking him."

"What? That's crazy."

"He didn't want to go back yesterday. He wanted to stay with me."

"But you took him back, right?"

"Yes, of course. What was I supposed to do?"

"We all had a good time. He was just wishing. That's all."

"But what if he's run away?"

"When did she call you?"

"About thirty minutes ago."

"So he's been gone—"

"Going on eight hours. Oh my God! Where's he been since seven o'clock this morning?"

"Has Dora called any law enforcement?"

"I have no idea. I…I hung up on her. She was screaming at me that I took him."

"This will be Sheriff Norwich's jurisdiction. You need to call her. See if she's been contacted."

"Okay."

"If she wants to question you at her office or meet you at Dora's, I can be at either place."

"No, that's okay. That's sweet, but you don't have to do that."

"I don't have to. I want to do it."

"No, Jason, you can't."

"What do you mean, I can't?"

"Jason, I appreciate your help, but we're just dating. This isn't your problem. It's not like we're in a relationship or something."

What was wrong with her? She had spent the night tossing and turning and coming up with ways to push him away, but maybe right this minute was not cool.

"I didn't mean that the way it sounded. I just…I need to handle this."

When he still didn't respond, she added, "Okay?"

"Okay. Sure."

"I'll call you as soon as I know something."

She hung up before he said anything that might make her feel guilty. All she cared about right now was Will and finding him. Jason had to understand that. Nothing else mattered.

49

Pensacola Beach, Florida

Maggie checked into the Margaritaville Hotel on the beach. She'd stayed here before. By now, she was bone-tired and needed something familiar, even if she afforded it on her own dime. But more importantly, gut instinct told her Gregory was here.

On the beach.

What better place to hide out than an empty vacation rental where no one would expect him to be? However, it might be impossible to figure out which one.

Okay, not impossible, but difficult.

Especially since he had obviously switched the Mercedes for another vehicle. Did he suspect they were following him? She didn't think so. It would be too easy for him to simply toss the GPS tracking device or attached it to an eighteen-wheeler headed across the country. And he hadn't done that.

No, he was here. And if Alonzo was correct about him having family in the area, it made perfect sense.

As soon as she got to her room, she headed to the balcony and took in the stunning sight: the emerald waters, sugar-white sands. The waves were alive, and the rhythm of them lapping against the shore, had an instant soothing effect.

Before she ordered food and took a shower, she made a phone call. She wanted to hear his voice. Being this close, she *needed* to hear his voice.

"Hey," Ryder answered. One word filled with that smile that hitched up at the corner of his lips.

"You'll never guess where I am."

"You decided to come down early?"

"Not exactly. Remember, you told me to go get the killer."

"He's in Pensacola?"

"Long story, but—yes. We spooked him. He ran. I followed him to Jacksonville. But he didn't stop until he got here. One of the few things we know is that he's an investor and executive at a management firm in Miami."

"Miami? But he's here in Pensacola?"

"Alonzo thinks he has family here. But his company owns and manages luxury vacation rentals."

"You think he's hiding out in one? On Pensacola Beach?"

It surprised her sometimes how much they thought alike. But both of them had been chasing killers in one way or another for too many years.

"Yes. Well, maybe." Now she sounded like Alonzo. It was just such a long shot.

"You might call Hannah. She knows a couple of people who manage some rentals on the beach. You know their listings overlap. You get credit just for advertising the house on your site."

"I didn't think of that."

"They'd at least be able to go in and tell you which properties are currently being rented. He'd have to be staying in an empty one. In December, I can't imagine it's a busy time."

"You are so smart."

"I get it from the dogs."

She laughed. Wanted to add that he was also very humble and not very good at taking a compliment.

"You sound tired," he told her. "Were you driving all night?"

"Most of it. Had a little detour. You sound tired, too."

"We spent the night waiting for a flight with some of the dogs from Afghanistan." He paused, then said, "There were only three on board."

"When are they sending the others?"

"That's just it. They're not. Dr. Avelyn's still trying to find out what happened. My guess is the Taliban realized the dogs were valuable to us. Maybe they'll ask for some kind or ransom…or…"

"Or?" Maggie prompted.

"Or they've already killed all the others."

She heard his sigh of frustration. The thought made her sick to even consider, but she knew he could be right.

"Let me see if I can find out anything," she offered.

"How?"

"My old assistant director sent me on wild goose chases all the time for his D.C. friends. I've unwillingly done enough favors I should be able to ask some questions."

"Military brass?"

"No. Politicians. Although these days there isn't much difference. Everyone in D.C. seems to be a politician. Do you have time for dinner tonight?" she asked.

"I wish." He dragged out the word, and she knew he really did wish it. "But I can't. We're packing up. We just found out a little boy is missing."

"I thought you said he was a teenager?"

"No, that was last week. Jason got a call. Actually, you met Taylor Donahue. Her seven-year-old son didn't come home from school. She shares custody with Will's grandparents. Sounds like he didn't show up for school this morning."

Maggie did remember Taylor. She'd ended up in the middle of a murder investigation last June. Maggie had met her mother-in-law, too, though she couldn't remember the woman's name offhand.

"Let me know if I can help."

"Likewise. You don't happen to have an item from this guy that would have his scent?"

She hadn't thought of that. Her mind immediately went to the canvas bag underneath the bridge and the pair of shoes back at Quantico.

"I never thought of that. Would it actually work?

"If he's out walking around the beach, yes. If he's only driving, no."

An incoming phone call interrupted. She glanced at the I.D.

"I've got to go. It's Alonzo."

"Be careful."

"You too."

She tapped over to Alonzo, her impatience blurting out, "What do you have?"

"You said you wanted to know more about the homeless woman."

It wasn't at all what Maggie expected. For the moment, she'd allowed herself to forget about Nessie. She wanted to ask how she was, but that wasn't the information she had told Alonzo to get for her.

"Metro took her fingerprints."

"Wait. That's sort of unusual."

"One of their own was almost killed. Kuszak thinks they're treating this as a target hit."

"What are you talking about? They think he meant to kill Racine, and Nessie just got in the way?"

"No. They think he meant to kill Racine, and Nessie lured Racine to where he wanted her."

"That's not what happened! Nessie was helping me."

"Eventually, you'll probably need to tell them that. In the meantime, Kuszak ran her prints."

"Are you saying you already know her real name?"

"It actually was very easy."

"Her prints are in the criminal database?"

"No. But they are filed with the federal government since she had classified clearance."

"Classified clearance?"

"Her name is Vanessa Sambrook. Up until five years ago, she was employed by the State Department. More specifically, the Bureau of European and Eurasian Affairs. She speaks Russian, German, French and Italian. Never married. No listed close relatives."

Nessie had joked about it, and Maggie waved it off as the imagination of a mentally challenged homeless woman.

"So what happened? How did she end up on the street?"

"Looks like she handed in her resignation. No indication whether it was forced. I haven't dug that deep. Do you want me to?"

"No. Not right now. It's more important we make sure she's okay. And that she's definitely not treated like a co-suspect. Please tell them she was working with us. With me. As an informant. Tell Detective Sheldon. Can you do that for me?"

"Absolutely. I'm on it."

Maggie clicked off the call, then walked back out onto the balcony. She rubbed at the knot of tension between her shoulder blades. Unsuccessful at dismantling it, she sighed and stared out at the water.

What a mess. And the fact that she had caused it was eating away at her. Maybe she could counter her mistake with a good deed.

She scrolled through the contacts on her phone. The number was here, though she had never used it. When the senator gave Maggie her private cell phone number, the woman was genuinely humbled and beyond grateful for what Maggie had done for her and her family. At the time, Maggie knew she meant it when she told her, "If there's ever anything I can do to repay the favor, please call me."

Maggie tapped the number. It was worth a shot.

50

Linden Estates
Santa Rosa County, Florida

Taylor had met Santa Rosa County Sheriff Francis Norwich back in June. However, it was only weeks after the sheriff had suffered a heart attack and was still on the mend. It was difficult to match that convalescing woman with the person who waited on Dora's portico. Dressed in uniform, she looked every bit the authoritarian figure Jason talked about, lean with square shoulders and sleek gray hair.

She watched and waited as Taylor parked along the Ramsey's circle driveway behind the sheriff's SUV. She continued to wait for her even as Dora opened the door. Unfortunately, Taylor wasn't close enough to hear the exchange. But she did see Dora's expression. Her mother-in-law looked surprised to see the sheriff, then her face turned into a scowl when her eyes found Taylor making her way to the front door.

Nevertheless, Dora led them into her formal living room, then sat down without offering them to do the same.

"Is your husband here? It would be a good idea for him to join us."

"He was in Biloxi today for business. He's making his way home as quickly and safely as possible. Besides, I've already taken care of things," she said to the sheriff, avoiding even acknowledging Taylor.

"You've taken care of things?" Sheriff Norwich continued standing, and Taylor followed her lead. "Because my office hasn't heard from you. Or are you saying your grandson is not missing?"

"I called Kevin Perry. He's handling the situation."

Taylor looked from Dora to Norwich as the two women seemed to stare each other down.

"I don't understand," Taylor finally said. "Who is Kevin Perry?"

"He's an FBI agent," Norwich answered, her eyes not leaving Dora's. "From what I remember, he's with the Jacksonville office. This isn't his jurisdiction."

Now Taylor understood why Dora hadn't called Sheriff Norwich. She'd already called the FBI.

"I'm the one who decides if and when to call the FBI, Mrs. Ramsey."

"Well then, I made your job much easier. And kidnapping is a federal offense."

"Kidnapping?" The sheriff shot a look at Taylor, truly confused now. "You know your grandson has been taken? Has someone contacted you?"

"She thinks I took my son."

This time Norwich let out a long sigh before confronting Dora. "And why do you think she'd do that?"

"Ask her. And then ask her where she's hiding him."

"In my experience—my twenty-eight years of experience—the parent who's kidnapped the child isn't the first one to call law enforcement."

"Unless she's afraid she'll lose her custody rights."

"We had an argument," Taylor told Norwich, but just like the sheriff, she didn't take her eyes off of Dora.

"It was a discussion."

"What if Will heard us?"

"Then you have that to feel guilty about as well."

"Hold on." Norwich put up her hands. "Ms. Donahue, did you take your son?"

"No. He was with me for the weekend. I brought him back here last night."

A knock at the door startled all of them. Norwich stepped back into the entrance. "My deputies are here." She held up a finger to tell them to wait. "Whatever happened between the two of you, I need to hear about it. But right now, it's my understanding we have a young boy who didn't make it to school this morning and hasn't come back home. Is that true, Mrs. Ramsey?"

"Yes."

"Do you remember what he was wearing this morning?"

Norwich pulled out a small notebook and pen, and Taylor saw Dora twitch at the question. She couldn't remember. Hadn't she even noticed? Will said the housekeeper usually helped him pick out his clothes and had breakfast ready for him.

"Miss Rosa could tell us," Taylor offered.

"And who is Miss Rosa?"

"She's not here right now." Dora gestured as if the woman was out running errands. Except Taylor remembered Will saying she hadn't been to work for a while.

"You don't remember what he was wearing this morning?" Norwich looked up at Dora, waiting.

"He's at that age where he wants to pick out his own things."

Norwich waited for more, then finally asked, "Did you see him this morning?"

"Yes, of course. We had breakfast together. I don't remember exactly. You should ask her when she picked him up." She pointed at Taylor. "And just for the record, I will be filing charges of kidnapping when Agent Perry arrives."

"Do you drive him to school?"

Dora was still staring at Taylor. Maybe she thought the questions were done. She glanced back at the sheriff as if irritated by such mundane details. "The bus picks him up."

"And where is that, exactly?"

"At the entrance to the neighborhood."

"He walks there?"

"Yes, of course, it's only a few blocks. That must be where she intercepted him."

Another glare at Taylor.

"Tell me again, how old is Will?"

"He's only seven," Taylor spoke up this time and hated that her voice had been reduced to a whisper. How could Dora not remember what he wore? Was she lying about breakfast? Had she even seen him this morning?

"You're wasting precious time," Dora told Norwich. "You should be questioning where she took him. Where she's hiding him. The fact is —"

"No, Mrs. Ramsey, the fact is when a young child goes missing, the early hours are critical. Each hour decreases the likelihood that he will be found. Your insistence that he was taken by his parent will hamstring my efforts to determine if he's in immediate danger and even the ability to issue an Amber Alert."

"You don't need an Amber Alert. For God's sake, just look in her apartment above that marina."

"Mrs. Ramsey, are you refusing to cooperate with this investigation?"

Dora crossed her arms over her chest, clearly upset that Norwich wasn't listening to her. Finally, she said, "I'll cooperate with Agent Perry's."

Another stare-down. Then Norwich shook her head and turned on her heels. "Ms. Donahue, if I can have a word with you outside."

Taylor followed her out.

The two deputies waited at a vehicle parked behind Taylor's. She continued to walk silently alongside the sheriff until they were standing at her SUV.

Norwich pulled out a business card and wrote a number on the back, then handed it to Taylor.

"I need you to send me a photograph of Will. Something casual and something recent would be best. It would be tremendously helpful if we knew what he was wearing this morning."

"The housekeeper usually helps him get dressed. Will told me on Friday that she hadn't been around for over a week. But I can tell you he doesn't go anywhere without his red backpack."

Norwich slipped the notebook out of her pocket and jotted that down. "Anything special about it? Logos?"

"No. It just always looks too big for him. He is tall for a seven-year-old. He had a growth spurt this summer."

"How tall?"

She put her flat hand on her chest next to where she estimated the top of his head came. Norwich wrote in the notebook again.

"His hair is a little darker than mine. Short. A crazy cowlick makes it stick up." She caught herself smiling, remembering just yesterday trying to help him comb it. "Oh, and he has a new pair of sneakers we bought this weekend. He loves them. I'm sure he wore them this morning. They're Under Armour. Blue with lime green soles."

"That's good," Norwich nodded. "That'll help a great deal. Does he have a cell phone?"

"Yes, but he's not answering. Or the battery is low." She gave Norwich the number. "It's new to him. I don't think he's in the habit of using it or charging it. He hasn't even added a personal message for voice mail."

"Did you buy it for him, or is it under his grandmother's account?"

Taylor felt a sting at the realization, dropped her chin, and closed her eyes for a couple of seconds. "His grandmother's." She knew getting access to his account would be a challenge without Dora's help.

"Do you know any of his friends at school? Or in the neighborhood."

As she said it, Norwich looked around the street, and Taylor's eyes followed. Linden Estates had huge empty lots in various stages of progress. There was a half dozen finished, sprawled across the wide open space. Well-manicured lawns had palm trees and ferns, but there were no bicycles, trampolines, or red wagons. Nothing to signal a child lived in any of the houses.

"Will told me that he has a couple of friends in the neighborhood across the highway, but he's not allowed to ride his bike there."

"He has a bicycle. Do you know where he parks it?"

Taylor felt a twinge of hope. Of course. If Will ran away, he would ride his bicycle."

"I think the garage."

Norwich nodded, glancing back at the massive four-car garage and scribbling another note to herself.

"I'm going to have you talk with one of my deputies. And we'll need to see if Will's bike is still here. You don't happen to have anything of your son's in your car with you? An article of clothing? Or a blanket he may have used?"

"I still have his old sneakers. They're on the floor in the backseat."

"Those would be perfect. Could you check and get those for me?"

Norwich looked up and waved at another SUV winding its way into the neighborhood. Taylor glanced, then did a double take when she saw Jason. She didn't know whether to be angry or glad that he hadn't listened to her.

The sheriff noticed Taylor's expression and said, "I called them. Dogs can cover twice the ground my entire force can in half the time."

That's when Taylor saw Brodie in the passenger seat. A second, almost identical SUV turned in behind Jason's.

51

Creed waited. He told Jason to do the same. Sheriff Norwich was introducing Taylor to one of her deputies. He knew Jason was already going against his first impulse to go to her and see how she was doing. It would probably be Creed's impulse, as well. But the best thing they could do for Will right now was get to work. Comforting his mother wouldn't speed that up.

Taylor pulled something from the backseat of her car. She handed it to Norwich. A deputy joined them, ready with a notepad and pen.

The sheriff gestured for them to park across the street instead of pulling into the circle drive. Three lots stood empty, ground dug up, excavator and backhoe parked at the rear of the properties where the woods began.

He left the Jeep running with the windows down and the fan sucking in the cool, fresh air for Grace. He met Norwich at the driver's side of Jason's Jeep. They were far enough away that their conversation couldn't drift across the road to reach Taylor or Dora Ramsey. Although he hadn't seen Mrs. Ramsey come out yet. Still, Norwich threw a look over her shoulder as though she needed to make sure.

"Dora Ramsey insists Taylor took Will and is hiding him."

"Taylor told me that," Jason offered.

"What do you think?"

"I think it's crazy."

"Even if her custody battle might be going south?"

Creed stood quietly and watched the exchange. Jason Seaver had struggled to overcome more challenges than men twice his age, but he was loyal and probably to a fault. Yet Creed knew he wouldn't let his emotions interfere with the safety of a seven-year-old boy.

"Part of the reason she's in a custody battle is because she thought she was doing what was best for Will by having him live with his grandparents."

"So she wouldn't take him?"

"No, she wouldn't. Unless…" He paused. Gave it some thought. A long sigh, then he added, "Unless she believed he might be harmed or in some kind of danger."

"Has she ever mentioned anything?"

"No. I just had lunch with the two of them yesterday. They were laughing and having fun."

"Well, her mother-in-law is convinced that Taylor's taken him and has hidden him. Whatever her reasoning, she's not cooperating. I have to operate on the facts. I have a seven-year-old who didn't show up at school this morning. With a child this young, the first two to four hours are crucial, and we're already eight hours behind. The school said he didn't show up. I'm waiting for one of my deputies to tell me what the bus driver knows."

"But he was here this morning, right?" Jason asked. "Taylor took him back last night?"

"Dora said they had breakfast together, and he walked to meet the school bus at the entrance to the neighborhood." She craned her neck to look in that direction. Houses and a couple of trees blocked the view.

"So PLS is the Ramsey's house?" Creed asked. Place Last Seen. It helped to have a starting point.

"Yes, until we have a witness who says otherwise." Norwich looked over at the Ramseys again. Creed could see Dora's behavior wasn't sitting well with the sheriff. "She couldn't tell me what the boy was wearing. That's not as critical as it sounds. Some people just don't pay attention. Can't even tell you what they had for their last meal. Minds get occupied. However, this woman is extremely hostile, not just to her daughter-in-law, but to me."

"Do you two have a history?" Creed asked.

"Not that I'm aware of. I've seen her at a few different events, but this is the first time we've spoken to one another. For whatever reason, she doesn't respect or trust our department. She's already called an FBI agent she knows from the Jacksonville field office."

"Doesn't the FBI have to be requested by local law enforcement?" Jason asked.

"Yes. But not if there's evidence a child has been kidnapped and possibly or potentially taken across state lines."

"Does she have evidence?" Creed asked.

"No, not that she's presented."

"So, are you thinking she's a control freak? Or does she have something to hide?"

"Maybe both. Right now, I can't care about pissing contests." She handed Creed a plastic bag. "Taylor had an old pair of Will's sneakers in her car. I'm hoping you can do your thing without access to his bedroom."

"How long has it been since he's worn these?"

"She said she just bought him a new pair over the weekend."

"These will work."

"I need to get my deputies started with a door-to-door canvasing."

"We'll start at his house," Creed told her. "We're going to run two dog teams with Brodie coordinating. Kids have higher metabolisms, so they shed more skin rafts. But since this is his neighborhood, there'll be a lot of his scent. It'll be difficult to determine whether it's from today or yesterday or even last week."

"Sounds like you can't just follow his route from this morning?"

"Afraid not. But if he hasn't been here all weekend, today's scent will be fresh."

"A thunderstorm went through early this morning," she said, her eyes flashed the question.

"Shouldn't be a problem. It might actually play in our favor." He didn't mind her going through the list, even though she already knew the answers.

"We're checking to see if he took his bicycle," she continued. "That could make a difference, right?"

"A little, yes. But the dogs will still be able to follow. If he got into a vehicle, though, the scent would stop there."

Norwich took in a deep breath. Her eyes darted around to take in the other houses on the street. "I'm hoping one of these neighbors has a security camera that'll show us exactly what happened. The Ramsey's camera will only show him leaving."

From what Creed could see, the massive house that blocked everyone's view of the entrance was still under construction, with Tyvek walls and hollow window wells. When Norwich looked back at him, he could see she might be thinking the same thing he was. There would be no security footage of the school bus pickup.

"All this construction," Norwich waved her hand. "Do me a favor and have your dogs do a quick check of the Dumpsters. I counted three. There may be more." Then she locked eyes with Creed and asked, "They can do that, right? Or is it too confusing?"

She was delicately asking if the dogs could switch from search and rescue of a missing person to recovery of a body.

"Grace can," he assured her. Sometimes Grace found things he didn't ask her to find. She was a multi-task dog and couldn't help it if other scents she was trained to find happened to show up on the trail. And if he asked, she could easily go from search and rescue to recovery.

"We're long past two hours." Norwich didn't take her eyes from his.

"I know."

She gave him a quick nod.

He didn't dare glance at Brodie or Jason, but could feel them watching, wondering. Maybe he should have prepared them better. He already knew if they didn't find a missing child within the first two or three hours, the likelihood of finding him alive decreased with each passing hour.

"You all have radios?" Norwich asked.

"Yes, ma'am," Jason answered.

She told them what frequency to use. "I'll assign Deputy Trevor as your liaison. He's worked with K9s before. Of course, if you find something you aren't comfortable advertising over the radio, call or text me directly. I have my cell phone." She waved to another police cruiser as it turned onto their street.

"Sheriff, I know this isn't the best time, but I have to ask, what about Caleb Monroe? This morning we talked about a new search for him?"

"Oh, yeah." She raked her fingers through her hair. "His parents insist he's staying with friends. Of course, they won't give me names or present any proof. I'm weighing all my options, including arresting them both. But a fifteen-year-old who's known to have run away a time or two is a bit different from a seven-year-old who didn't make it to his bus stop three blocks from his home."

Creed nodded. "We don't have much daylight left."

"Your dogs can still search after dark?"

He felt himself bristle. He glanced at Jason and Brodie. Both already knew his stance. Whether they agreed or not, they would never say so. Jason was still a new handler and respected Creed's experience. As far as Creed was concerned, darkness counted as its own obstacle. One that was impossible to predict and prepare for. And he knew he was prejudiced on the issue because of his experiences in Afghanistan.

Technically, nighttime was better for scent detection. Scent pooled downward after the sunset. Moisture refreshed particles dried out in the light of day. But a handler couldn't see the dangers lurking in the shadows, and dogs hardly paid attention when they were following a trail.

"They can," he finally told Norwich. "But it's not safe, and I've never felt comfortable taking the risks. Remember, some of those garbage dumps we saw in the woods? In the daylight, it's just trash that we have to navigate a dog around. In the dark? That trash becomes dangerous and toxic.

"Also, because of the development in this area, a lot of the wildlife gets disturbed. Keep in mind that we're close enough to fresh water. We'll need to watch out for alligators. And these woods are dense enough that there could be black bears."

A session of blinks and what looked like a hard swallow told him Norwich hadn't thought about either of those obstacles.

"Then let's find this boy as soon as possible," was all she said.

52

Brodie had never done this before. Not outside a training session. This was for real. A boy's life depended on her getting it right. Not just any boy. Will.

Basically, she would be the communication between Ryder and Jason and law enforcement. At the same time, she'd also make sure both teams had everything they needed: water, medical assistance, maps, updates or even transportation. She'd be the one hoofing it back to the Jeep for items not already in her pack.

And no matter how much Ryder hated night searches, he'd given her a couple of flashlights, along with extra batteries. She knew both he and Jason had Maglites and headlamps in their own packs. He'd also tossed her a couple of rolls of Cyalume Cyflect tape. The flexible, lightweight vinyl was photoluminescent and glowed green in the dark. They could easily and quickly tear strips and adhere them, not only to the dogs' working vests, but also to their own shirts.

She wasn't sure how many of the items Ryder included were standard for K9 handlers or stuff that he used as a Marine. Because the last of the "just in case" items were high-tech night vision goggles that Brodie found fascinating, but Ryder winced at.

"Let's hope we don't need to use them," he'd told her as he handed the contraptions to her earlier.

"But they're so cool," she insisted.

His only explanation was a shrug and, "Too many bad memories."

It felt odd to think of her tall, strong, invincible, big brother as having weaknesses or triggers. Then she remembered what he looked like a couple of months ago in that hospital bed back in Nebraska. The doctors had relied on her—his sister, his advocate—to make decisions when he bobbed in and out of consciousness. Up until then, Brodie hadn't been responsible for anyone other than herself. That is, if you didn't count Kitten and Hank.

Now she would be responsible, not just for helping to find Will, but for making sure her handlers and their dogs were safe and had everything they needed.

She'd come prepared with maps and notebooks so she could keep track of each area or sector as they searched. She'd record anything they found. Anything suspicious. And any alerts or interest the dogs might show. She'd mark those places and highlight sectors that might require a second sweep or a narrower grid. She'd be responsible for documenting each as they cleared a sector and moved on to the next. Her notes and navigational coordinates needed to be accurate.

Also, any questions or new information from law enforcement would come through her.

She could do this. She knew she could do this.

Still, she looked to Hank for reassurance. He stared at her expectantly, waiting and ready to go, and so handsome in his vest. Of course, she saw "handsome," but she knew other people looked at Hank and saw "terrifying." The American Staffordshire terrier was big and muscular, with a jaw that looked like it could rip a man's arm off.

Before they left, Brodie had filled Hank's zippered pockets with basic medical supplies. His vest resembled a dog-size saddlebag instead of the working vests Grace and Scout wore. Hank didn't necessarily run faster than she could, but he could maneuver through places she might not be able to navigate. Plus, he knew how to pick up Grace and Scout's scent and track them even when they were far out of sight. A mile through Blackwater River State Forest was Hank's longest record.

They'd practiced those drills over and over in case one of the dogs got hurt. Hank found them every time. But they'd never trained in neighborhoods with asphalt streets, strangers in and out of houses, vehicles driving by or other dogs barking behind fences.

Right now, Brodie remained grateful that this area had more houses under construction than completed. Dozens of empty lots surrounded them. The thick woods bordered the back of the neighborhood. Fewer neighbors meant fewer people walking around, leaving more scent or simply distracting the dogs with their presence.

Norwich left as more of her deputies arrived along with the State Patrol. Uniformed officers walked from house to house, knocking on doors. Residents were coming home from work. Brodie watched a couple of vehicles slow down on the highway and hesitate before pulling into their own neighborhood. A Santa Rosa County Sheriff's department vehicle blocked the entrance with a deputy checking each car and turning away a couple that couldn't prove they were residents.

While Ryder and Jason finished prepping, Brodie turned her back to the commotion. She laid out the first map on the hood of Ryder's Jeep, smoothing the accordion folds. Assorted items from her pack anchored down the corners. The slight breeze felt good, but it would add a chill to the air after the sunset. Hannah had reminded her to take extra layers. This time of year, the day's temperature could be seventy and easily dip into the forties at night.

The thick humidity left a damp sheen on her skin, and the scent of pine overwhelmed. She put a K9 CrimeScents ball cap over her short, spiky hair and added a button-down collared shirt over her T-shirt, leaving the tails out and the buttons undone. Then she rolled up the sleeves like Jason and Ryder did.

Back to the map, she began dividing up sectors with a highlight marker and giving each a number. She was so focused she didn't notice Jason standing next to her. Then Ryder came up on the other side.

"How far can a seven-year-old travel on his own?" Jason asked, his voice low and his eyes darting over his shoulder.

Brodie didn't need to look to know he was checking on Taylor. He'd been doing that since they arrived.

"Will's smart," Brodie reminded him. "He's probably not a typical seven-year-old, right?"

"He's also got a big lead on us," Ryder said. Then, he asked Jason, "You sure you're okay doing this? It's hard when it's a kid, but it's even tougher when he's someone you know."

"I'm okay. It's not like Taylor and me are in a relationship or something."

Brodie glanced at Ryder. He met her eyes and raised an eyebrow. Neither said anything.

Jason continued, "You always say it's best when handlers don't know too much about the case or we might make our own assumptions. We could influence our dogs and guide them in a direction we think they should be going based on what we think we already know. But this time, it might help to know what Will is or isn't capable of doing."

"Okay. So what's your gut reaction?" Ryder asked. "Do you think he ran away?"

"How do we know Dora Ramsey isn't hiding him?"

53

Creed didn't want to give any validity to Jason's theory, but he couldn't help thinking it was odd for a grandmother to act the way Dora Ramsey was. What grandmother wouldn't be out here front and center giving details? Or digging for more? Demanding more.

For Creed, all of this brought back too many memories of when Brodie went missing. After she disappeared, his mother dragged him along for months, checking out every tidbit of information as it surfaced. Her world—and his, by extension—became a scavenger hunt.

A witness claimed he saw Brodie in a Memphis diner, and Olivia James didn't wait for the police report. She packed up her son and went to question the man herself. A tip came in on a hotline about a little girl matching Brodie's description going in and out of a hotel outside of Kansas City, and off they'd go again.

When Jason had asked how far a seven-year-old could go, Creed avoided telling him just how far. Because he already knew if no one had seen a little boy playing hooky—over the course of eight going on nine, hours—there was a good chance Will had been taken. And if it wasn't a parent, Will's odds weren't good. Unfortunately, Creed knew that kidnappings by strangers usually resulted in murder. Sometimes within the first three hours. Most likely, within the first two days.

When he and Hannah had started K9 CrimeScents, it was a direct extension of his search for Brodie. His mother had given up years before, but Creed found he still needed answers. And although he expected to find only remains, a small pocket of hope bloomed deep inside him. It had been enough to keep him going. And sometimes late at night when he couldn't sleep, when old demons still haunted him, he shuddered to think what would have happened to Brodie if he had given up. Like his mother had given up.

He kept an eye on Brodie, looking for glimpses of how much this situation might shake loose her own memories. After all, she knew firsthand how far an eleven-year-old could get in a matter of hours. The woman who had taken her from a rest stop would have driven across two state borders in a matter of eight hours.

Now Brodie pointed out what she considered red flags on the map. She was a stickler for details. This would be a good assignment for her. She had incredible instincts and saw things others overlooked.

In the last several months, he'd realized that if anything or anyone was holding her back, it was her overprotective big brother. Sort of the same thing he was doing with Grace. But the incident in Nebraska had taught him how strong his sister really was.

"We're not used to working with radios," Creed said as he leaned in closer to see the map. "Just a reminder." He glanced at Brodie. There were a lot of balls she'd be juggling.

"I remember," she told him. "No sudden outbursts. Gentle. Calm. Slow and easy, so I don't surprise the dogs."

"We'll both start from the house. Give me and Grace a head start. Chances are, Scout will follow the exact route she does. But my guess is Will's scent will splinter into two or three well-worn paths."

"Do you think he would have gone into the woods?" Brodie asked. Both of them looked over at Jason for the answer. Then all three of them glanced at the forest.

A yellow monster bulldozer sat at the edge after having plowed down a swatch of pine trees. The debris piled off to the side.

"He's a kid," Jason finally said. "What kid doesn't think the woods are an adventure? Maybe he just got lost."

Creed looked back at the map. He had a bad feeling about this. Maybe it was simply the reminder of those heartbreaking searches for Brodie. Maybe it was something else. Eight hours was a long time for a seven-year-old to be missing. But Jason made a good point. The boy could have gone to explore. Maybe went farther than he meant to and lost his way. He hoped that was what happened.

He forced himself to concentrate on the map and get some bearings to their surroundings. This was the third time in less than a week that he'd been to the area. Each time, he'd noticed something different.

As recent as the map was, it couldn't keep up with all the new construction. His eyes darted away and took in the wide strips the bulldozes had plowed into the dense woods. Somewhere on the other side, they'd caught the guy dumping concrete just the other day. How far away was that? It had to be close enough or connected by a back road.

"What's bothering you?" Brodie asked.

He did a double take at her question. He thought he was pretty good about hiding his emotions from his dogs, but lately, his sister was able to pick up on his discomfort.

"I don't like all this new construction. It disrupts natural habitats." He pointed to the map, blue lines delineating creeks and streams. "We really will need to watch out for alligators. And bears."

Brodie stared at him. Jason's jaw clenched tight.

He tried to ignore their reactions and looked over at Jason. "Does everyone call him Will?"

"I think his grandparents call him Willie."

"Any everyone probably calls him William when they're upset with him," Brodie chimed in.

"That's a good point. Let's call him Will with the dogs. Just in case he hears us, he won't automatically think he's in trouble."

Creed used different trigger words for different searches. Telling your dog to "find drugs" in a crowded airport sent out an alarm, so he used, "go fish" or "find fish." But when searching for a missing person who they still believed might hear them, Creed instructed his handlers to use the person's name. Now, he thought of Caleb Monroe and realized that approach could backfire with a missing teenager if he had run away and didn't want to be found.

Behind them, Creed heard more vehicles arriving. The neighborhood was filling up with all kinds of scents that would be trampling over the one he wanted his dogs to follow.

He held up the plastic bag Norwich had retrieved from Taylor and said, "Let's get this started."

54

The dogs could feel the urgency. Creed knew Grace definitely sensed his anxiety. It reminded him to stay positive, not only for Brodie and Jason, but for the dogs, too.

As he finished securing Grace's vest and leash, she subjected him to a full facial tongue-bath.

"I'm okay," he whispered to her with his back to the others. Between Grace and Brodie, he'd need to learn to hide his emotions better.

Already on the ground, Scout did a hotdog twirl that signaled his impatience. He could almost hear the dog telling Jason, *Come on. Come on. Let's go.*

He let Grace and Scout exchange greetings, then he squatted in front of the Jack Russell. "Grace, this is Will." He held open the plastic bag, inviting her to sniff what was inside.

Immediately, her nose twitched. Her small head dived into the bag, and he simply pulled the opening wider. He heard her snuffling and snorting as the bag moved around. When her head popped out, she was ready to go, waiting for his command.

Before he passed the bag over to Jason, he held it up for her to see, then he said, "Grace, find Will."

He kept her on a long lead. There were too many vehicles and people to let her run loose. There were no sidewalks, so they had to stay in the street. Creed expected to start at the Ramsey's, but Grace bypassed their circle driveway and headed for the rosebushes at the far corner of their property line. Her nose skimmed over the leaves, careful not to get close to the thorns. She sniffed the pine straw underneath.

Inhale. Snort. Sniff.

She threw back her head, testing the air. She wasn't interested in the rest of the plants and weaved around them. She skipped across the street, ignoring a state trooper who stopped to watch.

Out of the corner of his eye, Creed saw Norwich waving for other law enforcement officers to step back or move out of their way. He was grateful to have someone experienced like Norwich to lead the efforts. Already she had deputies stopping and assessing vehicles before allowing them into the neighborhood. Highway traffic had been stopped as well. Blockades rerouted to detours well out of sight to avoid on-lookers.

Creed had been on dozens of searches for missing people, but the ones looking for children were different. There was a tension, an anxiousness that filled the air like a heavy fog physically weighing on their shoulders. In the beginning, optimism and adrenaline would help drive them.

Just when Creed expected to cross another street to get closer to where the school bus usually picked up Will, Grace turned. No hesitation. Her head bobbed, then wagged side to side, pulling in air, separating scent and following the particles she knew only as "Will."

This time, nose in the air, she wanted to run. She tugged and pulled, but settled to a steady lope as Creed picked up his pace beside her. But again, instead of going anywhere near the highway or the school bus pickup, Grace took them in the opposite direction. She was heading to the trees.

A couple of the construction site lots had pallets of supplies stacked and sitting in the dirt. The plastic wrap covering them had torn and flapped. Grace slowed. Creed took note. He glanced back at Brodie, who followed ten paces behind. She nodded and scribbled in a small notebook. But even as the two of them evaluated the various housing materials strewn across the front yards, Grace decided there was nothing here.

She bounded to where the landscape was torn up and where a massive bulldozer sat. Deep tread marks crisscrossed, making it difficult to keep a steady footing. Creed slowed Grace down. There had been enough rain that morning, the clay now caked his hiking boots. None of it affected Grace.

He expected her to lead him to the woods beyond the gaping hole left by the bulldozer. Nose still in the air, Grace didn't go any farther than the huge yellow machine, stopping between the blade and the crawler tracking.

As she turned to catch his eyes, Creed saw another set up footprints. Footprints half his size.

55

Brodie radioed in the alert, and the four of them waited.

Ryder had given Grace her pink, squeaky elephant. While she tossed her reward toy, Hank sat by Brodie's side, simply watching. Ryder called up to the cab, explaining to Will who they were, and that he wasn't in trouble.

He talked in such a convincing manner, Brodie expected Will to peek out and wave down to them. But she noticed Ryder kept glancing over at Grace as she pranced around. He was looking for some indication from his dog that Will might actually still be up there.

Grace cocked her head at the word. For her, "Will" was a scent she was asked to find, and she had accomplished that. To Grace, Will was not a little boy they hoped would come crawling out of the bulldozer's cab. Ryder had explained how the dogs didn't have emotions for the people they searched for. To Grace, Will was simply a scent on a worn pair of sneakers.

Brodie jotted notes. She wrote down the time and took photos of the footprint, especially its proximity to the machine. On her sector map, she carefully placed an "X."

She looked back at Ryder to see he looked miserable, waiting for Sheriff Norwich. Patience was not one of his strengths. Brodie knew he wanted to climb up and see for himself. He took two steps back instead, making sure he didn't disturb the smaller footprints.

Evidence at a crime scene.

Both Ryder and Jason had drilled it into her at every practice session. Any search could risk disturbing a possible crime scene. Suddenly, that thought struck her. She had prepared herself to help look for a missing boy. Maybe a lost boy. She wasn't ready to find a dead boy.

Jason's voice came over the radio, jolting her back. She turned up the volume so Ryder could also listen.

"We're across from the entrance. Scout pulled me through the ditch. We came up onto the other side of the highway. Back behind some trees, there looks like fresh footprints. Deep treads like new shoes and small enough to be Will's. But Scout really wants to continue into that Woodriver neighborhood."

Ryder clicked on his radio. "Hold up a few minutes, okay?" he told Jason. "We need to check something here." Then he waved as if he could see him.

But instead of Jason and Scout, Brodie turned to find Sheriff Norwich marching diagonally across lawns, not wasting time by sticking to the paved streets. A tall deputy accompanied her. It was just the two of them.

"Brodie, Ryder, this is Deputy Lucas Trevor. That's Grace. And Hank."

Brodie watched him take in the dogs before his attention came back to them. She thought he looked awfully young to be a deputy, but when his eyes met hers, she recognized an old soul even in those brief seconds.

He tipped his ball cap to her and Ryder, a polite acknowledgment or perhaps simply an excuse to wipe back the sweat off his forehead. The air was cool, but the humidity had ticked up. Brodie hated the damp chill. It easily brought memories of a cold basement floor that smelled of mildew.

While Norwich and Deputy Trevor discussed the best way for him to climb up, Brodie used the pause in their search to offer water to Hank and Grace. Then she got a drink for herself. She didn't realize that in the back of her mind she'd started a mantra that now drummed against her temples.

Don't be dead. Don't be dead.

It continued as Deputy Trevor pulled on latex gloves. It seemed to pound louder as his long legs climbed up the huge trackers. His fingers grabbed the first rung on the metal ladder. In seconds, he stood on the platform and hesitated as he peered through the dusty window on the machine's door.

Brodie couldn't help wondering how a seven-year-old boy had managed to climb up. Though Deputy Trevor didn't need to use them, the grooves in the tracker could possibly work as footholds and fingerholds.

Don't be dead. Don't be dead.

Why was he taking so long? The cab wasn't so big that he couldn't see what was inside.

"Nobody here," he finally said.

Brodie heard a collective sigh from Ryder and the sheriff.

As he opened the door, he said, "But he might have been inside."

The hinges screeched, then the door caught the breeze and slapped against the metal side of the machine before the deputy secured it.

All of them waited as he snapped photos of the interior, then handed the phone down to Norwich. He stayed on the platform, waiting for her instructions.

Ryder came alongside the sheriff to take a look, so Brodie moved in close on the other side.

Mostly, it looked like someone had left their trash on the floor: several candy wrappers, a couple of empty water bottles, and a Kool-Aid juice pouch with the straw still sticking out. There were also crushed pieces of paper with what looked like colorful marks.

"I'll check with the construction company, but this certainly looks like it could have been a seven-year-old."

"Maybe he played up there," Brodie suggested. "It would be a cool hideaway."

"Who knows how long ago he was here, though?"

"It doesn't look like the bulldozer has moved in a few days," Deputy Trevor offered.

"And the footprints are fresh," Ryder pointed out. "At least since this morning's rain."

"So maybe he skipped school and hid up in the cab. But where did he go from here?" Norwich looked at Ryder.

He jerked upright. Her question reminded him of something he'd forgotten. Then he grabbed the radio attached to his shoulder.

"Jason, sorry. Hang on a couple more minutes."

To Norwich, he said, "Scout found fresh footprints on the other side of the highway."

"That's where the kids wait for the bus."

"The prints are back in the trees. And Scout wants to go into that neighborhood."

"I have deputies and state troopers canvassing over there, too. So far, no one noticed a boy wandering around after the bus picked up the kids."

"If he skipped school," Brodie said, "he wouldn't want to be seen."

"Let's see what Scout can find," Norwich said. "I'm going to go update a very frantic mother. Deputy Trevor, collect those items as you would evidence."

"Jason," Ryder called into his radio, "I'm sending Brodie and Hank to assist you and Scout." He checked Brodie's eyes to make sure that was okay with her.

"Roger that," Jason told him. "Sheriff, do we know yet if he's on a bicycle? I'm not seeing any tire marks here, but there are a whole lot of pine needles and fallen leaves that could be hiding them."

"The bicycle is gone. I just found out. Mrs. Ramsey let us check the garage. She's giving us access to their home security cameras, too, while she waits for Agent Perry. I'll let Brodie know as soon as I know anything else."

Then Norwich caught Brodie's eyes and asked, "Do you have your cell phone on you?"

"Yes, ma'am." She pushed back the shirt tails and showed her the holstered phone on her belt. It was next to the bear spray.

"I want you to have direct access to me." They exchanged phone numbers and tapped them into their contacts. "And don't hesitate to ask me anything. You need something. Let me know. Right now, these dogs and handlers are my number one tool. So anything they need, you just holler. And if I learn a piece of information, you all need to know, I'll dial you directly. Are you okay with that?"

She said this last part with a smile, and Brodie nodded. As the sheriff left them, Brodie checked her radio and tried to ignore the weight of that responsibility. When she realized Will might not be lost—that something awful may have happened to him—something had shifted inside her.

She should have been the first to know what kinds of things may have happened. Except she couldn't relate to that little girl anymore, the one taken from a rest stop. She had willingly gotten into a stranger's RV. Followed another little girl up the steps just to see a new puppy. Could something like that have happened to Will?

"I'll be joining you and Jason on the other side," Ryder was telling her, bringing her attention back to the present. "Say in thirty minutes. I want Grace to check if there's any other paths Will took around here."

She looked up to see him glance back toward the woods. Already the sun had sunk behind the treeline. At the mention of Will's name, Grace came back to Ryder's side and surrendered her squeaky toy. She was ready to get back to work.

Brodie took a deep breath, and Ryder noticed. Trevor had disappeared inside the bulldozer's cab, but Ryder stepped to the side, blocking the deputy's view.

His eyes latched onto hers, then he said, "No worries. You've got this."

56

“He’s always been fascinated by those machines,” Taylor told Sheriff Norwich as she looked at the photos of the trash left inside the bulldozer’s cab. “Can I look at the drawings?”

“In a little bit. My deputy’s bagging them. Can you tell if any of this might have been Will’s?”

“Juice pouch, yes. I sent him back with some. He loves the Kool-Aid grape flavored, but his nana only gets him cherry Gatorade. And Sour Patch Kids,” she pointed out the wrapper, “they’re his favorite. He doesn’t usually throw away his drawings, though.”

Norwich raised an eyebrow and pursed her lips like she hadn’t realized that Will may have left them on purpose. “We better take a look at those.”

The sheriff’s phone interrupted. She held up a finger to Taylor as she fished it out of her pocket. “Excuse me just a minute. This is Norwich.” She listened, then turned her back and took a few steps away. “Yes, that’s exactly what I asked. No garbage collection, at least for the next two days.”

Taylor swallowed hard, trying to keep the acid in her stomach from coming up. She could not—would not—think about why the sheriff wanted to delay the garbage collection.

Norwich finished on the phone and stood in front of her again. “Why do you think Will skipped school today?”

Taylor felt the sheriff's gray eyes pin her down. She blinked too soon and had to look away. She hated this. All she wanted to do was find Will, scoop him up, and never leave him here again. The sun was setting. As soon as it was dark, it would be chilly. Did he think to pack a jacket?

"Ms. Donahue, there's something you're not telling me," Norwich said, bringing her back. "If you're hiding this boy—"

"No," Taylor said quickly. "I didn't do that." She looked away at the organized chaos. Dozens of law enforcement officers were searching the area. More on the highway were still arriving. She hadn't been able to unclench the knot in her stomach since Dora's phone call. When her eyes came back to Norwich, the sheriff was watching her. Waiting.

"I didn't take him," she told her. "But I wish I had. I think he ran away. And it's my fault." For the first time, she could hear the panic in her own voice.

"Okay. Help me understand that."

Taylor glanced over her shoulder. Dora's front door remained closed, though a shadow passed by the front windows.

"When I picked up Will on Friday, Dora and I argued. I told you that, right?"

Norwich nodded. "Care to tell me what that was about?"

"Custody stuff. She doesn't like that I'm dating. I've been dating Jason Seaver." She paused, checking to see if there was disapproval. He was younger than Taylor. That mattered to some people. It obviously mattered to Dora. She hoped the sheriff understood. She didn't want to share the part that her mother-in-law had called her a slut.

"I think Will overheard some of it. He's been anxious to come live with me full-time, and that's supposed to happen after the first of the year. I keep telling him we just need to be patient." She steeled herself. She would not cry. Maybe anger could get her through this.

"Dora told you she doesn't want you dating Jason?" Norwich prodded.

"She didn't say that exactly. But it was clear she didn't like that I was dating. Period."

"And she threatened that it could affect your custody terms?"

Taylor tried to remember Dora's exact words. Everything else got clouded in her mind after she called her "a slut."

"She reminded me that I left Will with her and gave her the right to decide what was best for him. She made it sound like she could delay the full custody if I wasn't living up to that. I think Will heard the part about the delay. He asked me over the weekend…"

Oh god, did she really want to admit this? As soon as she did it would be the end of her ever getting custody. Dora would convince the courts that Taylor's actions could cause her son to run away. And all the dangers.

"He asked what would happen if he just didn't go back."

"What did you tell him?"

"I told him we needed to be patient for a little longer. That he needed to finish the school year at his school over here." She shook her head. Bit her lower lip. "I made it sound like there wasn't another option."

"Was there another option?"

Taylor shot another look over her shoulder. There was no way Dora could hear them this far away in the street. Still, Taylor lowered her voice. "Do you know my mother-in-law?"

Norwich looked like she was holding back a response. Then she shook her head. "By reputation only."

"Then you know, she and her husband have a lot of influence in this community. If she wants something to happen, she can make it happen."

As if on cue, a rumble in the distance grew louder.

"Son of a bitch," Norwich hissed under her breath.

"What is that?" Taylor looked up, trying to find the sound in the sky. "What's happening?"

"Your mother-in-law."

The helicopter came into view, or rather, its searchlight did first. The bright beam cut over the houses like a laser, lighting up the shadows from the setting sun. It swooped low just over the trees and sending leaves, pine needles and pieces of trash airborne.

Over Norwich's radio came a woman's voice, urgent and angry, "Get that helicopter out of here! It's scattering the scent."

A tall woman waved at Norwich as she jogged toward them. It wasn't until Taylor saw the big dog alongside her that she realized it was Brodie. She was fast even with a backpack, shirttails flying behind her, one hand holding down her ball cap.

Norwich had her cell phone to her ear, barking orders.

"The downwash," Brodie was yelling to be heard over the heavy whomp of rotor blades. Now, as she stood in front of them, she still had to shout. "It's lifting the scent. It'll scattered it away from its original positions."

Taylor realized it was Brodie's voice that had come over the radio. Norwich was nodding at Brodie even as she and Hank continued jogging up the street. Norwich still had the phone to her ear. The noise was so loud, Taylor could barely make out the sheriff's words as she yelled instructions.

This time, when she glanced over her shoulder, Dora stood in her open doorway, arms crossed over her chest. Despite being at the end of the circle drive, Taylor could see the woman smiling as her head pivoted, watching the sky. She seemed to pay no attention to the chaos and only cocked her head to get a better look up above.

The helicopter disappeared on the other side of the trees. But within minutes, the tops of the pine trees began waving wildly again. The rumble grew. It had looped around and was returning. Now, it came lower. A gust of downwash dismantled anything not anchored down.

Taylor could feel the pull, the swish of her hair and the flap of her scrubs. She put a hand over her eyes to avoid the blinding searchlight. She couldn't help thinking that this would get Will's attention, and her eyes scanned the edges of the woods back to where the bulldozer was.

Then suddenly, the helicopter banked to its side and took off across the highway to do the same thing to that neighborhood.

Taylor saw Norwich turn. The phone was still pressed to her ear, but now she noticed Dora standing at her front door. The sheriff glared at Dora like she wished her death-ray stare could make a difference. Taylor wanted to tell her it would take more than that to pierce an ice-cold heart.

But now she could clearly hear what Norwich was telling the person on the other end of the phone, "I don't care what you have to do. Get me the governor on the line. And do it now!"

57

Peter Gregory worried the hallucinations had taken over his mind. He fought to determine what was real and what was only a figment of his imagination. All these law enforcement officers and vehicles amassed in the streets. Were they real or imaginary?

It took him a while to realize they weren't looking for him. After he'd safely ditched the blue pickup, he became an ordinary man walking the neighborhood. His work clothes and boots helped him fit in. A tattered old ball cap he found in the glove compartment completed his camouflage.

He heard bits and pieces from their radios and their shouts to one another. Door-to-door, street-to-street, they marched. An invasion that stirred up electricity and tension in the air as thick as the humidity.

It wasn't until he saw them checking the garage that he realized it was the boy they were looking for. He was close enough to hear the discussion about a bicycle.

He wondered why they were so far behind. Why hadn't they started looking sooner? Now, in their urgency and turmoil, they'd even left the garage door unlocked.

They'd never find that boy.

When Gregory heard the helicopter approaching, he knew his mind had not conjured up this chaos. He could feel the vibration of the machine when it skimmed the treetops.

But this chaos and urgency that made all these people reckless also kept them from noticing the obvious. And it all played right into his hands, aiding him instead of driving him away or driving him to madness.

It was a good thing. Because for several weeks, he'd questioned his sanity. What was real? What was created by the demons in his mind? Demons, or what his mother called his "overactive imagination."

She had drilled it in over and over again after that night. She insisted what he *thought* he saw had been influenced by different factors.

That's what she told him. It's what she told everyone.

She insisted that a young child's mind could be easily manipulated into believing things that simply were not true.

That was her answer when his description of the events that took away his father didn't coincide with what she had witnessed or reported. The situation was "too traumatic" for him to remember correctly. That's what she told the authorities.

"He's still in shock. He just lost his father," she said. "Trauma can tangle memories and details until none of them make sense."

Plus, her older son had a vivid imagination to begin with. He always had his nose in a graphic novel or a comic book. She sometimes thought he got reality mixed up with the made-up stories he read.

And she could be so convincing.

She'd even convinced him.

So much so that for years, he believed his nightmares about that night were convoluted by his wickedly vivid imagination.

But not anymore. Those same nightmares had finally revealed the truth about that night.

Now, after he'd walked by countless law enforcement officers, he casually entered the unlocked garage. Only one vehicle filled the huge space. Someone wasn't home. Though Gregory had gotten a glimpse of the woman standing in the front entrance. She had flung open the door, and watched the helicopter passing overhead with a flicker of a smile. For some reason, its presence pleased her.

The rotors' whomp-whomp masked Gregory's attempt to check the knob on the door between the garage and the house. It, too, was unlocked. Such a safe neighborhood. It probably rarely got locked when those huge garage doors were down.

The helicopter noise concealed his entry into the gleaming white kitchen, where no one greeted him. Or blocked him. He kept the knife tucked inside its holder, hidden by his shirttails.

He passed through the dining room. In the living room, he slowed, then stopped to look at the photos on the mantle and on the walls. He shook his head. Chided himself for being disappointed.

When he finally stepped into the hallway, the helicopter sound was fading. She was closing the door. There was a whisper of the smile still on her face before she turned and gasped at the sight of him.

"What in the world?"

"Hello Mom."

58

Twilight had turned to dusk by the time the helicopter left, robbing them of the last hints of light. Grace had taken Creed on several paths, but stayed out of the woods. That surprised Creed. He thought for sure Will might have gone off to play in the forest. And now he felt a dread weighing down on his shoulders. As they continued to cross off all the reasons for a boy playing hooky on a day of adventure, all that remained were more sinister situations on the list.

When Creed and Grace finally made it over the highway to find and join Jason and Brodie, it was dark. A sliver of moonlight peeked through the canopy of trees, then disappeared behind clouds.

Darkness.

Creed could feel it like an ominous presence ready to undermine every decision and exaggerate every shadow as a threat. Experience nagged at him, told him their search got tougher without the benefit of daylight.

This neighborhood was completely different from the large estates across the highway. Here, small houses sat tight together with narrow driveways between them. And those driveways were filled with a variety of vehicles and trailers sometimes overflowing with other parked vehicles along the curbs.

Small front yards kept the front porches and front windows close to the streets, so that the yellow lights from inside leaked out and created shadows in the front yards. There were few sidewalks and even fewer streetlights.

Screen doors slapped. Dogs barked from behind chain-link fences. Somewhere an engine revved. The night birds and insects began their symphonies. The smell of someone's dinner, greasy and partially burnt, wafted on the humid night air. A block over, Creed smelled cigarette smoke before he saw the cherry-red tip bobbing under the dark shadows of a carport.

He remembered parts of this neighborhood from when he and Jason had driven to Caleb Monroe's house. The teenager's parents weren't the only ones not welcoming strangers. He had felt that from inside his Jeep that day. And it was even more unsettling walking through these streets now and in the dark. Though he couldn't see them, he could feel their eyes following.

He was grateful he and Grace weren't the only strangers drawing attention. Police cruisers dotted several streets as troopers and deputies knocked on doors. Some searched between the parked vehicles, sweeping beams from their flashlights to check the underbellies of trailers and pickups.

The one thing Creed noticed was that very few residents had come out to see what the commotion was or to offer help.

Now Jason explained how Scout had gone around in circles for several blocks.

"He kept going back to the same two houses," Jason explained. "Only he was taking me there from different directions. At one of the houses, he led me right to the front door."

"I contacted the sheriff," Brodie told Creed. "A couple of deputies talked to a woman who lives there. She admitted her daughter knows Will from school. He'd ridden his bike over, but that was about a week ago."

"What about the other house?"

"Scout wanted to go into the backyard. The gate was left open."

"A deputy reported nobody was home. At least not yet," Brodie said.

"I didn't let him go into the yard." Jason's eyes darted around before he added, "I think we need to be careful. Just the looks we've been getting. These people don't like having this kind of police presence in their neighborhood. And they consider us a part of the police."

"Let's stick close together, then. But give Scout a rest. I'll see if Grace picks up the scent." As Creed said this, he saw her nose poking the air and her head swaying back and forth. He didn't need to ask her to find Will. She was already working the scent of him.

Before he followed, he glanced back at Brodie. "Is Grace headed in the same direction?" He didn't want to repeat the circles Scout had just finished.

She checked her map again, then scanned the surrounding houses. "No, that was to our left. About three blocks over."

Grace's nose twitched now. She was ready to go, looking back at the two of them and impatiently tugging on the leash. She darted from street to curb, taking in any foliage—mostly patches of lawn and a few shrubs—then weaved up and down into front yards. She ignored dogs barking in her wake, as they clawed and jumped to get out of their fenced backyards.

Creed realized his fingers were checking for the pepper spray on his belt in case one of these dogs managed to get out. Tension prickled at the back of his neck. There was something familiar about this street.

It didn't take long for Grace to race up a long driveway. She stood on hind legs and sniffed the back of a large crew cab pickup, then abruptly and calmly came to a halt. She sat down and looked up at Creed just as a voice behind them came out of the dark from the house's front porch.

"Get that dog out of my driveway. And get that Pit bull the hell out of here."

"Hold on, sir," Brodie said from the street. "We're searching for a little boy. A seven-year-old named—"

"Yeah, whatever. He isn't here. Now get those frickin' dogs off my property."

"No problem," Creed told him. "Come on, Grace." He stalled, digging out her squeaky toy from his daypack. To Hank's credit, he stood calmly at Brodie's side, but Creed could hear a low, quiet growl as his eyes stayed on the man.

Creed tossed the toy for Grace to catch. Her prancing gave him enough time to get a good look at the pickup. A load of fertilizer bags stacked high in the bed. Then he noticed the sign on the vehicle's door: MONROE LANDSCAPING.

59

Creed stopped Brodie when she started to call in Grace's alert. With his back to the man on the porch, he held up his open palm as a signal for her to stop. Her fingers left the radio before she pressed down the button. This was one of the few times he appreciated her ability to keep her face blank without emotion or question.

They left, continuing up the street, walking side by side, not saying a word. Grace still had her toy, the squeaks filling the silence between them.

Lately, the dark tended to throw Creed off. His eyes pivoted to bundles of shadows, expecting them to come to life and charge straight at them. Was he always like this during night searches?

He didn't want to admit to Brodie that his sense of direction was messed up or that his anxiety level kept climbing. And especially not now when she was watching him with long glances, waiting for an explanation.

To simplify things, he stopped and asked Grace to surrender the pink elephant. Ignoring the dog drool, he slipped it back into his daypack, then he said, "Grace, take us back."

She immediately turned them around and headed in the other direction.

Finally, when they were out of earshot of the man he presumed was Mr. Monroe, Creed nodded an all-clear sign to Brodie.

"Why didn't we call in the alert?"

"It was my mistake. I think she was alerting to the fertilizer in the pickup's bed. When we were back with Jason, she started picking up a scent. I thought it was..." He avoided using Grace's name and Will's. "I thought it was the boy's. I didn't ask her to specifically find him. But she's a multi-scent dog. If I don't ask, and she smells something else that she's trained to find, she will alert to it. She's done it before when I haven't been careful."

"Why fertilizer?"

"A lot of the same ingredients are used in making explosives."

"You and Grace have searched for bombs?"

Creed shot her a look to keep her voice down, not just because Grace noticed, but because residents might.

"We haven't in a while. But it is one of the scents she's trained to detect. And she's alerted me to it a time or two."

"That was what you and Rufus searched for in Afghanistan."

"Yes."

"I never considered that you'd still be doing searches that dangerous."

"We haven't. Not in a long time. Grace and Bolo are really the only ones, and I would never take an assignment that would put them at risk."

"So Scout—"

"Search and recovery. I don't train dogs for apprehension either, but Bolo has a crazy instinct to protect me. Kind of like Hank with you. Certain dogs...we train them, but they still have their own instincts."

"I trust Hank's. And he sure didn't like that guy."

"Remember the missing teenager Norwich had us looking for? I think that was his father."

"I'd run away from him, too."

Creed glanced at her. He had said the teenager was missing. Brodie immediately said, "run away." It made him think of Sully wanting to protect the boy.

Grace led them to where they had started. Jason and Scout had moved to an empty parking lot across the street, where he was helping a couple of people set up a large canopy tent. An SUV had parked close by, its tailgate up, displaying cases of water, battery-operated lanterns and several coolers.

Scout noticed them first but waited for Jason before crossing the street.

"Volunteers," Jason said, waving a thumb over his back. "They brought some water and sandwiches for all of us."

Creed was surprised Jason didn't already have one of the sandwiches in his hand. The kid had an insatiable appetite, and all they had in their packs were protein bars.

"Find anything?" he asked.

Creed told him about the fertilizer.

"I want to take Grace by the houses that Scout alerted to. Something tells me that trail is fresher than a week ago."

Scout and Jason took one side of the street. Creed and Grace took the other. Brodie and Hank followed. Creed asked both dogs to "find Will."

They weaved around parked vehicles, trying to avoid going up onto front lawns and keeping out of driveways. Both dogs went into tracking mode at the same time, and Creed knew which houses before Jason pointed them out. But Grace didn't stop. She slowed to wave her nose over the weeds in an alley, then moved on. Tree roots buckled the concrete of a common area and drew her attention. But again, she moved on.

On the other side of the street, Scout wanted to run. Jason strained to keep up. Despite each dog's different stops and starts, it became clear they were headed not only in the same direction, but to the same place. A small park with a playground took up half a block. It looked well maintained but poorly lit. Obviously intended for daytime use only. The area was more sand and clay than grass, with a couple of huge live oaks.

Creed could make out the shadowed forms of a swing set, slide, and merry-go-round. As soon as they all stepped into the park, he could tell where both dogs were headed. Far off in the corner, on the edge of the square, was a Dumpster.

60

When Deputy Trevor handed Will's drawings to Taylor, she felt like finally she could help. The overwhelming sense of having no control over the situation nagged at her. However, she wasn't prepared for the emotion that swept over her at seeing his illustrations now displayed as evidence.

She tried to ignore the slight tremor in her fingers. Tucked a strand of hair that had come loose from her ponytail. Then she carefully took both Ziplock bags. Each contained a piece of paper that had been crumpled but was now smoothed out.

She knew instantly they were Will's, though they were rough sketches. She recognized the energy and action of bold lines, some pressed down so hard she could see the indentation in the paper. She'd seen him do this before, almost manically getting the visual down on paper before it could leave his imagination.

"They're definitely Will's," she told him.

"Do any of these scribbles mean something to you?"

Taylor stopped herself from correcting Deputy Trevor. These were sketches. At worst, rough drafts. But never scribbles. This wasn't the time for a lesson, but she could still hear Will. The memory of him schooling her tugged a smile at the corner of her lips.

In the first drawing, a blue pickup roared down a road. The marks symbolizing speed followed behind. Those were the deep pressed lines of different lengths with puffs of dust in between.

"Do you know anyone who drives a blue pickup?" the deputy asked when she took too long to answer.

"No, I don't."

Taylor stared at the driver Will had drawn. He emphasized the man with his head poking out the vehicle's window; the head disproportionately larger than the pickup to make the figure look more menacing.

Then she added, "He does a lot of action adventure scenes. And sometimes they include villains."

"But this looks like the driver is a vampire." Impatience slipped into his voice as if he was handed an assignment he'd already warranted as a waste of his time. "I mean vampires. Why would he draw a vampire? Is that just all a part of his imagination? Does he draw them a lot?"

Will had definitely made the driver a vampire with a prominent widow's peak and the mouth open to expose bloody fangs.

She shrugged. "He does have an active imagination. But no, that's not a familiar figure. At least I haven't seen him draw a vampire before."

She remembered the surfers riding the waves at sunset. He'd created that one while they had dinner on the beach watching. He did that a lot, sketching what was in front of him, almost unaware that he was doing it. But then there were the stunning illustrations of the superhero he'd created, crafting him from Jason. The action scenes were pure fiction. Picking up a vehicle with his mechanical arm and flinging it into an evil army descending on a helpless village.

Yes, her son had an amazing imagination. And that's why she almost gasped at the next drawing.

It was a little boy running away. Yellow hair, lime green and blue sneakers. He carried a red oversized backpack. Will had drawn himself. In the distance was a forest, thick green blotches atop black tree trunks. And off to the side…a bright yellow machine. The bulldozer.

"Do either of these make sense to you?"

She felt Deputy Trevor staring at her. Maybe he could see that they did, indeed, register something. He was waiting for an explanation.

"He sometimes draws single frames of action."

"Frames of action?"

"Like graphic novels or comic books. And he tells a story."

"Okay. So, the little boy running away, is it Will?"

"Yes, I think so." She pointed to the machine in the far corner. "He's running to the bulldozer."

"Running away from a vampire?" The deputy didn't bother to hide his skepticism. In his tone, she could hear his disappointment. That these were just the idle scribbles of a little boy who was bored after skipping school.

She didn't want to ask the question that now pounded against her temple. The question that suggested her son was in danger. It seemed so obvious to her.

"Has anyone reported a blue pickup in the neighborhood?" she asked. "One that maybe looked like it didn't belong?"

He looked from Taylor to the drawing, then his head shot up to scan the surrounding streets as if it just occurred to him the significance of what she was asking.

"You think he's showing something that actually happened?

"Yes. That's exactly what I'm saying."

He stared at her for a beat longer, then grabbed at the radio on his shoulder just as a voice came over. Despite the static, the words were loud and clear.

"K9 alert. Dumpster."

She saw the expression on his face before he could hide it. He left the radio in place but took the Ziplock bags from her fingers.

"I need to let Sheriff Norwich know about these." He turned his back to her and marched out into the street.

She watched him all the way to his SUV, then noticed a commotion with other officers responding to the radio message.

K9 alert. Dumpster.

The dogs had found something. It could be anything. She remembered Jason telling her how the dogs could find the smallest of things that would make a huge difference. Yes, that's what they had discovered. That was all it was. A piece of evidence. She told herself that as she grabbed a sweatshirt out of her car and headed in the same direction, the new motion was taking the others.

She walked past the huddle of neighbors outside Dora's house. She weaved through the array of law enforcement vehicles. When she made her way across the highway and into the other neighborhood, no one paid attention. She followed the wave of energy.

Voices squawked over radios. In the streets, officers shouted instructions to each other. Dogs barked in backyards. People sat in the shadows of their front porches. Kids peeked out windows. The dark made ordinary items look menacing.

Taylor just kept walking.

61

Pensacola Beach, Florida

Maggie had been walking the beach for hours. Looking for him. It felt like a futile effort while she waited for more information from her team. Her time would probably be better spent resting, but she was restless and had ended up pacing her hotel room.

She weaved her way around the streets closest to the water where most of the luxury house rentals were. Alonzo had provided a couple of photos of Peter Gregory. Headshots of an ordinary-looking man, his widow's peak and slicked back dark hair the only defining characteristics. But she remembered the tall man running away from the crime scene. In her mind, she conjured up his lean frame beneath the long, black coat billowing out behind him.

She figured his complexion would be pasty after spending months in snowy D.C. Maybe he'd stand out on the beach. So far, she'd seen no one who came close. Late on a December day, there weren't many to choose from.

The horizon had faded from reds and oranges to deep blue. It was dark now as she walked back along the beach to her hotel room. This was ridiculous. They'd never find him like this. He could already be on the road again. Just because the Mercedes sat in a storage unit, didn't mean Peter Gregory was anywhere nearby.

She decided she needed to sleep at least for a few hours. She'd tried earlier after her shower, but her mind wouldn't shut off. Every time she closed her eyes, she saw Nessie in her hospital bed, then Nessie in that huge canvas bag at the edge of the swamp.

When her phone rang, she automatically expected Alonzo, hoped it would be Ryder, but was pleasantly surprised to find it was Gwen.

"I heard you skipped out on us," her friend said. "How are you doing?"

"Tired. I spent all night following him and I still might have lost him."

"Your instincts are usually spot-on, so hang in there."

"They weren't this time. I think I really screwed up."

"Racine makes her own choices. Even she will tell you that. And Nessie? She's going to be okay. She's conscious. I just talked to her, and goodness, that woman can talk. But more importantly, she is a survivor."

"They let you talk to her?"

"You forget, I still have hospital privileges. As of a few hours ago, I am officially one of her consulting doctors."

Before working with the FBI, Gwen had her own successful practice as a psychiatrist. She still saw a few clients on a regular basis.

"I have an amazing team," Maggie simply said.

"You got that right."

Her phone vibrated with another call.

"Speaking of my team," she told Gwen. "Alonzo is calling."

"Get your mind off Nessie and get some rest. We'll get this guy."

"Thanks."

She clicked off and tapped on Alonzo's call.

"I might have something," he said immediately.

"Good, because I have nothing."

She paced. Stopped to grab a cold French fry from the room service tray she had abandoned a few hours earlier.

"I'd been coming up empty-handed because I was using the wrong name."

"You found another alias?"

"No, not an alias. Peter Gregory was adopted when he was eleven. It wasn't until years later that he went back to using his birth name of Gregory. He actually grew up outside of Pensacola in Milton. That's where he went to elementary and high school. Left to go to Florida State in Tallahassee. Didn't graduate. When he turned twenty-five, he inherited money his biological father had left him in a trust. The man died when Peter was ten, but he had a family trust fund. Looks like it was something he'd inherited from his father. The fund has built up over twenty years. It's worth over ten-million dollars."

"This doesn't sound like our guy."

She couldn't add up a profile of a millionaire traveling from city to city and bludgeoning homeless men to death. She'd seen photos of the victims. There was too much passion. The murders looked personal.

"Hang on a minute. This might help. I went back to see what happened to his father, Thomas Gregory."

"Go on."

"The family was going home late one night and stopped to help a motorist stranded on the side of a country road. The motorist started attacking Thomas Gregory. Get this…with a crowbar. The wife sped off to get help. Said her husband gestured and called out for her to go. Headlines emphasize that she saved her boys.

"By the time sheriff's deputies got back there, the vehicle was gone and so was Thomas Gregory. There was blood at the scene. But Thomas' body was never found. Newspaper reports called the motorist a transient."

"Okay. That's pretty…incredible. How many years ago are we talking about?"

"Nineteen, almost twenty now."

"Something triggered him to start killing," she was thinking out loud.

"Or he's been killing for a long time but getting away with it, because he's a rich, smart bastard."

"Have you checked if his mother still lives around here?"

"I did, and yes, she does. She remarried. Usually it takes five years, but because of the circumstances, she was able to have Thomas Gregory declared dead in about a year."

"What was Peter Gregory's adoptive name? The one most people know him by?"

"Ramsey. His stepfather is Carl Ramsey. The man owns a major construction company in Santa Rosa County."

"Carl Ramsey. That name sounds familiar. I think I may have met him. What's Gregory's mother's name?"

"Isadora. Looks like she goes by Dora."

"I need to pay them a visit."

"I knew you'd say that. I have their address for you."

62

Santa Rosa County, Florida

Creed paced. He hated waiting. But this time, not as much as Jason.

"I could just open the lid. Take a quick look."

"No," Creed had to tell him. "We can't risk messing up fingerprints."

The dogs were already enjoying their reward toys: Grace with her pink elephant and Scout with his double-knotted rope toy. Even Hank got his bouncy ball, throwing it up high and catching it before the ball touched the ground.

Creed hoped this wasn't the end of Will's trail, but both dogs alerted to the Dumpster. Grace wanted to continue, pulling and tugging and pointing toward the forest on the other side of the chain-link fence. Creed didn't want to risk the dogs getting hurt if Will was here, and only a piece of his clothing had been discarded in the woods.

He hated to even think about that possibility, but unfortunately, he'd seen it happen before.

When he stopped Grace and insisted they wait, Brodie and Jason exchanged glances. He could see it in both of their eyes. They were steeling themselves for the worst-case scenario.

Brodie took notes and photos. Creed gestured to Jason to take the dogs back further into the park area where there was more grass and a lone streetlamp.

"Hey, guys." Brodie stopped them.

She was doing a walk around and now stood shining her flashlight between the Dumpster and a section of fence.

Tucked into the tight space was a bicycle. In the dim light, it was easy to tell it wasn't an old rusted one that someone had attempted to throw away. Instead, it looked like it had been placed carefully against the fence in an attempt to hide it. On the other side of the chain-link, the forest began again. No one would see it except from this slight angle.

Creed looked to Jason for an answer. "Do you have any idea what Will's bicycle looks like?"

"I think it's his."

Jason fumbled his own Maglite out of his daypack, his fingers scrabbling to turn it on. He shot another beam across the frame, checking out the brand, then settled on the handlebars. Light reflected back off the rearview mirrors.

"It's his. Taylor bought him a new one for his birthday. He had a growth spurt this summer and his knees were hitting into the handlebars. She also bought some rearview mirrors. I installed them, but it was tricky because Will wanted grip shifters instead of trigger shifters."

He pointed the light to where the pieces fit in.

Brodie took a photo. "I'll text it to Sheriff Norwich."

That's when headlights appeared on the other side of the park, coming around the corner. Norwich was looking at her phone even as she got out of the vehicle. The road didn't come back this far. She had to walk across the park. Behind her, Creed could make out a mobile crime van jockeying its way for a closer position, then finally parking.

"So what does this mean?" Jason asked. He was looking at Creed, eyes filled with as much hope as dread.

He wished he had something, anything to offer, but right now, the only ones who could answer that question were the crime lab technicians. There were three of them, and despite wasting no time, it seemed to take forever.

"You found the bicycle." Norwich said.

"It's Will's." Jason explained how he knew for sure.

"A woman in this neighborhood said she saw a boy on a bicycle today. She doesn't know what time but remembered thinking he should be in school."

"The houses that Scout alerted to earlier," Creed said. "He may have ridden by or even stopped. Jason said Scout took him up to the front door of one and wanted to go through the backyard of the other."

Norwich nodded. "I heard about that. This is a working community. It sounds like not many folks are around during the day on a Monday." She paused as she watched the techs unloading their equipment. "I also just got a message from Deputy Trevor. He showed those crumpled drawings we found in the bulldozer to Will's mother. She thinks the boy might have been sketching what happened to him."

"What was in the sketches?" Jason asked.

"A little boy with a red backpack running away from a blue pickup." She paused for a moment. "We're checking to see if any security camera footage caught anything like that, or even a blue pickup that doesn't belong in that neighborhood."

"You sound skeptical, Sheriff," Creed said.

"It's hard not to be. Will drew the pickup driver as a vampire."

63

Tuesday, December 5
After midnight

No one had tried to stop Taylor. They didn't even notice her. She walked in the direction she'd seen the CSU van drive. The streets were clogged with response vehicles and law enforcement officers. It had to be midnight and almost every house in the neighborhood still had lights on inside.

K9s alerted. Dumpster.

She wouldn't let her mind go there. They had found something, but it was only evidence. Will was okay. He'd just gotten lost. Maybe he'd tried to ride his bike to…where? He had to know her house on the beach was an impossible ride from here. And yet, it was Taylor's first thought when she heard he was missing.

He rode his bike. A man in a blue pickup scared him. He could be hiding. Yes, he was hiding somewhere.

She rubbed her arms. Even with the sweatshirt, she felt the chill, and she winced at the thought of Will huddled and cold, not wanting to go back to Dora's house.

Regret tied knots in her stomach. All of this was her fault. For leaving him in the first place.

Buddy, just be safe.

She turned a corner and followed the beams from spotlights. A block away, there was a park area. In the far corner, she could see figures climbing over the top of a Dumpster. A wall of trees grew close behind it, the spotlights shooting high enough she could see the branches swaying. Back here, the sound of birds and insects drowned out the human voices calling to each other.

The dogs spotted her first. Of course, they did. Scout and Hank knew her. Grace, she'd met only once. But all three heads jerked in her direction, anxious and excited before their owners noticed and looked over.

She didn't care that she might not be allowed. What could the sheriff do? Arrest her?

She was too far away to hear their exchanges. All the light was on the Dumpster, so it was too dark to see their expressions.

Jason left the group. He stopped to attach a leash to Scout, and the two of them started toward her. She hadn't spoken to him since she rudely told him she didn't need him. Watching his steady gait, an easy air of confidence and competence, she realized she'd have a slew of things to regret by the time all this was over.

Scout greeted her first. She offered her hand. He licked and nudged it. Jason tipped back his ball cap, a familiar gesture she recognized. She'd seen him do it many times when he greeted friends, a polite courtesy, a way of giving them his eyes and his attention.

She wanted to know what they had found. But at the same time, she didn't want to know. She was suddenly standing on a fine line that separated hope from despair. Did she want to breech that? Was she strong enough?

"We don't know yet," Jason said as if he could read the anxiety vibrating off her body. "We found his bicycle back behind the Dumpster."

"Someone tried to throw it away?"

He shook his head. "It was carefully tucked into a narrow gap."

"I don't understand what that means."

"Sheriff!" One of the crime lab technicians yelled to Norwich, and everyone stopped. All movement came to a halt. Even the dogs went still.

Taylor held her breath. A few minutes ago, she was prepared to walk right up to them. Demand what they knew. What they were seeing. But now? She doubted her knees would hold up that far.

Norwich and the technician were silhouetted against the beam of light. Their heads came together in conversation. There were no gestures. No body language for Taylor to read. Then Norwich turned, said something to Ryder and Brodie and started toward Taylor and Jason.

This was news she had to deliver herself.

The sheriff's face was shadowed. It was impossible to see her expression. By the time she got close enough to speak, Taylor felt a sheen of cold sweat sliding down her back.

"He's not in there," Norwich said, hurrying to close the distance between them.

"Oh, thank God!" Jason's arm looped around Taylor's waist before she realized she was falling. He held her against him, keeping her upright.

"They're still checking to see if any of Will's belongings may have gotten tossed inside. So far, it looks like the dogs alerted to Will's bicycle."

The relief lasted only a few minutes. Taylor found her footing and asked, "Why would he leave his bicycle like that?"

She looked from Norwich to Jason, then pushed away from him enough so she could watch his face and Norwich's when she asked, "Do you think someone took him?"

"At this point," Norwich said, "We have to consider every possibility."

"The man in the blue pickup."

Before the sheriff could answer, her radio came alive.

Taylor didn't recognize any of the codes they used. She wished she hadn't been able to understand the rest of it. Wished the words had been garbled or the static so pronounced she might have mistaken what was said. But that wasn't the case. The voice came strong and clear.

"We have an alligator sighting in the area," a man said.

Even Norwich's eyes went wide when the voice added. "And it was dragging something large."

64

Creed insisted Jason and Scout stay with Taylor and ride back with Norwich. He suggested the volunteers' tent at the neighborhood's entrance. Norwich agreed. Said they had coffee and food. Creed told Jason that he and Brodie would join them after he let Grace check out the woods behind the Dumpster.

He told Jason they wouldn't go far. It was probably easy for Jason to believe him, since he knew Creed didn't like the dogs out in the dark. And knowing there was an alligator running around out here, he couldn't believe he wasn't following his own instincts.

But what if Will had ditched his bike and ran into the woods because some guy was chasing him?

That's what Grace seemed to be telling him. Now that she knew Creed was ready to go, she pranced and tugged, leading him around the length of chain-link. He slowed her down, wanting to wait until Norwich had driven away and the CSU technicians were out of earshot. Then he turned to Brodie, who was still watching the SUV's taillights disappear around the block.

He pulled at his daypack and his fingers dug around inside. He brought out a flare gun. Being at the edge of the spotlights allowed him to see a cannister was loaded in the gun, and the safety switch was in place. He tucked it into one of the outer pockets, leaving it more accessible.

"Are you worried we'll get lost?" Brodie asked, noticing the flare gun.

"No, Grace can always get us back to where we started. Have you ever heard one of these?"

"No."

"It's pretty loud. Has an annoying scream. I've never used one to scare a bear or an alligator, but I'm guessing it might do the trick. If I need to use it, you and Hank need to be fast and high-tail it in the opposite direction."

She stared at him, and he waited. But instead of nodding, she said, "You were right about the dark. It makes everything so much scarier." Then she asked, "What about our bear spray?"

"I have no idea if it works on an alligator."

The idea of an alligator, whether it was dragging a kill or not, worried Creed. Not because it could be Will. He couldn't even go there. He had to stay positive. But alligators were quick. People thought the reptiles moved slowly because their legs were short and they slithered on their bellies. But they were actually very fast in short bursts. And in the dark, if they didn't see it coming, an alligator could snatch Grace in just a few seconds.

"This is sounding more like a very bad idea," Brodie told him.

"But what if Will is out there? Maybe hurt? Maybe just lost?"

The dogs were waiting. Hank leaned against Brodie's legs as if to nudge her into action. Grace's front paws were tapping the ground.

"Okay," she said. "Let's go do this."

Any semblance of natural light quickly was gobbled up under the canopy of pine trees and live oaks. Grace jumped over fallen branches and disappeared in and out of shrubs, despite Creed keeping a tight leash on her. In several places, she stopped completely. Once, she stood on her hind legs to sniff the top of a plant that stretched over her head.

She huffed at it. Turned to Creed as if to say, "not here," before taking off again further to the right of the misleading plant.

It didn't take long, and Creed heard the crunch under his feet. He winced and stopped immediately, calling for Grace to stop as well. They had come upon one of the dreaded garbage dumps. In the daylight, the debris had made him cringe about Bolo's unprotected feet. Now in the dark, the sound felt like a sucker punch.

"What's wrong?" Brodie asked, stopping in her tracks. She and Hank were several paces behind.

"Garbage," he told her.

"Garbage?"

"Some people dump their trash out here. Bolo and I ran into some the other day. We're kind of in the same vicinity."

He shot his flashlight across the floor of the forest. Broken glass glittered. In looked like a couple of tires were lobbed on top of a debris pile that animals had still gotten into and scattered. Every nerve in his body told him to pick up Grace, turn around, and go back.

Of course, the Jack Russell terrier didn't notice any of this as a threat. She waited impatiently, her nose still taking in scent.

As Creed waved the beam over the ground, something caught his attention on the other side of the trees. He angled the light up, raising his arm high. Through the tree trunks, he could see a long stretch of open grass. That's exactly where Grace wanted to go.

They navigated the garbage as best they could. When they cleared the woods, Creed stopped Grace again.

"What is this place?" Brodie asked.

Acres and acres of pristine grass extended for as far as the flashlight's beam. The area was still under development, but Creed could tell what it eventually would be.

"I think it's a golf course."

He didn't remember any public roads that drove by this. It looked like the equipment came through a dirt road along the edges of the forest. He couldn't investigate that right now. Grace wasn't finished.

She led him to a stretch of new sod not even fifty feet from the forest. There was nothing here out of the ordinary. No equipment or leftover piles of anything. Just the pristine grass. She sat down and looked up at him. Directly up at him. Her eyes meeting his.

"Ryder," Brodie said from behind him.

He turned to find that she and Hank hadn't followed all the way. Brodie was on her knees and shined her flashlight at Hank's front leg. There was blood.

"The garbage," she said. "The glass must have cut him."

He could hear an unfamiliar panic in his sister's voice.

He yanked Grace's reward out of his pack, but the Jack Russell was already headed over to lie down beside Hank. Creed continued digging in his pack for his first aid kit as he came over.

On his knees, he could see the cuts.

"Shine your flashlight here," he told Brodie. He gently took Hank's foot. He could already feel glass embedded in his paw. Creed's hand came away bloody.

"Oh, no!" Brodie whispered, hugging the big dog to her body even as she kept the flashlight steady.

It took Creed about fifteen minutes to carefully remove the pieces he could see and feel. He told the dog how brave he was as he tweezered and dabbed alcohol. Hank let him do what he needed to do without a flinch. Creed had saved him once before, and the dog trusted him.

"He's gonna be okay," he tried to reassure Brodie even as he noticed her biting down on her bottom lip. "But I don't want him walking all the way back or putting pressure on it until we know all the glass has been removed."

The bleeding looked like it had stopped. As he wrapped it, he told her, "I'll call Jason. He should be able to find this access road and come get us."

"What about the spot where Grace alerted?"

The Jack Russell sat beside Hank, her eyes not leaving Creed's hands or Hank's paw.

"It looks like fresh sod. I want to say it's probably fertilizer again. Did I ask her specifically to continue with the boy's name?"

"I don't remember."

Then she looked fully at him, concern flashing across her face. Not just for Hank. Now, it extended to him, too.

"Are you all right?" she asked.

"Yeah, I'm fine." But maybe he wasn't. He'd made the same mistake twice within hours. "I'll take down the coordinates. We can tell Norwich about the alert."

"I should be taking down the coordinates."

"Stay with Hank."

Creed stood and pulled out his flashlight. He wanted to give Jason more than a GPS coordinate. He slid the beam along the dirt path. The tracks were cut deep and recent. They must connect to a main road, but he couldn't see any of that in the dark. Just as he swung the light to the other side, something reflected back.

Brodie turned to see what had his attention. She added her flashlight. A pickup was parked just off the road and close to the trees.

"No one inside?" Brodie asked as she waved her light over the windows and the windshield.

"I don't think so." It was pulled up on the grass. "Looks like someone was trying to hide it."

"Didn't the sheriff say Will sketched a pickup following him?"

As if synchronized, both of them doused the vehicle's frame in light. There was no doubt. It was a blue pickup.

65

She offered him food. Gregory wanted to laugh. Wasn't that so motherly? They hadn't seen each other in years, and the first time they reunite, she wanted to feed him.

Or maybe poison him.

When he hadn't responded, she simply walked around him and headed to the kitchen. She started taking items out of the massive refrigerator. Mayonnaise, cheese, slices of ham and pickles.

His mother hadn't been much of a cook. It looked like she hadn't changed. His father, on the other hand, created masterpieces even with leftovers. Gregory remembered the aromas coming from their small kitchen. It was half this size.

He welcomed the change of scenery. At least this room didn't have trophies and photographs of his brother.

"What are you doing here, Peter?" she asked casually as she opened cupboards for bread and maybe a sharp knife.

"You invited me to join you for the holidays."

"A little heads up would have been appropriate."

In the kitchen window behind her, the sky lit up. A rumble of thunder followed. She turned to glance out, and the corners of her mouth curved downward. It was an expression he recognized. The weather was disappointing her. All those things she just couldn't control.

"Where's good old Carl?"

Her eyes darted to a clock on the wall, then back to the sandwich makings spread across the countertop.

"He's away on business. He's trying to get back as soon as possible."

"Because of the boy?"

Now she turned to look at him. He finally had her full attention.

"What do you know about him?"

"That's who they're all looking for, right?" He waved his hand in the direction of the front of the house. "Mickey's boy. I didn't even know he had a kid."

"Maybe if you came around more often, you'd know things."

"He looks exactly like him."

There was a flicker of panic in her eyes. He saw it before she put it away.

"You saw the photographs." She probably didn't think he could hear the relief in her voice.

"I thought I'd seen a ghost."

"He does resemble his father." There was a smile now.

"Does he know about me?"

She glanced up as she slathered a slice of bread with mayonnaise. "He's probably seen your picture."

"Doesn't look like there are any of me."

She shrugged. Not concerned. No guilt. No regret.

"He didn't seem to recognize me."

Her head jerked up, and her eyes darted to his. The panic mixed with anger now. "You? You took him! Peter, what did you do?"

"What did *you do* to my father?"

Noise came from outside the kitchen. The garage door was going up.

His mother's eyes flew to the connecting door, then back to Gregory. She froze. Though clearly, she wanted to run, yell…do something to warn the person coming.

No, he was wrong. She expected to be saved. Yes, of course, that's exactly what she was thinking. He could see it now. There was even another smile, a smirk.

When the man came through the door, Gregory was surprised how small and diminished—how old—her hero looked. Especially compared to Gregory's memory of the man. Thin with broad shoulders now a bit hunched, he yanked off his ball cap to reveal a shock of white disheveled hair. His arms were still long and lean from days of physical labor. They still looked just like Gregory remembered in his nightmares. Even the tattoo was the same. A blue anchor on his left forearm.

Carl saw only his wife as he said, "Damned I-10 traffic. I almost—"

His mouth stayed open. His eyes went wide despite the fatigue and wrinkles.

"Well, if it isn't dear old step-dad. You're just in time."

66

It wasn't until Maggie hung up that she remembered why Carl and Isadora Ramsey sounded familiar. She'd met the pair last June. They were Taylor Donahue's in-laws. After a battle with a madman obsessed with controlling the young nurse, Maggie had helped explain the situation to the Ramseys. Back then, the couple had sole custody of Taylor's son, and she worried they would try to blame her for what happened.

The meeting would have been uneventful except for the formality of it. Dora Ramsey seemed more concerned with how she served her FBI guest. There was tea to be had. Iced sweet tea presented in a crystal pitcher with matching glasses. Lemon slices aligned perfectly on a small porcelain plate alongside a bowl of sugar cubes and cookies. The aroma permeated the house of the fresh-baked cookies.

She appeared fascinated that Maggie worked at Quantico, as if that elevated her stature in Dora's eyes. Ever the profiler, Maggie could tell the woman was only interested as she tried to figure out how she might use this new connection in the future. At the time, Maggie didn't care if it meant Taylor would be left in good standing with her in-laws and have access to her son. She had no idea that six months later, Taylor would still be battling for custody.

Before she left Pensacola Beach, Maggie tried to call Ryder. His phone went directly to voice mail. Of course, he and Grace must still be out searching. Then she tried to call Sheriff Norwich. Again, directly to voice mail. This time, she left a detailed message and contact number.

She was about to barge into the middle of an active search. She didn't want to alert Dora Ramsey, but she did need to notify law enforcement.

When her cell phone rang, she grabbed it expecting Norwich. It was Alonzo.

"We have a match," he said.

She let the silence hang between them as her mind switched gears.

"How sure are we?" she finally asked.

"Agent Warren's team got a treasure trove from the outside and inside of the canvas bag. Gregory may have been overly confident that the alligators would take care of his carelessness."

"They match what Kuszak has?"

"Yes. She's searching through the New York and Jacksonville cases for any prints left behind at those crime scenes. He's never been fingerprinted before. He thought he was safe."

"I'm headed over to his mother's now."

"It's kind of early in the morning."

"I'm counting on the element of surprise." She wondered if Dora Ramsey would recognize her six months later.

"You're thinking he might already be there. You have backup, right?"

"Her neighborhood is crawling with law enforcement. Her grandson has been missing since yesterday morning."

"Now that's an interesting twist. Coincidence?"

"By my calculations, the boy disappeared right about the time Gregory arrived in Pensacola."

67

It didn't take long for Jason to find the old dirt road. Creed watched the Jeep bump and wind its way along the trees. Clouds blocked the moon. A fog had set in, hugging the ground. A rumble of thunder threatened in the distance.

Headlights followed Jason's. Norwich. Creed could see she brought with her only Deputy Trevor.

When he called the sheriff, he used his cell phone instead of the radio. It was simply easier for him to explain all the details, but Norwich's voice seemed strained, extra anxious. She thanked him for keeping this off the radio, then asked him and Brodie to continue to stay off. There was something in her tone that troubled him.

Jason barely stopped the Jeep, and Taylor was out the passenger door and headed straight for Norwich. Jason came over to Ryder and Brodie.

"I didn't tell her," he said in a low voice with his back to Taylor. "But when Norwich followed us, she figured something was up."

He looked from Brodie to Creed. "What did you find?"

"I think Grace alerted to more fresh fertilizer. They obviously laid sod in the last week."

Jason's eyes stayed on Creed's, waiting and expecting more.

Creed ran a hand over his jaw and let out a sigh of frustration. "I might not have used the boy's name when I asked Grace to continue the search."

He hated admitting it to himself, let alone everyone else.

"I called Dr. Avelyn," Creed said, wanting to get back to business. "She can meet you at the Waffle House on Avalon. You won't have to go all the way back to our place. She'll bring her first aid kit. Take a good look at Hank." He didn't want to tell Brodie that Hank was finished for this search, even if Dr. Avelyn didn't find any more broken glass in his paw. Creed wouldn't risk him getting an infection.

"You guys get yourselves something to eat. Feed the dogs. I'll join you when we finish here."

"Wait. You're staying?" Brodie asked. The look she gave him was one of concern. There was no mistaking this time,

"I just want to make certain Grace is finished"

When he glanced over, Taylor was headed back to join them. Norwich was on her cell phone. Deputy Trevor waited. The sheriff must have been convincing that there was no new information. Taylor looked disappointed and frustrated, but not terrified that her boy could be buried under freshly laid sod.

Jason and Brodie carried Hank to the back of the Jeep, where he would settle in next to Scout.

"I know she's not telling me everything."

Creed startled at Taylor's voice. He thought she had gone back to the Jeep and didn't realize she was standing behind him.

"You never dream that cops would be looking for your little boy in Dumpsters and ditches." Her eyes were scanning the woods. "You can't imagine him being lost and frightened or…or taken."

She rubbed her shoulders. He could see she was shivering.

Her eyes came back around and caught his, holding him there as if to seal the promise she was about to ask for. "Please bring him home. I know you've done it before. I don't deserve rescuing. But Will does."

Then she turned and walked back to the Jeep.

He watched them leave. Norwich watched them leave, too, then she tucked away her cell phone and came over.

"I just talked to Maggie O'Dell," she told him. "She's been following a serial killer all the way from Washington, D.C."

"I talked to her earlier today." It was now long past midnight. "Actually, yesterday."

"She thinks he might be involved in all this."

"I thought he targeted homeless people?"

"She just found out his mother is Isadora Ramsey. She's on her way to talk to her. Seems like an odd coincidence that this guy gets to Pensacola right about the time Will went missing."

"Did she mention if he was driving a blue pickup?"

He turned and switched on his flashlight. Off to the side of where the sheriff's SUV headlights marked, he shot a stream of light across the pickup tucked close to the trees.

"I don't like this," Norwich said. "I don't like this at all."

When he glanced back, he saw Deputy Trevor coming over to join them. Only now, Creed noticed the deputy was carrying a shovel in each hand.

68

Gregory couldn't believe this. His mother showed more concern about her poor husband's bump on his head than she ever showed about his father. He zip-tied the man's semi-conscious body to one of their heavy-ass dining room chairs. The frame was made of wrought iron.

She was whining. "You can't do this, Peter."

It took him a while to realize she wasn't protesting him wounding her husband.

"What did you do with Willie?"

"Heaven forbid I hurt Mickey's mini-me."

"I swear—"

"Tell me what you two did to my father."

"Your father was taken and killed by a transient. You know that."

"I know what you told me. But that's not what I saw. And I've been seeing it very clearly lately in my nightmares."

"In your nightmares. Listen to yourself, Peter. I've tried to help you. I've tried—"

"To brainwash me. To drug me."

"It was to help you get through your nightmares."

"I saw the man who killed him. I recognized him."

"No, you imagined—"

"Stop it! Just shut up and stop for once!"

Even after all these years, she wanted to control the narrative. But it didn't matter anymore. He had figured it out. After all these years, the dreams, the nightmares told the real story over and over in vivid detail. He could just never quite see the man's face. Only the crowbar coming down on his father's skull. The crowbar being held by an arm tattooed with a blue anchor.

"Whatever you believe, Peter, you must not take it out on a poor little boy. Where is he? What did you do with him?"

He couldn't believe her. She hadn't changed one bit.

"That's what you care about right now? That's really all you've ever cared about is your precious Mickey. And now, his precious offspring. I know that Carl was the man stranded on the side of the road that night.

"No, you're wrong."

"I know he killed my father."

"Your imagination—"

"I couldn't quite see his face until recently."

"Of course not, because you're wrong. You're projecting—"

"But I clearly saw this." He grabbed Carl's arm and yanked it up. The man was fully awake, grunting in pain as the zip-tie dug deeper into his wrist.

"Oh, Peter." The condescension…she still had it down pat. "You know how many men have that same tattoo?"

"His body was never found," Carl said through gritted teeth. "Your father left you boys and your mother. He left."

Gregory dropped the man's arm and walked around behind the chair. He didn't want to look at his face. He'd seen it too many times, shadowed in his dreams, the features blurred by his mother's lies.

But he knew he was right.

He'd been right since he was a boy and confessed to his mother. Now, all these years later, he understood. Why she worked so hard to convince the authorities that her son had a habit of lying, making things up. *A wicked and vivid imagination.*

Carl shifted in the hardback chair, readjusted, sat a bit straighter. Gregory's mother stood in the middle of the room where she faced him. Her eyes dropped to the knife now in his hand, but she didn't appear concerned. She planned on winning this discussion. And why not? She always won. She was always right.

"If he chose to leave, why did he create a trust for me weeks before? Did you know his family had all that money?"

"Your father was a silly, weak man. He made us live in a ramshackle house."

"So you knew. I remembered how you two argued about money all the time. Your arguments made Mickey cry. I just plugged my ears. Went off in my mind to somewhere, anywhere else."

He watched her now. "But you didn't know he put it in trust funds. For me. None for you. A small portion for Mickey. But not as much, because he knew you'd take good care of him. Your favorite. And you did. Anything he wanted, including medical school. But dear old dad knew you wouldn't give a damn about me."

"That's not true. You always make up such lies." But she stared at him. And for the first time, he saw her bristle at his words.

"Then Mickey was killed in Afghanistan. The remainder of his will eventually go to Will. That's the way mine's written. If we have any heirs. But you…you still didn't get any."

Her nostrils flared with what? Indignation? Anger?

"Or did you discover a way to get your hands on it?"

"You're being ridiculous. Willie will get his father's when he turns twenty-five, just like you did. Just like Michael could have."

Funny, she seemed to display sadness only about Mickey. Everything was still about Mickey. He and his father were always a distant second and third.

"I almost didn't recognize this area," Gregory said casually, waving the knife and gesturing toward the back patio doors and the woods that met the backyard.

"Interesting that you chose to live out here," he continued. She'd even named the development Linden Estates. Mickey's middle name. He couldn't be distracted. Not now. "The country road is now asphalt. The forest used to come all the way up to the road. But that curve…that curve brought back a flood of memories."

She tilted her head. The movement was slight, but he noticed it. She was trying to keep emotion from her face, but it was becoming a challenge. Still, she didn't interrupt. Maybe she wanted to hear what he knew. What he remembered. All these years later, did her version still hold up?

"Good ole Carl bought all this land. To develop. You bulldozed bunches of trees. Piled on dirt. Built houses. That's quite a nice pool back there."

His mother's eyes glanced down. There it was. The tell. She and Carl exchanged a look. He was on to something.

"Somewhere on this land that you own, all this property that you control—whether developed or still a part of the woods—somewhere close by, you buried my father."

Her eyes lit up with as much surprise as anger.

Then suddenly, all three of them startled at a knock on the front door.

"Get rid of them," Gregory told her. He came up close behind Carl and raised the knife. It took every ounce of restraint to not slit the man's throat right here, right now.

Instead, he shoved Carl's chair until the man's belly wedged up against the table, incapacitating him even more. No one would see his zip-tied hands down below if his mother was stupid enough to invite them inside. They would think Carl was simply sitting at the table.

Except for the bump on the head.

She understood. He saw her put on her "we have guests" face before she disappeared around the corner to the entrance.

"Mrs. Ramsey," said a woman's voice. "I'm with the task force to find your grandson. I have a few questions I need to ask you."

"This isn't a good time. My husband and son just got home. We're all exhausted. Can it wait a few minutes? Maybe twenty or thirty?

Gregory smiled in spite of himself. His clever mother was giving *him* a deadline. Not the person on the other side of the door.

How much of who he was—of what he had become—had he learned from her? In the past, she could destroy him in much less time than half an hour. He doubted she had any idea of what he was capable of doing.

69

"This sod looks freshly laid," Norwich said, examining the spot Grace had alerted to earlier.

"Give me a few minutes, Sheriff," Creed told her. "I need to check something."

The clouds lit up around them. A roll of thunder moved closer.

Creed took Grace aside, then asked her to "find Will." He winced when her immediate response was to take off across the golf course. She wanted to continue to the woods on the other side. Those were thicker than the stretch they'd come through. He reined her in.

Now he knew he'd made another mistake. His mistake. Not Grace's.

Will had crossed this field of grass. Maybe someone was chasing him. Grace insisted he had run to the woods. To escape?

Creed glanced back at the place where the Jack Russell had alerted. He couldn't shrug it off as fertilizer. Just because it didn't make sense to him, or because he hadn't given her the correct command, didn't mean she was wrong. Grace was rarely wrong. Sometimes she found things. Other scents she'd been trained to find. And she did it without Creed asking.

He hated to stop her now, but he needed to check her previous alert.

"Let's take a break," he told her.

She recognized the phrase and relaxed. It didn't matter that they had already been standing down and waiting. That was different. They were tending to Hank. She understood that. She was quiet and at his side, knowing the dog had been hurt.

As they walked back, Grace dragged her nose through the dew-slick blades of grass. Instinctively, she was keeping her nose wet. A wet nose helped to collect and navigate scent. She knew she wasn't finished.

When they got back to Norwich, she asked, "Does that mean this is a false alert?"

"I'm not sure. It was a solid alert. I think we need to check."

"You mentioned she alerted to the bags of fertilizer earlier. Didn't you say it was Mr. Monroe's landscaping truck?"

Creed nodded.

"Sod, fertilizer," Norwich said, her face tense but her voice hopeful. "It could just be more fertilizer, right?"

"It could." But he no longer believed it was.

"This section doesn't seem as flat as the rest." Deputy Trevor poked around the grass where Creed had tossed down a red flag.

Norwich swept her high-powered flashlight along a seam in the sod that buckled up. Creed grabbed the other shovel. He and Trevor started carefully peeling back rolls of sod as the first drops of rain began to fall.

Underneath the grass were chunks and clods instead of smoothed out dirt. As they rolled up another area, they could see a mound begin to emerge. It stretched about six feet by two feet. Not only was the earth disturbed here, but there appeared to be an obvious hump.

Something was buried here.

Both Creed and Deputy Trevor hesitated. Creed glanced over at Grace. She sat calmly, her eyes going back and forth from the mound to Creed's eyes, almost as if she was telling him it was about time he took a good look.

When he glanced at Norwich, she was watching Grace, too.

"You'll need to be careful," she reminded the men.

Creed stood back and let Deputy Trevor gently scrape off bits of dirt with the end of his shovel rather than stick the blade down into the mound.

Little by little, something red and brown and orange began to appear. Something sturdier than a piece of fabric. With only a small section revealed, Creed heard Norwich inhale, a long deep breath close to a gasp.

"It's a rug or a piece of carpeting," she announced.

Deputy Trevor skimmed the blade over an edge, and a corner flapped open. He stopped and without a word, checked with Norwich. She gestured for him to continue. He wedged the blade under the flap.

The rug sagged open enough for them to see a head of hair.

Norwich released a long, tired and disappointed sigh. She kneeled on the damp grass as she fumbled a pair of latex gloves from her trouser pocket. Gently and slowly, she pulled back the corner of the rug. Then she dropped her hand and shook her head.

Creed recognized the boy, if only from the photograph being shown during his search.

Lightning illuminated the sky, followed by a rumble of thunder, a soft groan reverberating above them. Rain came down harder now, washing the lifeless face of Caleb Monroe.

70

Linden Estates
Santa Rosa County, Florida

Maggie had no idea if Dora Ramsey recognized her. But she was certain the woman was telling her things were not okay in her house. Dora's eyes darted over her shoulder even before she mentioned that not only had her husband arrived home, but so had her son.

Peter Gregory was in the house. Right now. Dora made it clear she didn't feel comfortable inviting law enforcement inside or joining them outdoors for questions that could help find her missing grandson.

Confirmation of Maggie's suspicions came when Dora closed the door. She heard the lock engage, then immediately a whispered click followed as the lock disengaged.

Maggie walked back down the circle driveway to where she'd left the state trooper. Norwich had assigned him to accompany Maggie. She promised other resources. Whatever Maggie might need.

As she briefed Trooper Vargas, she checked her watch. Was Dora serious about the time limit she'd given? Did she expect something to happen?

Maggie was a profiler. A forensic expert. Usually, by the time she arrived, the crime had been committed. Victims were already dead. She tracked and hunted serial killers and sometimes it didn't end well.

But this?

She had little experience in hostage negotiations. She couldn't be sure what this was.

Trooper Vargas stood as tall as Maggie. A veteran law enforcement officer, his face wore well-earned lines. His eyes held the intensity of someone who didn't easily back down.

He began to tell her the options available for a situation like this.

From the street, Maggie couldn't see beyond the curtains in the front windows. The properties were sprawling. It'd be impossible to approach from any direction and not be seen by one of the security cameras. The other houses in the development were mostly dark.

Some of the law enforcement vehicles had left. Several in the last few minutes. Their sudden exit made Maggie wonder if there had been a break in the missing boy's case. But nothing had come over the trooper's radio.

She avoided looking back at the Ramsey's house.

"Right now, he doesn't realize we know about him," she explained. All the options Trooper Vargas outlined had the capability of producing fatal outcomes.

"That would actually make it easier to get a SWAT team in there," he told her.

Peter Gregory was her responsibility, but it would be Norwich's team executing the plan. Things always appeared worse and more urgent in the dark. Any time after midnight, nerves were frayed and adrenaline fading fast. All the ingredients for accidents and mistakes. Maybe what happened back in D.C. made her more cautious. Whatever the reason, she needed to wait.

She texted Norwich to call her as soon as she could. That the sheriff hadn't done so yet—coupled with the sudden exit of law enforcement—made Maggie think Norwich had her hands full at the moment.

She glanced at her cell phone. Then her watch.

Why would Dora Ramsey give her a time limit? What did she expect to change in twenty to thirty minutes? Was it just enough time to allow her son to escape?

"These properties." Now she strained to see behind the houses. She started walking up between the Ramsey's and their nearest neighbor. "Is there another street that runs along on the other side?"

"Everything on this street backs up directly to the woods."

Her pulse ticked up. "We need to check the backyard," she told him.

Just then, a series of loud blasts came from inside the house. It stopped both of them in their tracks.

"That sounded like gunfire," Trooper Vargas said. Then he grabbed his radio. "We have gunshots. The Ramsey's house."

Maggie was already rushing to the front door, her weapon drawn and down by her side. When she eased up onto the portico, the state trooper was right behind her.

She stopped and turned. Pressed her back against the bricks alongside the doorjamb and met the trooper's eyes. She gestured to him that she'd open the door. Held up three fingers, telling him they'd go in on her count. She poked her thumb to her chest to let him know she'd go in first.

He nodded, and she grabbed the doorknob. It twisted easily in her fingers and the heavy door slid open. She waited three seconds, then entered in a crouch.

The long entry was lit only by the light coming from the living room. The wall worked to their benefit. Maggie couldn't hear anything except Trooper Vargas's soft steps behind her. She kept her eyes focused forward. At the end of the hall, she crouched even lower and peeked around the corner.

Across the room on the floor, a man's body sprawled on his back. She could see blood pooling underneath him. On a nearby sofa, two figured sat side by side.

Maggie stood slowly. She entered the room cautiously as she announced, "FBI. Don't move." She kept her weapon on the Ramseys, and chin-pointed at Trooper Vargas to check the man on the floor. Only now did she notice the gun hanging from Dora's hand.

"Mrs. Ramsey, drop the gun."

She sat with her elbows on her knees. The white-haired man had his arm around her back. Maggie recognized Carl Ramsey.

"He was going to kill us both," Dora Ramsey said.

"Put it down. Now."

Dora placed it on the edge of the rug at her foot. Maggie couldn't help but notice the woman was comfortable handling the weapon.

"Where did you get a gun, Mrs. Ramsey?"

"It's legal and registered," Carl explained. "I bought it for her. I'm gone so much, I wanted her to have something for protection."

"He was like a madman," Dora said. "He may have done something with Willie."

"Did he say that?" Maggie asked. She kept an eye on the couple as she sidestepped closer to the body.

"Yes. He talked about how much he looked like Michael." Dora's eyes slid over to the fireplace mantle and the array of framed photographs. "Peter was always so jealous of his brother." She shook her head as if that explained everything.

Trooper Vargas squatted over the body, two fingers on the man's neck. He shook his head at Maggie. A knife lay close to the dead man's fingers. When Vargas stood up, he grabbed his radio and started reporting what they had found.

It wasn't hard to recognize Peter Gregory. But Maggie jolted at the gunshot wounds. They had hit him in the chest. Center mass.

71

Waffle House
Avalon Boulevard, Milton, Florida

Lightning pulsed through the clouds, but the rain had stopped by the time Creed pulled his Jeep into the parking lot. He was tired and wet to the bone, though he'd tried to towel off himself and Grace. The heater blasted warm air, but it didn't help dislodge the chill.

He parked in the far corner where he'd left his Jeep the other night, halfway between The Red Roof Inn and the Waffle House. The headlights streaked across the woods before he switched them off. The hotel's section of the lot was half empty.

Jason's Jeep and Dr. Avelyn's SUV were parked with a half dozen other vehicles clustered close to the restaurant's entrance. In a few hours, the morning breakfast rush would pack the place.

In the dark, Creed dug out a clean T-shirt and another button-down oxford from his duffel bag. He should have changed into the dry clothes when Deputy Trevor dropped him off back at his Jeep, but he wasn't thinking. Still, wasn't. Adrenaline long spent; he was operating on instinct.

He stripped off the wet shirts and pulled on the dry. Now, as he shoved the duffel onto the floor of the backseat, he noticed another bag already there. A plastic bag tied loosely at the top and lodged between the driver's seat and back bench. He didn't need to look. He already knew what was inside.

Creed glanced up at Grace. She stretched out on the Jeep's folded down bench right outside her open kennel. Without raising her head, her eyes watched him, moving from the bag, then back to him. When she noticed his attention, her tail wagged a soft tap-tap. He had fixed her a meal before they left Linden Estates. Exhausted and with a full belly, she still didn't move from her place.

He held up the plastic bag to her and said, "You were searching for both of them."

Another wag.

Of course she was.

Urgent to find Will, Creed had forgotten about Caleb's sweatshirt. It was still here after his search with Bolo.

He scratched behind her ears. Told her what a good dog she was. Promised he wouldn't be gone long. She could rest and get some sleep now.

He tilted the moon roof open for fresh air, closed the door gently, then locked the Jeep and started across the parking lot.

When he was still with Norwich, Creed had texted Jason, knowing Taylor was still with him and Brodie. All he said was,

Found a body. It's not Will.

His cell phone vibrated against his chest. He pulled it from his shirt's pocket.

"Maggie, are you okay?" They had missed each other several times.

"I'm good. What about you?"

"Tired. A little bit dryer." He managed a laugh. Dryer didn't mean warmer.

"I heard Grace found that teenager."

"Yeah. But we still don't know where Will is."

She was quiet too long.

"Do you know something?" he asked, stopping in the middle of the parking lot, waiting for her response. It was almost as if he was too tired to talk, to listen, and to walk at the same time.

"My serial killer was at the Ramsey's. Mrs. Ramsey was his mother."

"Was?"

"Evidently, he threatened her and her husband. While I milled around outside their house trying to figure what to do, she shot him."

"She shot her son?"

"Yes."

He heard so much emotion in that one-word answer.

"He wasn't a good guy," Maggie said. "We have evidence that connects him to at least three murders. Maybe more. Mrs. Ramsey thinks Peter Gregory did something with Will."

"There were drawings left in a bulldozer cab. Taylor said they were Will's." He couldn't see into the Waffle House. There were no windows on this side. Still, he thought about Taylor, what she had asked of him. He hadn't been able to deliver. "It looked like someone in a blue pickup was chasing Will."

"Sheriff Norwich told me you found the pickup. We'll be able to tell if Peter Gregory had driven it out here."

"But how do we find out what he did with Will?"

More silence.

Creed rubbed a hand over his bristled jaw, trying to unclench it. He stood still. Looked up to see a sliver of moon peeking through the clouds. That damn statistic drummed at his temple. A child taken by a stranger was usually murdered within the first three to twenty-four hours.

"I don't know right now," she finally said. "I'm still at the Ramseys'. Are you able to go get some rest?"

"I'm meeting Jason and Brodie…and Taylor. Dr. Avelyn's here, too. She's checking on Hank."

"Is he okay?"

"Yeah, sounds like it. He ran into some glass."

"What about you?" she asked.

"Me?"

"How are you holding up?"

He couldn't deny that he was exhausted, that maybe he'd made some mistakes because of it. But Grace had made up for them.

"I'm holding up." That's all he would concede when others were in worse shape. "How about you? You've got to be running on empty about now."

"Definitely close."

"We'll be here for a little while longer. Check to see if we're still here when you're finished."

"I will do that."

He slipped the phone back into his pocket. He hadn't gotten farther than thirty feet away from his Jeep. Before he headed for the restaurant, he saw Grace standing and looking out the window on the opposite side. There was movement in the woods. But Grace wasn't barking.

He walked slowly back toward his Jeep. That's when someone came out from behind the trees. Creed recognized the man's silhouette. He met him at the back bumper.

"You keep crazy hours," Sully told him.

"I could say the same about you."

"I saw another Jeep with dogs. Thought it might be you."

The old man's forehead was sweaty and creased with worry.

"Is everything okay?" Creed looked around and realized Sully didn't have his dog with him. "Is Gunner okay?"

"She's fine. Can you come with me?"

"You mean out into the woods?"

"To my camp."

Creed glanced at Grace. He put his palm up against the window, meeting her paws. "It's okay, Grace. Lie down. Get some rest."

He started following Sully before he realized the man didn't have a flashlight. Maybe he knew the way so well he didn't need one. But Creed almost tripped a couple of times. The old man was quicker and more agile than Creed expected.

"You okay back there, Jarhead?" Sully glanced over his shoulder, but he didn't slow down.

He wanted to tell him about Caleb, but he knew he couldn't. Right now, all Creed's brain concentrated on was the chill in the air. How the dampness seemed to cling to him. How the branches appeared out of nowhere at the last minute.

They started downhill, and he skidded on wet leaves. He grabbed onto a sapling before he fell. More frustrating was the chuffing sounds Sully made in front of him. The old man almost seemed pleased that Creed wasn't able to keep up.

Finally, he could see the outline of a tent. A rope was tied between two trees with pots and pans hanging from it along with a couple of battery-operated lanterns. Two metal folding chairs sat in front of a firepit surrounded by rocks. Wet ashes in the middle.

The lantern light didn't reach all the way around, and Creed couldn't make out some of the other items. There was movement in the trees beyond. Another tent. Maybe a flashlight.

Sully stopped and turned, staying in front of him. His face was serious and glistened in the streak of moonlight that finally made its way down.

"You know how I let that boy stay with us out here?"

He knew. How did he already know about Caleb? Creed met his eyes as best he could.

"Whether it was for the best or not, I don't know," Sully shrugged.

Creed wanted to tell him he had done a good thing, but Gunner came wandering out of the tent. The dog looked fine. There was a big yawn, then she shook herself. She wagged, coming to greet Creed.

"You probably saved him." *For a little while longer.* Creed stopped himself from saying anything more.

Sully nodded. His mouth twitched like he still wasn't sure how to tell Creed what he'd brought him here for. "I'm real glad to hear you say that." He shuffled his feet. Hesitated. "Because I did it again."

Before Creed could ask what he meant, Sully went over to the tent and bent down to look inside. He told someone, "It's okay. It's safe to come out. This is the friend I told you about."

In the dim light, a small thin figure crawled out from between the canvas flaps. His hair was tousled and sticking up straight up in places. His face smeared with dirt, and his new sneakers caked with mud. But otherwise, Will looked unharmed.

Unharmed. And alive.

72

Wednesday, December 6
Florida Panhandle

Maggie woke up and rolled over. The spot next to her was empty. She sat up, and in the dim light, looked around. She had fallen asleep in Ryder's arms, but now she couldn't see him anywhere in the loft apartment.

"Ryder?"

The only sound came from the floor next to the bed. Rufus was snoring. Another glance around, and she realized Grace was gone, too. Darkness filled the windows. She checked her wristwatch. One-thirty. They had fallen into bed just as the sun was setting. Both of them were exhausted. It was their first opportunity for sleep, after too many hours of piecing together the events of the last several days. After trying to answer the remaining questions.

But the most important question had been answered: Will Donahue was alive and safe. He was with his mother back home in her apartment above the marina, and if Sheriff Norwich got her way, the boy wouldn't be returning to Dora Ramsey's custody any time soon.

Maggie hadn't bothered to drive all the way back to her hotel room on the beach, borrowing a T-shirt and boxer shorts from Ryder. She was chilly now as she padded barefoot around his place, looking for any sign of where he'd gone.

Her clothes were left on one end of the sofa, neatly folded. It made her smile. She hadn't left them neatly folded. Her holstered weapon and cell phone were arranged on top of the nearby side table. Even her shoes were placed on the floor in front of the clothes, nowhere near where she had kicked them off.

As she passed a window that overlooked the property, lights caught her eye. Hannah's house looked dark. So was Jason's doublewide trailer. But every single light appeared to be on at the medical clinic.

Her first thought was an emergency with one of the dogs. She grabbed her cell phone and tapped Ryder's number. Ringing came from the kitchen counter. He hadn't taken his phone.

She changed quickly into her clothes and checked on Rufus. He was still snoring. Instead of rousing all the dogs downstairs in the kennel, she took the back exit. The night air was wet with the scent of pine trees. A breeze made her wish she had her jacket, but she wasn't sure where it had ended up.

As she crossed the property to the clinic, her heart started to race. Why didn't he wake her up? If one of the dogs was in trouble, she'd want to help.

She'd never been inside this building before. When she opened the door, she could already hear voices. She followed the sound down a long hallway, glancing inside the rooms she passed. The place was impressive. No surprise there. She couldn't imagine Ryder cutting any corners for his dogs.

Finally, in the last room at the end, she found them. The area was large, with two walls lined with kennels. The light was low, so she had to squint to see that only three of the spaces were occupied.

They hadn't heard her come in. Although Hank and Grace certainly had. Their eyes were already on the open doorway before she came into view. It wasn't until tails thumped against the floor that Ryder and Brodie looked up. The two of them sat crossed-legged on the floor. Brodie had a book in her lap with a light attached.

"Hey!" Ryder kept his voice almost a whisper, but gestured for her to come in. "They're finally resting."

As she tiptoed closer, she got a better look at the three big dogs. Their heads were down. Only one squinted a look up at her without moving anything but the eyes. Soulful eyes that made her want to reach in and touch him. Instead, she sat down on the other side of Hank and gave him a rub on his chest. Grace snuggled back down beside Ryder.

"The Spaniel's had a tough time settling," Ryder explained. "He's not sure yet if this is only a temporary reprieve." She gathered he was the one with his eyes still open.

"I read to Hank," Brodie said, nodding to the book. "After his surgery. He didn't trust anyone either for a while."

"Looks like it's working again. What book is it?"

Brodie smiled. "One of Ryder's favorites. *The Princess Bride*."

Maggie raised an eyebrow at him.

He shrugged. "What's not to like? It has pirates, giants, fire swamps and rodents of unusual size."

"And true love," Maggie added, but then was taken off guard by the intensity of Ryder's eyes when they caught and held hers.

"So you've read it?" Brodie asked, not paying attention while she placed her marker between the pages and turned off the book light.

"No," Maggie admitted. "But I saw the movie. I liked it a lot, too. Please keep reading. Don't stop on my account."

Brodie glanced at Ryder. He smiled and nodded. She turned the light back on and began again. Her voice was soothing like a warm blanket, the inflections and genuine emotion tucking up around her audience, lulling them with a sense of security.

Maggie continued petting Hank, missing her boys, all the while feeling at home right here. She'd never experienced this before, feeling suspended between two places, not wanting to give up either, but still searching for a balance.

She'd scheduled a flight for Wednesday afternoon. Alonzo and Kuszak continued to build a convincing case against Peter Gregory, despite his demise. The investigation into his death, if there was one, would be up to Sheriff Norwich.

Maggie still needed to get back. There were too many obligations and responsibilities. The powerful U.S. senator who owed her a favor, the one Maggie had called on Monday—gosh, Monday felt like a week ago—had agreed to a private meeting at her D.C. residence. Maggie couldn't miss that meeting. She wouldn't miss it.

And there was the promise she'd made to her brother, Patrick, about building new traditions. They'd decorate that gorgeous tree he'd wrangled into her living room…their living room.

Alonzo had convinced Metro police that Nessie was an informant for the FBI and actually a hero. He said he told Detective Sheldon that the woman had helped them catch an active serial killer by putting her life on the line. Despite Alonzo and Gwen stepping in and taking care of things, Maggie needed to see Nessie. She needed to thank her. And she needed to apologize.

As for Racine? She wasn't taking Maggie's calls. According to her partner, Rachel, she wasn't talking much to anyone, basically pissed off that she was restricted to rest for the next four months. But Rachel also added, "Don't worry, she'll get over it."

Now Maggie watched Ryder, his attention on his three new wards. He was ready to take care of them, protect them, and help them heal. But she knew these three only reminded him of the others. The ones still left behind. He had confided in her hours before they gave in to sleep, that he couldn't stop thinking about them, worrying about what would happen to them.

She didn't try to talk him out of the concern. She knew she couldn't. He was a rescuer at heart. And deep down, she realized it was one of the reasons she loved him.

73

Friday, December 7
Santa Rosa County, Florida

Creed stayed close to Norwich as they entered the woods from the parking lot of the Red Roof Inn and the Waffle House. A week later, and here they were again. There wasn't the same urgency and no rush of adrenaline. But unlike their first trip with Bolo, this time Creed kept Grace on a leash.

Sully had left a message for Sheriff Norwich. Gunner had found more bones and maybe a grave.

Norwich stopped before they headed down the ridge and into the thicket. There was no visible path. Nothing padded down. No broken branches to mark a trail.

"I don't think I remember the way," she confessed. "Do you?"

The woods had been pitch-dark early that morning when Sully led Creed to his camp. Creed was so exhausted he could barely keep up with the old man. Sully took him and Will back to the parking lot, but even the beginning light of dawn didn't provide much guidance.

That morning, while the boy reunited with his mother, Sully hung back from the commotion. That's when he gave Creed his worn canvas bucket hat. Then he gestured to Grace, who watched from the Jeep's window. "When you decide to come over for some beans and rice, just use this. She'll find me."

Now, Creed pulled the canvas hat out of his daypack, showed it to Norwich, and said, "Better than a map. Sully gave it to me."

He bent down to Grace and presented it to her with the crown facing the ground. Her nose traveled over the underbrim. She gently put a paw on it to bring it down, so she could dip her nose inside. Then she sniffed the entire length of the sweatband. When she was finished, she sat and waited.

"Grace, this is Sully. Find Sully."

She started prancing, and he added, "We're going slow, Grace."

The dog understood. She didn't tug as she weaved and sniffed and panted. Holding back took added effort, even though she knew this search wasn't urgent.

Norwich kept pace alongside them, allowing them to go ahead when the path narrowed.

"How's the boy doing?" she asked when the ground leveled.

Creed knew Jason was giving Taylor and Will time together, but still checking on them.

"He seems to be doing well. He told Jason he's drawing a book about his adventures."

"Adventures?" She smiled. "Actually, that's probably a healthy thing for him to do. He told me Peter Gregory had chased him for hours. He thought he lost him when he climbed inside the bulldozer. But as soon as he got back on his bike, the guy was following him again." She shook her head. "When I think about him running around those woods…all the things that could have happened. We never did find that alligator."

"He's lucky he ran into Sully and Gunner."

"Yes, he is." She was quiet for a moment, then said, "I wish Caleb would have been as lucky."

"I heard you arrested his father."

"The mother turned on him as soon as we told them."

"You believe her?"

"Domestic abuse cases are often complicated. I'll leave it to the evidence. You remember Grace alerting to his work truck in the driveway?"

"Big four-door crew cab with bags of fertilizer stacked in the bed." At the time, he was certain it was the fertilizer that got Grace's attention.

"We found blood in the backseat. Evidently, there had been enough of it Mr. Monroe tried to clean it up."

They walked in silence through a narrow stretch. Creed tried to concentrate on the surroundings, so he wouldn't need a dog to guide him each time. He already decided he'd be checking on Sully from time to time. Hannah had warned him that not everyone wanted to be rescued. She had told him this before, but it was a hard lesson that he continued to brush aside.

"Sheriff, any idea who this person could be? The bones that Gunner found. That first one looked old."

"Maybe up to twenty years. That's what my forensic guy said."

"Any cold cases? Missing persons?"

He glanced at her just as she pursed her lips and shot him a look.

"It's probably nothing," she said. "Right now it's only a theory, and I haven't shared it with anyone else. I'm only telling you, because I trust the hell out of you, okay?"

"I understand."

"When Will went missing, we asked permission to access the Ramsey's home security system. It didn't help much, but we monitored it off and on throughout the time Will was missing. Lucky for Dora Ramsey, it most likely will validate her claim of self-defense. Her son did come in through the garage door unexpectedly. He roughed up Carl Ramsey and zip tied his hands. He had a knife he waved around. Knowing what he did to those homeless people back in D.C., we know he was capable of using it."

Creed wasn't sure what any of this had to do with his question about the bones Gunner had uncovered. Still, he stayed quiet and waited.

"There was an interesting accusation Peter Gregory tossed at the Ramseys. Dora married Carl when Peter and his brother were about Will's age. The family was driving home late one night and stopped to help a man with a stalled pickup on the side of a country road. When I heard him talking about it, it sparked a memory with me.

"About twenty years ago, I was a young deputy. Dispatch sent out that a motorist had been attacked by a transient. First deputies to get to the scene found blood and tire tracks, but no pickup. There was no sign of anyone. Thomas Gregory and the man he stopped to help were gone."

"How did they know he was a transient?"

"At the time, there were always men coming to the area for seasonal work. I pulled up the police report. Dora Ramsey used the term. There's no explanation how she could tell. But here's something interesting from that police report. One of the boys said he recognized the man. That he had come to their house."

"So the guy might have been stalking the family?"

"No. He said the man came to their house to fix things. His mother claimed the boy was too traumatized to remember. That he made up stories all the time. He had an overactive imagination."

"So they didn't check out the man who fixed things at their home?"

Norwich shrugged. "I haven't seen any follow-up. Only the note on young Peter's statement."

"Wait a minute. You're thinking the bones Gunner found might be Thomas Gregory?"

Another shrug as they climbed the rest of the way. "I told you. It's just a hunch I have. Definitely a long shot. But we have Peter's DNA. I can't remember what they need to do to get DNA from old bones, but it's certainly worth checking to see if we've finally found Thomas Gregory."

"You said on the security camera footage Peter accused the Ramseys of something?"

"He said his nightmares had revealed the face of his father's killer."

Creed stopped to give her his full attention as he said, "The boy with the overactive imagination who thought he recognized the man even back then." He knew before she answered.

"He claimed the man who killed his father was Carl Ramsey."

Creed's phone vibrated in his pocket. It surprised him. Usually, reception out here was spotty at best.

"Excuse me, Sheriff."

He fished the phone out, pleased to see Maggie's name. She'd left on Wednesday, but they had talked late last night. He hoped everything was all right.

"Hey, Maggie."

"I know you're out searching in the woods, but I couldn't wait to tell you. I have an early Christmas present for you."

Epilogue

Thursday, December 21
Kabul, Afghanistan

Creed watched out the plane's window as they descended through the dense clouds. The world below came into view, and he felt the knot in his stomach. There was snow in the mountains. The sight should have helped tamp down his memory of the dust. Dust so thick he could still taste it.

A tap on his shoulder, and he turned to find Maggie offering a bottle of water. She had been plying him with water the entire trip, making sure they both stayed hydrated. They'd be spending a ton of hours in the air. He appreciated her effort, but after the tenth hour, it only made him need to pee. He took the bottle anyway and thanked her.

It was hard to take his eyes off the landscape below. This godforsaken country had chewed him up and spit him out, along with so many others sent here to fight. Too many of them returned home like Jason without limbs, others with brain trauma and PTSD. All that they had sacrificed, only to watch the country be turned back over to the madmen they had fought against.

The last four and a half hours from Dubai had been quiet. So quiet it felt like they were all holding their breaths as they got closer. Before that, Dr. Avelyn's team of veterinarians had kept busy. Creed and Maggie worked alongside them, assembling kennels and attaching them to the floor of the large cargo space. They were expecting to take back with them sixty-six to seventy dogs. And this time, they were told, they would not be disappointed.

This jetliner had been converted during the pandemic in an effort to avoid bankruptcy. When passengers declined flying, the company decided to remove seats and make room for freight that still needed to move from country to country.

About two dozen seats had been left intact as well as the lavatories and the galley, which allowed them to refrigerate and prepare meals. And have a cup of hot coffee. The entire area was still climate controlled, though the vast space made it a bit chilly. Lights could also be turned up or dimmed for reclining passengers to sleep. Electrical capabilities allowed the veterinarians to set up and plug in equipment. They had even arranged an area for triage, if necessary.

They had no idea what shape the dogs were in, and it would be a grueling long flight back with a brief stop in Paris to refuel. But Dr. Avelyn and her team looked prepared. Several were military trained and had served in Afghanistan and Iraq. They had experience working with and treating K9s in the field.

From their attitudes and the way they prepared, Creed was impressed with the whole group. This was a mission they had dedicated themselves to since the fall of Afghanistan. Ever since the very first rumors began of military and working dogs being abandoned. Let out of cages at the airport. Destined to run the dangerous streets and fend for themselves. Dogs that were highly trained, but still dependent on their handlers.

Lately, memories flooded back to Creed. Just when he thought he'd stuffed them safely away where they couldn't hurt him anymore. Marine K9 units move from one platoon to another where they were needed. The men understood the K9 unit's importance, but Creed and Rufus were never anywhere long enough for them to get attached. They were the outsiders, respected for their magic, but kept at a distance because the K9 unit was the first out and first to die.

He remembered the exact minute he realized Rufus was alerting to an Afghan boy named Jabar. The boy was someone the platoon trusted and granted access to their camp. As soon as Jabar had reached under his shirt that day, Creed dived on top of Rufus, saving the dog but sending Creed to a military hospital and then home. Later, he didn't stop until he was able to bring Rufus home, too.

Now the knots twisted in Creed's stomach as they got closer. As usual, his jaw clenched. His fingers balled up into fists. He realized he desperately needed a distraction. He shifted in his seat, so he could keep his eyes out the window but glance at Maggie.

"You never mentioned what it was you did for this senator," he said. She'd only told him that Senator Ellie Delanor owed her a favor. This was a whopper of a payback.

She leaned in to look out the window with him. Took her time in answering. "I saved her children's lives." She paused, then added, "And sent her ex-husband to prison."

He glanced at her, expecting more, but she shrugged.

The Dubai businessman who provided this jetliner and assured their safe passage had also brokered a remarkable deal for the release of the dogs. Not just the ones being cared for by the rescue organization, but others the Taliban had been holding.

They learned that the Taliban had kept almost a dozen dogs caged or chained with their soldiers or at the airport, thinking it made them look tough. But they had no clue how to use the dogs for scent detection or security. All Creed knew was that the Dubai businessman was so well regarded the Taliban had scavenged the streets for any remaining dogs to please him and sweeten their deal.

"And what about the guy who owns this plane?" he asked Maggie. "Why is he doing this?"

Another shrug and a swipe at a strand of hair. He knew she was beyond exhausted. Finally, she said, “I suspect he owed the senator a favor.”

“That’s another big favor. Just because she’s a senator?”

“I think she has lots of other connections. Her ex-husband used to be the head of a Mexican cartel.”

“Choque Azul.”

She nodded. “Unfortunately, you know them well.”

The cartel had targeted Creed a couple of years ago when he and Grace found a payload of their drugs on a commercial fishing boat, buried under tons of tuna.

“When I told Senator Delanor what I wanted, all she asked was how soon. I got the impression they’ve already done this before, at least once.”

He felt the release of the landing gear underneath them and tried to ignore the tightness in his chest. He reached for Maggie’s hand, not bothering to hide his anxiety. She had seen it from the beginning. Knew what this would cost him. But also knew what it meant to him.

“I’m lucky to have you,” he told her.

“Yes, you are,” she smiled.

He brought her hand to his lips and added, “This is the best Christmas gift ever.”

Author's Note

Warning! There may be spoilers.

This is where I tell you what's real, and what's fiction. If you've been reading my novels for a while, you already know that I use tidbits from real life crimes and cases. It's also where I tell you how I came up with my ideas…or try to tell you. Sometimes even I recognize it's strange the way ideas and plots come together in my mind. And the twists? I'm not even sure I can explain how those emerge.

Back in 2021 and 2022, a serial killer murdered three homeless men in Washington, D.C. and two in New York City. I found myself fascinated by the case, and the fact that a killer could go undetected in two different cities. With the help of surveillance video and other evidence, law enforcement discovered that the man used the train to go back and forth. Ironically, when they captured Gerald Brevard III, it was at a gas station in Washington, D.C.

About this same time, I had an interview with the Radio Pet Lady. Tracie Hotchner produces and hosts an hour-long radio show called *DOG TALK® (and Kitties, Too!)*. It's the only NPR station on Long Island, interviewing pet experts and authors around the world. I've had the privilege of being on her show a number of times, and we always have a lively discussion. This time, Tracie mentioned how some homeless shelters didn't allow dogs.

All politics aside, it's hard not to see that the homeless situation across the country has hit crisis levels. Whatever the individual's situation and circumstances, it seemed a cruel blow that shelters wouldn't allow pets. I couldn't imagine how sad it would be to have to make that choice: a hot meal and warm bed OR keep your last companion in your life…your dog.

Also, going on about this time, Pensacola, Florida, was in the process of moving their homeless population out from under the downtown I-110 bridge. It shouldn't have been a surprise when some of these individuals moved out into the countryside.

The other news story that truly broke my heart was about the dogs left behind in Afghanistan. If you have any doubt that military and working dogs were left behind, I encourage you to look up a CBS news special with U.S. Army Platoon Commander Kristen St. Pierre who was a K9 handler. She was told she could adopt her military dog, Chase. He would be on one of the last flights out of Kabul. She waited. Then she was told the dogs weren't allowed to leave and were let out of their cages at the airport to fend for themselves.

Thanks to heroes like Charlotte Maxwell-Jones of the Kabul Small Animal Rescue, Chase was found and reunited with Kristen. Others have also been found alive and taken in by Charlotte and her team. Private organizations haven't given up in getting these dogs back home. But they still face many obstacles constantly placed in front of them.

I created Maggie and Ryder's rescue mission to bring some peace to my mind…as well as to Ryder's.

The panhandle of Florida continues to fascinate me. It's the one place on earth where pine trees meet palm trees. Where you can enjoy the forest and the Gulf shore. Where you'll find alligators and black bears.

To my friends in Santa Rosa County, Florida, my apologies for some creative geographical changes. Although I carved out and created Linden Estates and Woodriver, residents will still recognize the Red Roof Inn and the Waffle House on Avalon Boulevard. And if you find yourself in that area, consider stopping at The Oval Office for one of the best burgers you'll ever eat.

Likewise, you'll certainly find the Margaritaville Hotel on Pensacola Beach, but not Howard Johnson's Marina or Walter's Canteen. The latter is my tribute to real life U.S. Naval Commander Walter Carlin.

To my readers, thank you for waiting patiently for this one, for making these characters a part of your lives, and for allowing me to share my stories. Next up, is *Chasing Creed.*

The biggest compliment a reader can give an author is to tell a friend. If you've enjoyed this book, please tell a fellow book lover.

Acknowledgments

As always, thank you to my friends. You remind me that there's more to life than research and writing. Friends are the family we choose. Thanks to Sharon Car, Linda and Doug Buck, Sharon Kator, Amee Rief, Leigh Ann Retelsdorf, Pat Heng, Patti and Martin Bremmer, Dr. Elvira Rios, Ed Rief, Anne and Keith Brown, and Patricia Sierra.

Special thanks to:

Dr. Enita Larson, my friend and my go-to expert when I have questions about dogs.

Tracie Hotchner of Radio Pet Lady Network™ for planting the idea of including a homeless character (Sully) and his dog (Gunner).

Josh Mackey for being the voice of Ryder Creed.

Dedi Keenan Thorne, thanks to you my serial killer buys his shoes in secondhand thrift stores, making it difficult for my investigators to match his footprints.

Amber Allen, remember telling me about the rolled up carpet you saw tossed alongside the highway? You knew I was going to put a body in it.

Sue Jones and Wag N Train Terrier Rescue for bringing us our very own Grace.

Judith Barnes, years ago you suggested we use "Team Grace." Expect to see that phrase…a lot.

Lisa Black, author and forensic scientist, thanks for answering my questions about fingerprints inside latex gloves.

Deb Carlin, publisher extraordinaire, and truly the wizard behind the curtain. Thank you for all you do for the books, for the readers, and for me and the pack (Maggie, Huck, Finn and Grace). You make it possible for me to spend more time doing what I need to be doing…like writing!

My readers and VIR Club members: thank you for reading, sharing and recommending my books. I couldn't do this without all of you.

Finally, this book is dedicated to my dear friend, Marlene Haney. You've been on this journey with me from the very beginning when you told me, "Just do it!" Since then, you've allowed me to use your children's names as characters (and now grandchildren). When I asked to bury bodies on your family's farm, you simply said, "Dig in!" Thank you for cheering me on, reading every single book, and telling me I "keep getting better." Most of all, thank you for being such a wonderful friend.

Join Alex's Very Important Reader's Club to receive exciting updates on upcoming events, automatically be entered into contests, know when the next book is coming out...

and more!

Milton Keynes UK
Ingram Content Group UK Ltd.
UKHW012026081223
434064UK00010B/119/J